YET YOU CRY WHEN IT HURTS

NOTHING IS PROMISED 4

SUSAN KAYE QUINN

www.SusanKayeQuinn.com

Cover by BZN Studios

ISBN: 9798349228926

No AI programs were used in the creation of this story or associated artwork and audiobook. None of these stories may be used for training AI programs.

———

When the world is drowning, diplomacy is more than handshakes and headlines.

Nitara Desai has spent her life negotiating international agreements, easing points of conflict, and averting disasters. Worst-case scenarios belong in her nightmares, not the IEC's daily reports. On a calm day, being a director at the International Energy Consortium only requires fixing CarbonCon translators for flustered Brazilian delegates. A thankless job, but the world is still drowning in CO_2—there's no choice but to keep treading.

On a bad day, it's not just the Brazilians acting up, but the Americans walking out, and now the Governor of Southern California insisting on a clandestine meeting. Then a text comes from Matti, her solid rock in the stormy seas: *Guess what? We're getting married!*

Suddenly, an earthquake is slow-rolling through her personal life as well.

She waited too long: to tell Matti how she feels, to quit the unwinnable race to net zero, to grab hold of the things that make life worth living, not just trying to stay afloat. When the governor reveals an impossible technology that could save the planet, but it's in the hands of a murderously ambitious man, it's a catastrophe she can't turn away from. And it's almost enough to distract her from everything falling apart. *Work first*, always.

And maybe that's been the problem all along.

Yet You Cry When It Hurts is the fourth of four tightly-connected hopepunk novels in a near-future climate-fiction series. It's about our future, how the forces of greed are ever-present, how the fight for a just world never ends, and how it's not strongmen who will save us but the bright cords of connection that hold the world together.

ONE

NITARA'S TRANSLATOR WAS STRUGGLING TO KEEP UP.

The delegate from Brazil, Arminio Salles from the Ministry of the Environment, held the floor, making his impassioned argument in Portuguese as to why his country should not be penalized for the recent fires that had consumed 60,000 acres of the Amazon. But the AI whispering English in Nitara's ear garbled the translation somewhere around *"the outrage that we would roll back decades of incredible progress—"* The expressions of concern dancing around the room—delegate teams from all 35 countries of the Americas subcommittee—said it wasn't just Nitara's translator skipping words. *We've rebuilt—reserves —the Quilombolas who are—as you know...* a pause filled with static that sounded like an electronic cry for help... *should not be held against the great country of Brazil!*

Nitara lifted her chin to her assistant, gesturing to the water table. Sherri—a summer intern who'd only been with the International Energy Consortium for a month—jolted and hastened to slide on her gloves, grab one of the sterilized glasses, and fill it from the Sani-Water station. Nitara had been holding back, watching the proceedings. She was Director of the IEC's Office of Multilateral Funds and International Agreements and the head of this biannual Convention on Carbon Pricing. Fixing the CarbonCon translator wasn't her job. But diplomacy was more than handshakes and headlines—it was the careful cultivation of relationships, the wise stewardship of policy, and steady work toward common goals. Nitara had spent her entire career bringing experienced professionals together to manage points of conflict between the great powers of the world.

And right now, this translator was generating an unnecessary point of conflict.

Sherri wavered, slopping water out of the glass and looking to her for direction. Nitara tilted her head toward Mr. Salles, whose rant was increasingly translator-mangled. Her intern rushed around the perimeter of the large, circular table. Normally, Nitara would allow Salles go on, let him reveal why he was putting on such a show.

But something was off.

Brazil shouldn't be bringing up the fires at all. The Americas subcommittee of CarbonCon was *not* the place for it. Yes, the IEC was investigating the cause, but that was a separate division. CarbonCon was a perfunctory diplomatic dance on the IEC stage. Countries not meeting their emissions reduction targets argued for reducing the carbon tax; those ahead in the race to net zero argued for increasing it; some moderate change that satisfied no one was eventually reached. The underlying international treaty requiring carbon taxation to belong to the Climate Club had been in place for decades. Incentives for green energy were great, but every country had their own challenges, and the carbon tax was necessary to even things out.

Both carrots and sticks had to be used in the race to net zero.

The world was suffering too much to do otherwise.

Nitara could understand why Salles would be stressed about the investigation. The CO_2 release not only blasted through Brazil's annual emissions targets, but the Amazon was precariously close to a tipping point that would spiral the ecosystem down into a woodland savannah, not only wrecking the rainforest as a carbon sink but affecting the global water cycle. It was the worst kind of feedback loop and could get Brazil kicked out of the Climate Club, which would mean crippling across-the-board tariffs enforced by the D-10, the ten democratic nations who were the enforcement arm of the Club, officially known as the Alliance for Action on Climate Change.

That was the threat that hovered over Salles. More likely, penalties would be assessed, something proportional to the carbon cost of non-compliance, and maybe a probationary period. The IEC would investigate and make recommendations, but penalties and tariffs were political decisions, out of her hands or anyone else's at the IEC. So why was Salles sputtering on about the fires so intensely that he was befuddling the translator?

He seemed startled by Sherri appearing at his side, proffering the glass of water. Her intern shrank back a little.

Steady on, Nitara thought-commanded a message to her. She straightened and held out the glass. Having enhanced neural connections in Nitara's chip came in handy about a thousand times a day during CarbonCon.

Salles took the glass, muttered *obrigado,* then mercifully paused to take a long drink.

Whatever else was at play in the Brazilian delegation, Nitara also knew Salles had an ailing mother back home, struck down by the new hantavirus variant the World Science Organization had just identified. There was a Level Two alert over most of the country as the Pandemic Corps deployed a new proto-vaccine. This could be simply stress unrelated to the subcommittee, but it was her job to know the players and lend a hand when necessary, not letting the vast machinery of international politics get gummed up by anyone's personal difficulties, no matter how understandable.

Nitara strode across the room, using her command-by-thought messaging to instruct her intern, *Fix the translator,* as she retreated from Salles's side. Just having a pause would help. Nitara could bring down the temperature of the proceedings while Sherri dialed up the bandwidth on the translator. With any luck, the subcommittee would be back to the level of *boring* that earlier put the Guatemalan delegate to sleep. That embarrassment was the kind of minor diplomatic disaster she mitigated five times a day.

"I'm sorry," Nitara said at a measured pace, in English, sliding the microphone away from Salles. "We seem to be having some technical difficulties, which will be resolved shortly."

Salles paused his drinking to disapprove as she took the floor.

She gave him a wide smile. "I'd like to take this opportunity to commend Brazil for their responsible stewardship of the Amazon in recent decades." She nodded to the delegation seated behind Salles. He had a strong showing of indigenous leaders and the Afro-Brazilian residents of the Quilombo settlements, communities established in the 1800s by slaves escaping plantations. The Quilombolas had long ago adopted the indigenous forest-agricultural practices that kept the Amazon healthy. "Your Network of

Indigenous Forest Reserves has strengthened the resilience of the rainforest, reducing the number of naturally-occurring fires on previously disturbed lands. Which has been critical in meeting Brazil's waiver limits on natural fires, thus ensuring the continuous flow of aid money through the Amazon Fund."

Salles had opened his mouth to object but then hesitated at the mention of the Fund, which channeled contributions from the Climate Club to support forest sustainability projects, including wildfire response in remote areas.

Nitara pretended not to notice his almost-objection. "We owe a debt of gratitude to the people of Brazil—indigenous peoples, Quilombolas, citizens, activists, and civil servants alike—for the work you've done, adhering to the Forest Code and fighting the illegal fires that once plagued your great nation." That got a smattering of polite applause. "Whatever the source of the recent fires, we can all agree this has been an especially hard year in Brazil with El Niño exacerbating the dry season."

The fire could be natural in origin, but the size was suspiciously large. The more likely culprits were organized criminal gangs and illegal logging, stealing the wealth of the rainforest. The days when Brazil tacitly allowed the slash-and-burn of the forest had ceased decades ago. The cattle industry was gone, given their connection to the pandemic of 2030. The soy industry was still present, but they had a strong interest in rainforest health. The Amazon produced almost half of its own rain, evaporating and recycling water in the airmass above it. Without that giant, flowing river in the sky, Brazilian agriculture would die of thirst. Satellite imagery analysis would reveal the truth, but Nitara actually hoped it was thieves.

The worst wouldn't be that Brazil had fires set by criminals; the worst would be if they *didn't*. Spontaneous fires due to heat events and already-existing forest damage could destabilize everything.

Nitara understood stability. It was an elusive nirvana compared to the real world of compromise and diplomacy, but striving for it averted disasters on a grander scale. It was a thankless job, ensuring worst-case scenarios never became a reality, but she hadn't spent thirty years in public service for the *praise*. She was here to ensure the most terrible possibilities remained in her nightmares—and the IEC's extensive projections—and not in her daily stats reports.

Sometimes, that was enough to keep her going.

"I think we all understand," she continued, "the stakes are substantial for Brazil in the IEC's investigation of the recent fires." Salles was generally credible, and the Indigenous leaders were no fools. They knew their presence signaled a good faith effort. "While I'm not in the IEC's Office of Legal Affairs, I know the Division of Compliance is working closely with the scientists at the UN's IPCC to get the most accurate report possible of the source of the fires and the amount of carbon emitted. I can promise you, Mr. Salles and the entire Brazilian delegation, the investigation will be fair and will be seeking only the truth."

Nitara genuinely hoped Brazil could escape a punitive outcome. Otherwise, they could lose the Amazon Fund. Companies might divest from their fast-growing robotics sector. And unfair punishment for wildfires would feed Brazil's anti-carbon-tax movement, *Movimento Verdad*. The Movement of Truth was nothing of the sort. Every country had an anti-science, let-everything-burn political force, but Brazil's was a deeply cynical conspiracy-based movement that sought to isolate Brazil from the world, backed by the same criminals who were merely seething once-elites looking to reclaim their status. Their type always thought they could remain untouched by the climate crisis, with harm accruing solely to someone else. How could they be savvy enough to run a vast illegal operation yet make such a fundamental error in thinking? But she knew the answer: some people believed what they wanted, right until everything collapsed around them.

A message popped up in Nitara's peripheral view, where her chip floated the notifications she hadn't muted for the conference. *Translator bandwidth amplified!* her intern reported. Nitara hoped it would no longer be necessary.

"And while we await the investigation," Nitara said, gesturing Salles back to the microphone, "it appears our technology glitch has been fixed. Delegate Salles, I apologize for the disruption. Please continue with Brazil's position on this year's carbon tax adjustment." Never mind that Salles hadn't been discussing the carbon tax *at all*.

The man scowled but took the microphone. "As I was saying before..." His words were Portuguese, but slower now, and the translator in Nitara's ear easily kept pace. "...countries with unforeseen—and uncontrollable—natural emissions should not be punished, even when they rise above the waivers. The spirit of the Climate Club is violated when we do not recognize that we are all one Earth, each playing our part. Brazil has the riches and responsibilities of the Amazon. Right here in Southern California, you feel the effects of climate-driven drought and are beset with wildfires. We are not the only ones who struggle to stay under our natural emissions waiver. Understanding is all we ask. The burden of variable natural emissions does not fall evenly on every country. Adjustments to the carbon tax should take that into account." With that, Salles thankfully ceded the floor, and the subcommittee chair recognized Nicaragua.

Nitara expected no fireworks from the next few countries in the queue, so she eased back from the conference table and attempted to exit the room with as little notice as possible.

She had a busy schedule for the day.

With a short thought-controlled message to her slightly panicked intern—*Alert me if there are problems*—Nitara stepped into the hallway. It was empty except for the staff preparing food service tables, so she took a moment by the window overlooking LA to adjust her saree. The stunning blue and green piece from a new Indian designer married traditional cuts with a modern Earth-conscious aesthetic. Its provenance was impeccably fair-trade. She always endeavored to make a sartorial statement at CarbonCon, that they were all one Earth, bound together, responsible to and for one another.

Likely no one noticed.

Nitara closed her eyes and let the sun warm her face. Several deep breaths and a cleansing mantra brought her back to center. She could handle whatever CarbonCon might throw at her next. But when she opened her eyes, the sparkling reflection of the IEC's massive wave architecture captured her. It represented both the tumultuous ocean around the Power Islands and the waves of pandemic that originally drove the IEC's creation. The building was a wave that would never ebb: frozen, eternal, constantly threatening.

A deep weariness pulled at her soul.

She'd been in this fight her entire life. From basic training in the Pandemic Corps to serving in the refugee camps, from setting up the IEC to shepherding all the Power Islands that followed, she'd been engaged in the race for net zero for most of her fifty-five years on the planet.

And yet, they were losing. Not just the U.S. where she was born and raised, not just Brazil with its frantic desire to save the Amazon, but the entire world. She spent half her time on CarbonCon, the other half keeping the Power Islands afloat—and worked two more part-time jobs over-seeing Commissions on Climate Refugees and Emerging Science—but to what end? Carbon was still pouring into the atmosphere faster than it was being removed. The world was treading water, hoping not to drown, but the seas kept rising and the storms grew ever stronger. She'd thought the committees would give her a lifesaver of hope, but the world's steady drip of deadly heat events, deeper droughts, and inescapable floods kept coming. The entire population of the planet, human and animal, was shifting to the northern latitudes, a flow of living beings desperate to stay that way.

A few more pennies on carbon pricing, one way or the other, wouldn't make the difference. She didn't know, anymore, what truly could.

Yet there was no choice but to keep treading.

Which, for her, today, meant a half dozen subcommit-tees yet to visit and a special meeting with the delegate from China. They wanted an exemption from any future increases in the carbon tax, since *they* had reached net zero as a country five years ago, a claim largely verified by the IEC's Climate Tracker monitoring database. But *net* was still not *zero*—nor the negative draw down of carbon that truly needed to happen—and even China's claims of net zero relied on models that approximated the planet's natural uptake, which was constantly in flux precisely because of the ever-erratic climate. The world couldn't afford *any* emissions, regardless of borders, but try convincing a national delegate of that. They were all bound by negotiated treaties, but points of conflict could be managed or inflamed, and it was her job to keep the fires under control.

And now something had popped up on her calendar about a meeting with the Governor of Southern California. Which was heaven-knew-what, but the state was cooperative in hosting the IEC and CarbonCon, so she certainly could make time for the governor.

A message blinked in the corner of her vision. *Marked private.* She frowned and swiped the air to open it.

Guess what? We're getting married!

Nitara was genuinely confused until she saw who it was from: *Matti.* Then confusion became a slow-rolling earthquake through her entire body, starting with the twitch in her eyelid as she quickly scanned the rest of the message, climbing down her throat as it squeezed shut, compressing her chest as the wave passed, and finally landing in her stomach with such a thud it sent ripples of numbness along her limbs.

Not without you, of course! But we just decided, and we want to set something up for Saturday. Is Saturday good? I know the conference will be done, and you'll be tired, but we really want you there. Call when you can!

Saturday was impossible. Nitara knew that right away. Not because of the conference or any prior commitments, but because it was *impossible* Matti was getting married.

The shock wave bounced back from her extremities, and now this earthquake through her life was sending aftershocks through her stomach. She pressed a hand flat against it, willing it to calm, which did nothing. Suddenly, her private folder opened, and the pinned image of her and Matti in boot camp hovered in the air before her, summoned by her almost subconscious thought-command. Multiple other messages popped up in her peripheral vision, but they were all from Sherri, so Nitara jerkily swiped them away... and then the picture of Matti as well.

Married? How? Why? These were stupid questions formed by a brain that rejected the idea outright. Matti's boyfriend, Anthony, worked at the UN in New York. Matti was here in LA at the IEC, in the Office of Energy Technology. *Would Matti move?*

No. *That was impossible.* Only it wasn't, and that explained the tremors becoming more identifiable now: *fear.*

She'd waited too long. She'd taken everything with Matti for granted, spent too much time working, had *obviously* missed signals about the seriousness of her relationship with Anthony, and now it was too late.

Nitara barely heard the doors open behind her. It wasn't until the rush of heels-on-carpet headed her way that she blinked out of her shock enough to turn around. She expected to see the various subcommittees having gone on break and flooding the hall, but instead, it was just the United States delegation leaving the Americas subcommittee.

Sherri rushed up to her, eyes wide, voice hushed. "They're walking out!"

"The U.S. delegation?" she asked stupidly, her brain still spinning. She would have to park whatever was happening with Matti until after the conference, or at least until whatever crisis was happening right now was resolved, but her emotions were bleeding all over everything, draining through holes blasted open by the buckshot of five simple words.

Guess what? We're getting married!

"I don't know what happened!" Sherri was in a panic. "The U.S. delegate was going on about something, trying to upbid the carbon price—"

"Upbid?" That sharpened Nitara's attention. *Nothing* was making sense today. "But the U.S. is behind on its carbon goals—"

"I *know!*" Sherri's voice was hiking up, even though she was trying to keep it low. "It made no sense—*he* was making no sense—then suddenly, the whole delegation must have gotten a message or something because the delegate just stopped mid-sentence, conferenced with his team, and then they just stood up and *walked out!*"

"No explanation?"

"None." Sherri was throwing looks at the last of the delegation, which was already disappearing around the corner. "Should I go after them, Director Desai?"

"No." Nitara's instincts were kicking in. Decades of negotiating experience told her not to go running after people who had just metaphorically flipped tables, not without more information on what had just happened. "No, just carry on. Get back in the subcommittee and insist that we proceed without the U.S. delegation. They're still part of the Climate Club. If they don't want input into the process of determining the carbon price, that's on them. They can't expect everything to grind to a halt because... whatever this is." She waved vaguely down the hall. "I'll check back with the subcommittee soon. I've got a meeting with the governor—"

"Oh! I almost forgot!"

Nitara gave her a look. *Now what?*

But Sherri was spared responding because, just then,

the Governor of Southern California rounded the corner with a middle-aged gentleman of Asian descent by her side.

"The Governor... wanted to meet you... here." The last word was a whisper, and Sherri quickly retreated into the Americas subcommittee room.

Nitara worked hard to bottle up the mess she was. "Governor Kipo'mo," she said as the woman and her associate approached. "I just now received your message about wanting to meet sooner. I'm sorry if I didn't anticipate—"

"It's fine." The abruptness was less startling than the governor leaning in close and whispering, "We need somewhere secure to meet. This last-minute change is to throw off whoever might be listening in."

"I... see." Nitara ran a multinational organization that negotiated a tax that affected every country on Earth. She was quite aware that espionage and diplomacy were awkward cousins. Yet she also knew Southern California's first indigenous governor was famous for her directness, not her paranoia or even secretiveness. "I have a secure room." She was thinking of the interview room where high-level refugees were sometimes brought to debrief after escaping sensitive conflict points around the globe. The IEC essentially conducted a witness protection program for select refugees, but that required a certain security level to keep people safe. Nitara looked over the fifty-something man standing pensively next to the Governor. "May I ask who your associate is?"

The man bowed formally. "I'm Dr. Akemi Sato, Commissioner on the Southern California Public Utilities Commission."

Nitara's eyebrows lifted. Perhaps this wasn't the

Governor asking for a political favor of dubious legitimacy. "Well, then. If you'll follow me."

She led them through the IEC's main conference wing and toward the cluster of offices that comprised the Refugee Commission. They mutually refrained from small talk. Whatever this was, it distracted her—mostly—from the shock still trickling through her system. The Brazilian's antics, the Americans' walkout, and now the governor's insistence on a clandestine meeting. It was almost enough to keep her from falling to pieces over Matti's sudden betrothal and how that was about to blow up her personal life.

Work first. *Always.*

And maybe that was part of the problem.

TWO

"I'm sorry, Governor, you can't possibly be saying you've got an unlimited energy source."

"That's exactly what I'm saying."

Nitara blinked, her objections frozen in her mind by the static hum of disbelief. But she crossed the room to make sure the door's magnetic lock was still engaged, which signaled the security measures were active, and swiped up the monitor to double-check. Radio-frequency scans were clear, low-level audio jammer functioning. Their body heat signatures, as well as vibrations from speech and motion, would be muted by special materials built into the walls and the contoured, sound-absorbing sponge on the surface. The room didn't even have outlets or wiring—the lights ran on self-contained power—and the only furniture in the small, square room was a table and four chairs.

They remained standing.

"Just checking that the room is secure." Nitara wasn't at all sure what she was securing. Information about incredible world-changing technology? Or Governor Kipo'mo's reputation? The absolute cocoon of the refugee room meant

15

no one would be able to record whatever flavor of crazy Kipo'mo had brought to her. It would give all three of them room to disavow whatever was said here. Nitara was halfway hoping the governor would think better of this and just... leave.

She swiped away the security monitor. "What do you call this technology?"

"ZPE," Dr. Sato offered, a little too eagerly. "Zero Point Energy, the source of the power the reactor extracts from the universe. At the gigawatt level." He was a physicist and clearly excited about this.

"Right. Of course."

He scowled. "I have all the data. Video. I've *seen* it in action. We can prove *everything*."

"Well, that will help with..." Nitara struggled to place this clandestine meeting in any context other than *padded-room crazy*. The room's spiky foam walls certainly added that ambience. "What is it you think I can help with?" Would she need to call security? What kind of diplomatic disaster would *that* spool up? No. She mentally shook herself. There was something happening here, but half her brain was still swimming in shock from Matti's message. *Focus.*

"I didn't believe it at first, either." The governor folded her arms, like she would simply wait until Nitara had come to her senses, as if that were a process which would occur naturally with time. Nitara had spent hours in this room listening to harrowing tales of why refugees needed safe harbor, but this was something else. This was the already powerful trafficking in conspiracy. Maybe.

"It's... an extraordinary claim." Nitara mentally fumbled for an exit strategy while Dr. Sato pulled a small drive from his pocket.

"Everything's on here." His voice lowered. "Be careful where you upload it."

She took the drive. What did he expect? That she'd download the data to her base station right now? "I'm not a physicist, Dr. Sato—"

"The executive summary is brief," Governor Kipo'mo cut in. "But compelling. Miller Zendek and James Ellis have been secretly developing the ZPE technology for a decade, first on Power Island One, now moved to Renew Energy in Palm Springs. DARPA is involved, which means possible weapons development, in addition to their game-changing energy technology. I didn't have to understand the details of the physics to recognize the danger, especially given that Miller and Ellis attempted several murders, held the LA grid hostage, and sliced up a few citizens in pursuit of this technology."

"So, Miller, the wunderkind Power Island designer, is the bad guy here?" Nitara couldn't help the skepticism. She'd never met the man, but one couldn't be part of the IEC without knowing of his political savvy. He'd orchestrated the initial buildout of the Power Islands within USEC and eventually beyond it. Each country had its own partner organization that coordinated with the IEC, and Miller was a star inside and out of his.

"Without question." The governor was unnaturally sure of Miller's guilt.

"And James Ellis, the Nobel-prize-winning scientist, is his mad genius?" Nitara raised an eyebrow.

"He's not *crazy*," Dr. Sato protested, "but definitely a genius."

Nitara regarded the man and thought-commanded a search on him. There was incredible strategic value in gaining quick access to information during negotiations without revealing that act. It took her half a second, and the search throwing off two errors, before she remembered she was in a secure room and cut off from the gateway.

Nitara sighed. "Commissioner Sato, I'm sure you're well-regarded in your field—"

"Akemi has impeccable credentials," the governor interrupted again. "He was a professor at CalTech, set up the original fusion labs on Energy Island, and was a founding member of the Power Engineering Institute."

"Of course." Nitara vaguely remembered the name now. She'd been immersed in international issues for so long, she tended to forget the IEC was founded here in LA, the ground-breaking Energy Island project just offshore and tapping much of the local talent. If Akemi Sato's resume was as impressive as Kipo'mo claimed, he'd hardly be the type to rope the governor into some crazy conspiracy. Maybe Dr. Sato was playing 14th-dimensional political chess, setting up the governor to take some kind of fall? And using Nitara to do it? Or perhaps it was the other way around?

Things were never as simple as they appeared. A hundred machinations were always happening behind the scenes. Yet, often, those calculations were important only to motivation—they explained the *why* of certain actions, but the political outcome could still be taken at face value. If a treaty was well constructed, it would accomplish what it was negotiated to do, for better and worse, whether or not that bolstered one politician's power or quashed another's. If this ZPE technology was some ruse, anyone involved would suffer the embarrassment—reputations and money would be sacrificed, but the scope on that was limited. It wasn't like the harm Nitara saw every day by well-intentioned but misguided policies for climate refugee resettlement or wildfire abatement in the Amazon. Technology with "world-changing" buzz wouldn't get far without being exposed if it were mere fantasy. People with serious money and serious interests could be taken for a ride, but not for long.

But if it were real...

"So, Ellis has been working on this for a decade?" Nitara asked Dr. Sato.

"Yes. Before that, if you count the research in the fusion program that led up to it."

Nitara frowned. "The fusion program? You mean, on Power Island One?" Kipo'mo said that before, but now it pinged something in her brain.

"The original Energy Island, yes." Dr. Sato was nodding like he knew where she was going.

Nitara put up both hands. "Hold up. That work is covered under the original IEC charter." Her eyebrows slowly lifted. "That's why you came to me."

"*Yes,*" Dr. Sato gushed. "Exactly so."

"Plus, your jurisdiction is outside the United States," Governor Kipo'mo added. "Miller was entrenched in USEC. DARPA is involved. Akemi and I represent the interests of Southern California, but at the Federal level, I don't know how far up involvement in this project goes."

Nitara leaned slightly away. "You don't think this is a rogue scientist with fringe tech—you think it's a project of the United States government?"

Kipo'mo scowled. "Maybe not initially. The data suggests they started as a rogue project. But as it has proven successful—and deadly, with these bizarre murders in Palm Springs—yes, I think Miller's peddling it to the feds. If you were the Department of Energy, *or the Department of Defense,* wouldn't you be interested in a new unlimited power source that could be weaponized at a distance?"

Hairs raised on the back of Nitara's neck. *The U.S. delegation walking out of the Americas subcommittee...* "Yes, I would. In fact, if I had that in my pocket, I would be heavily in favor of jacking up the carbon price on every other country in the world."

Kipo'mo threw a puzzled look at Dr. Sato, who gave a small shake of his head.

"Sorry." Nitara rubbed her neck, telling the hairs to settle down. "Just connecting some dots. All right..." Where to even start with this? She glanced at the tiny drive still in her hand. "I need to check this out."

Dr. Sato—Akemi—seemed to melt with relief.

"I'll have someone in the IEC's Office of Energy Technology look into this—"

"Nitara." The governor's habit of cutting her off was annoying, but the sudden softness in her voice captured Nitara's attention. "You need to be careful. Make sure you can trust whoever you share this with. We took a considerable risk bringing this to you—not just for us, but for the people Miller has already tried to kill to keep this buried."

Nitara prided herself on being able to judge people, even with scant background: the governor's concern appeared genuine. But part of the reasoning didn't hold up. "You can only keep something like this quiet for so long. Its *use* is what brings power, money, and prestige. That can't be done in secret, not forever."

Kipo'mo and Sato exchanged another glance. The physicist spoke up this time. "Ellis has clearly been fine-tuning the reactor and gathering data for Miller to present to *someone*. We assume, since DARPA is involved, it's someone inside the U.S. government. But we don't actually know. We'd hoped *you* would be able to find out... without tracing it back to the people who originally brought this to our attention. Although I've verified all of it myself, including speaking with Miller and Ellis directly. They do not know I was investigating this. Or that we placed a bug in their laboratory."

"You have a bug?" Nitara's gaze dropped to the drive again and bounced up.

"Video and data." Akemi nodded. "You'll see. And I'll be happy to explain the technical details if you wish. Or the potential this technology has for the planet." He left that dangling, but she already knew.

"I've spent my whole life working to help the planet reach net zero, Dr. Sato," she said coolly, but her heart was racing. Some part of her already believed this. "I'm very much aware of the toll of not reaching that goal. An unlimited energy source... with that, we could *reverse* the warming of the planet. It would take time to scale up, but we've had the technology to pull down CO_2 in a serious way for decades. We just don't have the energy. It's almost impossible to overstate how radically that would change everything."

For better... *and worse,* the back of her mind whispered. Something like this would destabilize every international agreement on the planet. And not just the ones related to climate. The coordinated effort to battle the warming of the planet had also kept human rights abuses in check, not least regarding the refugees caused by the crisis itself. The world's precarious balance of power would undeniably shift —and it wasn't at all clear in what direction. "One thing I'm certain of: the U.S. cannot legally lay claim to exclusive use of a technology developed on Energy Island, I don't care how secretive they are about it. Nor can a single country be allowed to monopolize that technology, regardless of the actual legal position." Her pulse skipped a beat. If this were real, what would other countries do to obtain the technology? What *wouldn't* they do?

A few murders would be nothing.

"I think that's why the effort to keep it secret has been so dramatic," Governor Kipo'mo said quietly. "If they can erase the origins, bury Ellis's original work in obscure academic papers and abandoned lines of research, then they can present it as something the U.S. government developed in their own government laboratories."

"And then unlimited energy becomes a weapon." The full scope of this was unfurling in Nitara's mind. "Whether you use it directly as such or not."

The governor nodded, and Akemi stayed quietly pensive.

"All right, I need to... I need a little time with this." Nitara grimaced. Where to even begin? First, she had to make sure this was *real*. But then... how far was Miller down the path of exploiting this technology? She barely knew some of the players involved, much less how to grapple with or shape the fallout. How would the world react? Her mind boggled.

And she still had her conference duties, although CarbonCon—and the Americans' walkout—might be inextricably linked to this. One thing was clear: she wasn't doing this on her own. But Kipo'mo was right—extreme caution was warranted about who got read in.

"Thank you for bringing this to me. For *trusting* me with this. I'm not sure where I'll have to go with it. But I will do my best to protect the sources." She took a breath and then considered how the governor and commissioner had gotten into CarbonCon. The IEC building housed a range of organizations—the WSO, USEC, the Public Utilities Commission—so Akemi plausibly had access despite the conference's quasi-lockdown due to the outbreak in Huntington Beach. The governor must have pulled rank. "Meanwhile, you're welcome to stay here at the IEC in our adjacent quarantined lodging arrangements. Given the WSO's Level Two alert, we've created a containment zone for the conference participants. I'm assuming you passed the screening to get in, but it might be easier for you to stay inside our ecosystem for the moment. I'll set up a VIP suite for you to work remotely if that's acceptable to you."

"I think that's wise," Akemi said.

"And I prefer to stay involved," the governor added.

"Of course. I'll keep you updated." Then she activated the code to unlock the door and drop the security measures. "I'll be in touch." She bowed briefly as they left.

With the security down and the gateway reconnected, a flurry of messages popped up from her chip. Three were from Matti, a strange contortion of notes trying not to be urgent, yet that was belied by their rapid-fire nature. Normally, Nitara would already have her on a call, telling her all about the *insanity* that had just landed in her lap, but now... she was frozen. After twenty-five years of being inextricably part of each other's daily lives, suddenly she didn't know where they stood. That vast irony kept her teetering on the threshold of the secure room: she'd negotiated world-changing treaties but faced with a small change in a personal relationship, she was suddenly set adrift?

But it wasn't small. It was everything she had.

She realized she was staring at nothing when a call beeped through, yanking her back.

Matti. Oh, shit.

She accepted it, audio-only. "Hey."

"Nitara, honey, I'm sorry I'm bugging you. Are you in the middle of something? Just say yes, and I'll hang up, and you can call me back when you can."

Yes. But only to avoid talking to her. "No. I mean, yes, I've been offline, just got your messages, that's why I haven't—"

"Oh, good! I thought, *Oh, God, she's freaking out,* and *Why did I send that by message?* and most of all, *What the hell is wrong with me?*"

"Matti, it's fine." Nitara's stomach tightened.

"So, you're okay with it?"

Nitara swallowed. "The wedding? Saturday? Sure." She cringed.

"You're not okay with it." Matti's voice had dropped.

"No, it's just... short notice. And my head's full of the conference." *Lies.* She didn't lie to Matti. That wasn't their way. And yet here she was.

"I know. I'm so sorry. I didn't want to interrupt. But it's just killing me not to know. That you're okay with it. I mean, it's like *five days away,* and we need to plan things, and it's completely nuts, but the only thing I really needed... was you. To know you're okay with it. And that you can come."

"I can come."

"And Joffrey? Will he be in town?"

Oh, right. Her current casual, extremely hot photographer boyfriend. "I have no idea."

"That's not important!" Matti rushed out. "If he can make it, great. Totally welcome, of course. But I just had to hear it from you. Sorry to horn in on your workday."

Nitara's stomach somehow clenched more. She and Matti messaged each other every day, multiple times a day, no matter what was happening. Would that change, too? A desperate feeling surged up, a clawing need to pull Matti back in, as if she were out in dangerous waters, clinging to a floatation ring, and if Nitara didn't yank her back, *right the fuck now,* she would drown.

Only it was Nitara who was sinking. "You know, I could use your help on something."

"Yeah? Anything!"

"I mean... if you're not too busy planning the wedding." More cringe.

"No! Not at all. Besides, Anthony's doing most of it. What do you need?"

"It's IEC business, actually. A new technology I'd like to get your thoughts on." Matti worked in the Office of Energy Technology now, the Division of Basic and Emerging Science. And despite the sudden uncertainty in their relationship, there was no one on the planet Nitara trusted more. "But not over the phone. And I've got things I need to tie up here, first. Can you meet me later? I'll message you when and where, once I get that sorted."

"You got it. And yay, I'll get to show you the rings!" Matti gushed.

"Rings?" Nitara's stomach was solidifying into rock.

"Anthony had this really cute idea for rings—I'll just show you later! Now go do your Important CarbonCon Things, Ms. Director of International Agreements! I'll see you soon."

Matti clicked off.

Nitara tried to breathe out the tension gripping her entire body.

It didn't work.

THREE

Nitara was convinced.

It didn't take long to rush through the contents of the drive, given most of it was physics data she had no chance of understanding. But the video was compelling. And the accumulation of all the first-hand accounts, the narrative that wove the entire story together, the people involved...

This was real. And it would change everything.

Only it was in the hands of a man—Miller—who wasn't interested in saving the world, despite his reputation in developing the Power Islands. On closer inspection of Miller's public-facing records, Nitara could see the signature signs of an outsized ambition: early accomplishments paired with a handful of complaints about borderline abuse; his carefully crafted persona of a young genius that opened doors which might otherwise have been closed; the faux-modest retreat to being the designer of historic Power Island One, which she now knew to be cover for his larger plans to develop the ZPE. Miller had laid cable ten years ago specifically for the gigawatts of energy he hoped Ellis's invention would generate. He was a politically savvy man who planned ahead, and now he was probably naming his price to someone in the Department of Defense. Or was Miller after something more? Power? Prestige?

How do you stop a man with an invention that disrupts the world? And what if that technology might also be the world's salvation?

It was an equation with too many unknowns. She couldn't hope to come up with a solution, or even a strategy to find a solution, without knowing more about Miller's intent. And his next move.

Nitara swiped away the video she'd been running on a loop—Ellis and some blond woman conducting experiments with the large black egg that was the ZPE reactor—and reset the encryption on her base station. She'd already locked away the drive Akemi had given her in a hidden vault. Then she stretched, rose from her desk, and waved the windows to 100%. The sun put a blazing glare on downtown LA, and she had to squint against it.

Matti would arrive any moment, and Nitara needed to conjure the right frame of mind. *Keep it simple. Just business.* Matti's position in the Energy Tech division would be helpful in this thing with Miller. Matti was making a name for herself there, and Nitara couldn't be more proud. Long ago, Nitara had secured a position for her in the IEC's Climate Refugee office, just to anchor her again. That was after the breakdown, that dark time when Nitara wasn't sure if Matti would make it out of the Pandemic Corps in one piece. A year was spent fighting the PTSD, Matti sleeping on Nitara's couch until she was well again. That was years ago, but that time was seared into Nitara's soul as much as their time together in the Corps. Most people didn't understand what Matti meant to her, and it was none of their business, so she didn't bother to explain. Eventually, people stopped asking.

Nitara thought-commanded open her folder and the pinned picture. Her display automatically dimmed the brightness of the world so she could see the two of them, only three days through Basic and already *corps mates*. Grinning in their still-new fatigues, the caduceus of the Pandemic Corps stitched to their shoulders, ready to save the world first-hand. The sun on her face now was the same then—she could feel it. Maybe that's why she kept this picture, out of all the ones over all the years. This was where it started, and for her, it never stopped being *this exact feeling*. It wasn't easy to name, and she didn't think she had to, least of all to Matti. But maybe she was very wrong about that.

A light tone sounded at her door.

Nitara swiped away the image, dialed down the window, and turned as she thought-commanded open the door.

Matti came rushing in, all smiles, her dark brown hair highlighted these days and stylish, contrasting with her pale skin and light, no-makeup look. The IEC didn't have much of a dress code, and Matti liked her free-flowing, lacy dresses. Those combined with her tattooed hands gave her a bohemian look, an at-ease style she easily carried off, but that belied the trauma Nitara knew still rumbled softly under the surface.

"Look at you!" Matti gushed as she threw out her hands to take in Nitara's saree. "You went with the green and blue one. Were the delegates completely wowed?" She rushed up and hugged Nitara, an embrace she returned, although all the unspoken words bound up inside her were a physical pain in her chest.

"No one noticed." Nitara's voice was hushed.

Matti quickly pulled back and frowned. "Zero taste in that lot."

"It's fine."

Matti's expression turned to pity. "They should appreciate you more. Do they have any idea how much work you put into this?"

Nitara smiled a little. "The objective is to get a carbon price, not wow the delegates with my saree."

"They *should* be impressed by your fashion sense. Any idiot can see your diplomatic skills. Everything goes smoothly because of you." Matti disapproved with a blanket squint that covered all delegates to all conferences Nitara had ever run. It was the warm, automatic support she'd always had—that they shared without question—and it was both reassuring to feel it and terrifying that somehow it had turned precarious. "But forget all that. What did you need my help for?" Matti's eagerness was again that double-edged blade that cut Nitara even as she wanted to hold onto it.

"I, um..." Forcing her brain to switch gears took a moment. "Something landed in my lap that I need you to keep absolutely secret."

Matti's expression opened up. "Are there spies at the conference? Want me to run a counter-espionage program? I could honey-trap them into revealing their secret carbon-pricing strategies."

She shook her head but couldn't help the smile. "Anthony might not like that."

"I'll bring him along."

The smile grew. "You two are more adventurous than I suspected."

"Well, *I* am. Anthony is super boring."

"So boring, you're going to marry him." The smile faded, but Matti didn't seem to notice.

"Ah, he's the good kind of boring." Then her eyes lit up. "The ring!" She splayed her hand to show off the thin black band. "It's recycled tungsten, etched with our names." Hers had *Anthony* in a highly cursive font delicately encircling her finger.

"That's not very boring." Nitara worked hard to keep her voice neutral.

Matti searched her face, suddenly serious. "Tell me again, to my face, that you're okay with this."

"*Matti.* I've got something important to tell you."

Her face fell. "Okay."

Nitara steered away from that conversational abyss and back to the safer topic of unlimited free energy that would destabilize the world and cause massive international crises... and possibly save the planet. Rings and weddings were forgotten as Nitara rolled out the data, which Matti probably understood better than she did, with her background in technology, now refreshed since she'd been in the Emerging Science Division. It took some time to get through it all, but by the end, they'd taken a seat on the small settee at the end of her office, and Matti's serious side had shown up for work.

"Okay, this is bad," she said. "What can I do?"

"I'm not even sure where to start," Nitara admitted. "When survival is a matter of cooperation—which is what the race to net zero is all about—it has a way of sharpening up how well you behave. I've got these criminals in Brazil burning down the rainforest because they think their survival doesn't depend on cooperation anymore. If we let loose free energy on the world—if the U.S. announces tomorrow that they've got a monopoly on this ZPE reactor

—all international treaties might as well be tossed in the fire."

"But you said it's *our* IP," she said, meaning the IEC had jurisdiction. She'd been twisting her ring but stopped to throw up her hands. "How can they expect to just claim it's theirs?"

"They don't know we know, for starters." Nitara scowled. "But abiding by international intellectual property law is largely voluntary—and reciprocal. You don't break IP treaties because you don't want other nations to break them. The IEC doesn't have enforcement powers."

"No, but the Climate Club does. They'll get tossed out."

"Maybe," Nitara conceded. "But if you're in sole possession of unlimited energy, you'll quickly become willing to tolerate some extra tariffs to keep it. Which will destabilize *everything*."

"You're assuming the U.S. government is on board with this."

Nitara raised an eyebrow.

"I mean, *already* on board with this," Matti said. "Do we know for sure how far up the chain of command this goes? Is the President involved? The DOD? Congress? If Miller's still trying to pitch it to everyone, maybe he can be stopped. Or, I don't know, *re-routed*."

"You're right. We don't know. And we need some way of flushing Miller out. Or finding out who can stop him. Or at least slow him down." Nitara rubbed her temple. "I can't begin to imagine how to broker an international treaty regarding the use of something like this. There's no precedent. At all."

"If anyone can do that, it's you."

Nitara reached over to poke Matti in the knee, the little

thing they'd done since boot camp that said, *I see what you did there.* It was natural, like she didn't even remember there was a giant unspoken thing hanging between them now.

Matti poked her in the shoulder in return. "I mean it. Besides, you do all these media campaigns."

"The IEC has an entire media relations department."

Matti was unimpressed. "Which you orchestrate like it belongs to you. I hear what they say about you, you know."

Nitara pretended to be scandalized. "They *say things* about me?"

Matti snorted. "Like you don't know. But seriously: what are we going to do about this?"

The *we* in that sentence settled the tension between her shoulders a little. "The liaisons for every country-level IEC affiliate are here in the building, plus the world's delegates for CarbonCon. I can shake the tree, see what falls out. Specifically, I can make some noise about the U.S. walking out of the Americas subcommittee, see what rumors turn up. But I'd really like you to look into your contacts at the DOE about new energy technologies that are about to break out. If Miller's taking this out of the lab and into the world, word is going to leak. If we can trace the leaks, we can get a sense of how to box them in. Or slow them down. Something, until I can think through how to manage this, so it doesn't blow up the world. Metaphorically speaking."

"And maybe in reality?" Matti grimaced. "Sounds like it's still dangerous."

"There's that too."

"Are you going to tell the Executive Director?" That was the head of the IEC, two levels up from Nitara, who reported straight to the UN. In theory, the IEC was a specialized agency independent of the UN, the Climate

Club, and the D-10. In reality, the delicate balance of international relations was always a multilateral affair.

"Let's see what we can flush out first." Nitara sighed. "But you need to be careful what you say. Eventually, the entire world is going to know about this, one way or another. But how that goes down could make things dangerous really fast."

"Copy that." She stood up from the settee. "I'll let you know the minute I hear anything." Then she gently squeezed Nitara's hand. "I'm so glad you're coming Saturday. I know this takes precedence, but it means a lot to me that you *want* to be there. Even if you have to bail on us at the last minute to save the world."

"Of course." She smiled, but it was past a lump in her throat.

As Matti hustled out the door, Nitara had that feeling again, the need to yank her back. It was crazy because that wasn't how they were—they didn't hold each other back, they held each other up. Ever since they met in Basic, Nitara would instinctively drop everything and parachute out of an airplane to save Matti, and vice-versa. For Nitara, that intensity never faded. It wasn't sexual, not the kind of relationship you took to bed—it was way beyond that.

Maybe the intensity had waned for Matti. Maybe this thing with Anthony had filled up the space Matti always held open for her, all while Nitara was busy traveling the world and negotiating the race to net zero. Marriage had never come between them before. Nitara never had time or desire for that, but before and after Matti's first husband passed, their bond had never changed. They'd never questioned it. Never formalized it. Never called it something more than friendship, even though it was.

Nitara knew better than to leave important things to

unspoken intentions and vague promises that could be misunderstood. International agreements defined relationships, spelled them out in the agreed-upon language of the law. They were how the world stayed in balance. Somehow, she'd forgotten that in the most important relationship in her life.

She wiped away a tickle of wetness on her cheek. Emotions bleeding out of her again. She was an idiot—she should have talked to Matti the moment she walked in the door. But Nitara had no idea what to say. She just... needed a little time. To let the idea of the wedding settle in. Maybe it didn't *mean* anything. Approaching Matti could wait until she didn't feel so desperate, so clingy, like she might drown if Matti said... what?

She didn't even know.

But you don't walk into a negotiation with no idea what you want from it.

The right time in the right space would arrive. As soon as she was ready, Nitara would straighten this out. But *soon*. Before Saturday.

Meanwhile, stopping Miller was as good a distraction as any.

FOUR

"Wʜᴀᴛ's ɢᴏɪɴɢ ᴏɴ ᴡɪᴛʜ ᴛʜᴇ Aᴍᴇʀɪᴄᴀɴs?"

Nitara had been asking the same question, in various forms, for several hours. This time, it was directed at the assistant to the British CarbonCon delegate, so no translator was necessary—human or AI—which could inhibit the whispering of rumors.

"They're arrogant tossers." She was a slight woman named Poppy, about Nitara's age but with deep brown skin and African features.

"So, just the usual theatrics, then?"

"No." Poppy looked over her shoulder. No one in a crowded hallway between sessions was paying attention to them. "There's something brewing, Director. Everyone seems sure of that, but they don't know what. Do you know?"

She shrugged. "Just trying to figure out if they're closer to net zero than the reports suggest. Any ideas?"

Poppy surveyed the crowd again, then leaned closer and whispered, "You didn't hear it from me. But they've got some deal going with the Chinese, exporting their carbon in exchange for bumping the refugee lottery. And getting the UN to pull back the human rights monitors."

"That would make sense." Nitara waited but there was no more forthcoming.

Poppy stepped back into the flow of the hallway, apparently unwilling to get caught talking to her.

Nitara sighed. Low-level corruption in the refugee lottery was a known problem, but surveillance tech for carbon was so advanced—between satellites, a vast ground/air/sea sensor network, and the AI sniffing out everything—it was extraordinarily difficult to have undetected emissions. As the Brazilians had already discovered. But delegate teams at CarbonCon were always convinced someone was getting away with something. This wasn't the most outlandish rumor she'd heard. That would be the French delegate's girlfriend who said the Americans were using alien technology that harvested "vital essence," whatever that was, from poor climate refugees to power their grid. She further insisted this qualified as "renewable" because there would always be more refugees. Nitara had to refrain from physically assaulting the woman. Instead, she just smiled and insulted her intelligence, but in French and very politely, then moved on. She also made a mental note to check out the French delegate's personal life, which apparently was conspiracy-prone, and that was a serious problem. Perhaps the attraction was only in the bedroom, but still—understanding the vulnerabilities of the delegates was part of her job.

Her normal job. When she wasn't chasing her own conspiracies.

Nitara wove through the crowded hall. A queue of people stood outside her office, waiting to talk to her. She'd asked Sherri to round up lower-level assistants, people

Nitara could summon to her office without diplomatic incident, to see if there was anything she could flush out of them. She brought them in, one by one, and grilled them on unusual comings and goings at the conference. She'd manufactured a "breach" of the quarantine, and was using that for cover to see if the staff might let something slip. Secretive meetings between delegations. Individuals sneaking off for clandestine reporting to outside factions. But the questioning revealed little. It was a long shot anyway. Encrypted communication was secure enough. The American delegation could easily be talking to anyone in the world with minimal risk of detection.

She dismissed the assistants, and Sherri too, who was left apologizing to her fellow interns as they drifted away, chattering amongst themselves. Nitara had shaken the branches, but not much had fallen. Beyond the British delegate's assistant and the French delegate's girlfriend, she'd connected with reps from each of the D-10, plus an additional handful of countries from each region, and the Chinese and Russian delegations in particular, although that was mostly posturing. The Australians were convinced the Americans had some new energy technology they were developing, but when pressed, they were speculating. It made sense—the Aussies just had no idea the scope of what might be happening.

Nor did anyone else, except the Americans themselves. Which was why she had decided to summon the U.S. delegate directly. They'd surely been hearing about her inquiries—one can't whisper about rumors without creating a few—so it was time to make a more substantial move. The U.S. delegate himself was "unavailable" but pledged to send his deputy to Nitara's office. And they were late. When someone finally arrived, it was not the promised second-in-command, but a man so young-looking that Nitara had to check the register to confirm he was a legitimate member of the conference.

"Please have a seat, Mr. Green." Nitara kept her tone icy. The kid was barely old enough to vote. He swept his hand through his hair and smiled too much as he sat.

Message received, Nitara thought grimly. The Americans clearly knew what they had, were thoroughly unconcerned about ruffling the feathers of the director of CarbonCon, and were comfortable enough in their position of strength to insult her in the process.

"What can I help you with, Director?" the kid—Mr. Thomas Green—asked.

This boy didn't deserve the roasting she was about to give him, but she needed to send a message in return. She didn't want to tip her hand, but this kind of insult couldn't pass without consequence. And this pinged all her fears— that the imbalance of power brought by the ZPE technology was already tearing apart international norms of cooperation.

Nitara rose from her seat, swiftly, and watched the alarm trip across Thomas's face as she swept around her desk and towered over him, folding her arms and demanding, "Why did the U.S. delegation walk out?" She didn't bother specifying from *where*. There were no games in this except the one Thomas was unlikely to be aware of.

"Delegate Rodriguez sends his sincere apologies—"

"*Why?*"

"Be-because of a personal matter." Thomas leaned away from her but was trapped in the chair. "He didn't intend any disrespect—"

"Of course, he did."

"I'm sorry?" Thomas's expression morphed into horror that this was getting away from him so fast.

"Delegate Rodriguez is insulting this conference with his behavior."

"I... I... It was a *very urgent* personal matter."

"That's bullshit, Thomas. Try again." She unfolded her arms, sitting on the edge of her desk but leaning forward, further trapping Thomas in the chair but taking the hostility down a notch. He still looked desperate to escape, and the only way out was physically shoving the Director of CarbonCon aside. Nitara was pretty sure he would knock his chair backward to the floor first.

"Delegate Rodriguez meant no insult—"

"*Your presence in my office,* Thomas, is an insult. So, I need you to hear something very clearly. Tell Delegate Rodriguez that I don't need founding members of the D-10 acting like prima-donna dictators, flexing and flouncing off in a huff when they think they have the slightest advantage. Do you know how hard it is to keep the *actual* dictators in line and at the table, debating the carbon price? If the *U.S. delegation* can walk out as an unannounced negotiating strategy—because whatever the hell else this is, it's definitely that—then what's to stop any disgruntled autocrat from proving how mighty he is to the audience back home with the same antics? Nothing, Thomas. Nothing is going to stop that. Except that I'll start petitioning the Climate Club to move for censure, fines, and even suspension for countries that cannot abide by international norms and come to the negotiating table in good faith. Is that what Delegate Rodriguez wants? Because that's what he's going to get."

Thomas had visibly shrunk into the chair, his shallow breaths showing in the rapid movement of his chest under his thin, formal shirt. "No, Ma'am."

"No, Ma'am, *what?*"

"That's not what Delegate Rodriguez wants." He said it like a forced confession.

"So, I'd like you to try again, Thomas. *Why* did the U.S. delegation walk out?"

Thomas opened his mouth but struggled to form words before they were aborted by his brain, which was clearly working overtime to figure out which story to use.

"You don't know." Nitara leaned back, crossing her arms again. "Do you?"

He shut his mouth, and a flash of anger crossed his face, quickly disguised by panic again. But it gave away what Thomas didn't want her to know—that even the lowest member of the U.S. delegation knew *something*. And didn't enjoy pretending to be a flunky.

"It's all right." Nitara dismissed him with a feigned sigh. "I don't expect Rodriguez to send someone who actually knows what's going on." She took her time strolling back to her chair on the other side of the desk. When she got there, Thomas was still squirming, although it wasn't her holding him with her presence anymore. More like his own tortured ego. She gave him a look of surprise: *You still here?* "You can go, Thomas."

He leaned forward instead. "Delegate Rodriguez is doing the best he can with a bad situation."

Nitara waved him off. "I'm unconcerned with his imaginary personal problems."

Thomas lost his innocent affectation, although he was still absurdly young, so it wasn't so easily shed. "There's a rogue element in the President's cabinet. Someone who thinks the IEC is holding the U.S. back."

Nitara was genuinely unimpressed. It was a weak defense. "Not for the first time, I imagine."

"This is something... new." Thomas seemed to wrestle with his conscience for a moment. Nitara couldn't tell which side won, but he gave a look of disgust. "I'm not supposed to tell you anything. And I'm *not* going to breach any confidences. The truth is, I don't have any information you'd find useful anyway."

"Try me."

"There's crazy talk in the cabinet." Thomas had dropped his voice. "Things like the U.S. should invade Canada for more climate-friendly land. Like war is inevitable, and we need to start positioning ourselves now." At Nitara's skeptical look, Thomas held up a hand. "I'm not saying the President is contemplating any of those things. I'm just saying there's some crazy shit coming out of DC on the down low, and no one knows what to make of it."

"I assure you, *someone* does."

Thomas rose from his chair. "I don't know what's happening, Director. I do know Delegate Rodriguez is doing what he thinks is right. That's all I can tell you."

Nitara let out a real sigh. "All right. Go." He thankfully retreated. Maybe he would take her threats back to Rodriguez, maybe not. This business of a crazy cabinet member whispering war with Canada into the President's ear... that *was* the most absurd rumor she'd heard today.

And the only one that might be true.

Shit.

She closed her eyes and rubbed her temples. Should she take this rumor at face value? Was Rodriguez sending a flunky to plant disinformation? What was the end game with that?

She had no idea.

She opened her eyes and swiped to bring up Miller's folder. She needed a better idea of the man, what drove him, something to give a compass heading on where he was taking the ZPE. His position at USEC and his time setting up Power Islands all over the world were the perfect cover for an international arms dealer, if the ZPE could be considered a weapon. He'd spent a decade constructing a network he could exploit once the technology had been developed. Miller, if nothing else, was a man who planned ahead. But with DARPA officials on the ground at Palm Springs, he must have made promises to the U.S. Government that he wasn't taking it international—or perhaps that was the threat, if the Department of Defense didn't meet his terms. Renew Energy *was* an international company.

If Miller had proven out the technology, as Akemi's data showed, and the DOD had met Miller's terms, that would explain a nationalist cabinet secretary bringing new energy technology to the President, probably complete with a set of battle plans for exploiting its use.

But invading Canada? It sounded crazy, but fanning the flames of climate scarcity and promoting a zero-sum ethos when it came to international cooperation—*that* was familiar and dangerous rhetoric. It could gain traction if the ZPE proved to be unlimited power in America's pocket. Her rich and powerful country had a sordid past of hoarding all kinds of things—vaccines, medical supplies, scarce trace elements for green tech. There was a misconception about hate, that it created systems of inequality. In reality, systems of inequality created the hate, either justifiable anger against the colonizers and hoarders or a carefully crafted narrative to justify the colonizing and the hoarding. Unequal distribution of resources and opportunity were the root cause of, and justification for, conflict everywhere and throughout time.

America wasn't the only country with a long record of that.

But it also had a unique history of leading international efforts in cooperation and closing the gap between wealthy nations and poor ones. The formation of the IEC and the original Energy Island project were a shining example of her country's better nature. The D-10 took lessons from previous failed climate agreements and formed the Climate Club—a club whose membership required abiding by the jointly-agreed carbon price or be subject to tariffs on imports from Club countries. This "tax and tariff" system quickly made it untenable to be a modern nation *without* being in the Club. The carbon tax set by CarbonCon went to that country's tracking, surveillance, and green energy build-out.

Countries in the Club not only benefitted from avoiding the tariffs, the economic benefits of investing in a green economy were quickly obvious to everyone. The formation of the original Energy Island only accelerated that. The IEC levied a separate Global Energy Tax directly on member nations—which soon became every nation on Earth—to fund green energy research, but then that technology was available to everyone. Even the petrostates quickly saw the benefit of becoming electrostates. Membership became contingent on minimum human rights reforms as well. Cooperation wasn't just survival: it brought amazing rewards. The Climate Club was the first successful global climate treaty, and it ironically hinged on energy production becoming much more local, and the resiliency and security that inherently brought. It was also responsible for raising global living standards and an unprecedented stretch of peace. The Climate Club method of peacefully inducing cooperation brought stability to the world through soft power. And that was the only tenable kind of power on a planet slowly roasting in its own waste products.

What would happen if all that was disrupted by introducing unlimited free energy into the system? It was already destabilizing the Americans' behavior, regardless of whether their carefully planted rumor was true. Nitara had spent her entire life trying to stabilize a precarious world; Miller was undoing her life's work with a single technology. But what if the ZPE device were also their salvation? What if everything had to break in order to reform into something new?

Nitara had seen too much collateral damage in the refugee camps to ever think there were "acceptable losses." Those were counted in lives and suffering. Even the refugee treaties she'd helped broker were compromises written in blood. In the end, they reduced the carnage, and that was what allowed her to sleep at night. Maybe that was the best she could hope for now? Keeping a worse disaster from unfolding?

It was exhausting to even think about.

A message popped up from Matti. *I have something! Are you free?*

Thank God. Because I don't have the first idea where to go with this, she thought-commanded back. *Meet me in the secure room.*

Nitara hustled out, striding quickly through the conference hallways and dodging delegations, but Matti beat her there. She was vibrating from the need to spill her lead but waited until Nitara had the room locked down.

"Okay, what—"

"You remember Zahara from the Corps?"

Nitara squinted. "Skinny girl from Botswana who was a

kickass engineer? Refabricated solar panels for that refugee camp with the orthopox outbreak?"

"Yes! Wait—*that's* what you remember about her?"

Nitara lifted her hands. *How was this related?*

"She set up the contraband ring? With that Italian prince who was..." Matti trailed off at Nitara's mystified look. "Oh, right. I think we kept that from you. You were kind of... *you know.*" She gestured to the totality of Nitara's being.

"What?"

"The mole, Nitara." She was grinning. "You were the mole. And would totally rat us out to the brass."

She was speechless for a second. "I was not."

"Sure, sure." Matti was obviously laughing inside at how hopelessly strait-laced Nitara had apparently been in her youth, which Nitara would vehemently object to if she weren't so glad to see Matti had rescued some good memories from the camps. And that the two of them were being *normal* instead of having the impending nuptials hanging over them like a sarin cloud. "Okay," Matti went on, "this is either a crazy coincidence or totally a lead. I can't decide."

"Spill it, already. I'm completely tapped out."

"So, I keep in touch with a lot of people from the Corps. *You know.*" She shrugged one shoulder. Fellow Pandemic Corps "survivors" had been a lifeline for Matti when she was having her breakdown. "Zahara's part of this small group of us who... okay, that part is not important. What matters is that she's working now for NRCan, Natural Resources Canada, and her boss is heading out to this secret, last-minute, invite-only conference."

"Okay, that's odd, but—"

"It's sponsored by Renew Energy."

Nitara's eyebrows lifted.

"Right?" Matti gushed. "So Zahara's complaining to our group that she's had to find last-minute transport for her and her boss to the freaking *North Sea*. Because apparently this conference is being held at that creaky old floating island out there, not one of the Power Islands mind you, but the one they built for that wind farm Denmark put up in the 20's. You know, the one that proved out the capacity of offshore wind turbines in rough seas? And not only that, everything's booked going out there, and Zahara is losing her mind trying to find *something* because they're supposed to be there by morning."

"Holy shit."

"That's what I thought. It has to be related, right?"

"Has anyone in the IEC been invited to this?" Nitara asked, her mind spinning. "Do we even know what it is?"

"No one in the Office of Technology. I sent out a blast message. No one knows what it is."

Nitara ran a hand over her face. "Can she get me in?"

"Zahara?" Matti's expression opened. "Wait, you're going to go?"

"I need a way in—*not* as IEC. If this is Miller, he's moving fast for a reason. If it's not... then I'll waste a day crashing a party in the North Sea."

"Do you have any idea how hard it is to haul your butt out to fifty miles off the Jutland peninsula?"

Nitara cocked her head. "No, but Zahara does."

Matti's expression drew down into a scowl. "This is dangerous, isn't it?"

"Probably."

Matti surveyed her high-fashion, fair-trade saree. "You're going to need better clothes."

Nitara smiled.

FIVE

Nitara staggered down the boarding ramp, which heaved with the waves. She gripped the railing with one hand while towing luggage with the other. The autobag couldn't be trusted to navigate this on its own.

The fury of the storm whipped her hair, which had been tied back when they started this voyage of misery across the North Sea, two hours ago. The blowing strands blinded her so badly, she had to stop once she reached the dock. She clawed the useless hair band from its tangle, gathered up the mess, and secured it again at the back of her head. She'd managed to not get sick during the trip, but now that they'd debarked to the floating island, her head was still spinning. It might be too early to declare victory of mind over stomach.

"C'mon!" Zahara shouted to be heard over the wind, jerking her head forward, urging Nitara on with zero mercy for the state of her stomach. The Canadian Minister of Natural Resources, Jean-Yves LeBlanc, had been the first off the boat. He was now hurrying toward the row of utilitarian concrete buildings that must house the island's battery storage. Nitara was masquerading as their assistant, which meant she was stuck towing the minister's personal bag in addition to her backpack. The dock was steadier than the ramp, so she electronically tethered the autobag to her chip and trusted it to navigate the planks and not get swept off into the sea. Then she leaned into the wind as she trudged forward, slitting her eyes to keep them from watering. Zahara carried her own backpack of clothes plus the official NRCan briefcase. She was already halfway to the closest building, with the minister having disappeared inside.

To get to this clandestine energy summit in the angry North Sea, Zahara had somehow commandeered a trawler. Fishing Vessel Winter Queen had left its normal corridors to the south, picked them up in Torsminde on the Jutland peninsula, and brought them fifty nautical miles west to this antique floating island. The gale-force winds and seven-meter waves had punished them the entire way, and even in the slight shelter of the island's leeward side, it howled. The actual temperature wasn't terribly cold—it was mid-July, even in the North Sea—but the wind and ocean spray cut through.

FV Winter Queen was already pushing away from the dock.

The island and the wind farm surrounding it were a decades-old project of Denmark, intentionally placed outside normal shipping lanes. Five countries had maritime economic interests throughout the North Sea, and the inter-section point of them all was only a few miles away. The island's generated power connected to the underwater, transnational North Sea Offshore Grid, a critical part of the EU's supergrid. If you were going to site an experimental free energy source that could simultaneously feed power to dozens of nations, be difficult to reach, *and* maintain some ambiguity as to economic rights... this would be the place.

The island wasn't entirely neutral—Renew Energy and Denmark had a hand in convening this secret summit—but Nitara was already impressed with what Miller had achieved in staging this. *And concerned.* Was it already too late to stop whatever he had planned?

Her cover as assistant—dressed in rugged canvas pants, boots, and a sea-worthy jacket—should keep her anonymous while she poked around. The Canadian Minister hadn't yet recognized her from the IEC. On the ship, he hardly seemed to notice her, just periodically barked orders at Zahara then dropped into immersive. Satellite linkage was good, even in the storm, and the minister had spent half the trip in virtual, his body inured to the tossing of the waves. Nitara had seriously considered retreating into immersive as well, but Zahara had wanted to brief her. Plus, her body might have thrown up anyway, which would have been a disaster.

Now that she was nominally back on land—Nitara could swear the floating island rolled with the storm—she sent a quick message to Matti that she'd survived. Matti had assembled a small team of trustworthies, including Governor Kipo'mo and Dr. Sato, and they were monitoring her, as well as tracking down leads. Nitara had sent them a copy of Zahara's top-secret invitation: a very brief agenda that promised an "exclusive, international auction" for licensing rights to a "spectacular new renewable energy technology." No hint as to the nature of the tech, just the time and location and the requirement of in-person attendance at the auction. There was a *Come or be left behind!* vibe to the invitation and the secrecy surrounding it. Zahara said Minister LeBlanc was constantly on closed channel with higher-ups. The hush-hush urgency seemed spurred mainly by the hot air of speculation. That or Miller had teased out the technology on more secretive channels.

Nitara could only imagine what the Americans were thinking at this point. If they'd believed they had Miller in their pocket—if they had *paid* for that privilege—they had to be outraged at this turn of events.

Nitara had wired up before she left, so she could feed real-time video and audio to Matti's team. So far, all it had revealed was the inside of a fishing trawler and now the ocean-swept docks. The waves that roiled Nitara's stomach remained thankfully private.

She thought-commanded a message. *You getting all this?*

"Audio is a mess from the wind," Matti said in her ear, her channel coming in clear through Nitara's chip. "Should be better inside. The video from your earring cam is fine, but holy shit, those waves."

Copy that, she messaged back and kept trudging forward.

The island itself was much smaller than a standard Power Island—records showed less than half a square mile compared to a Power Island's fifty—and the entire surface was concrete and steel, unimaginative block structures built to endure the harsh weather and deliver power, not support a vibrant ecosystem of power engineers and green tech.

It was fitting such a utilitarian place would mark the dirty, underground debut of this new ZPE technology. In the last 24 hours, she'd tried to wrap her mind around how a radically abundant energy source could be *legitimately* brought onto the world stage. There had to be a way to negotiate this among the world powers that didn't lead to war or destabilizing riches for a few and poverty and dependence for everyone else. She imagined multiple, painstakingly managed conferences, with thousands of people doing the hard, thankless work of reducing points of conflict, until they reached an accord that would leave many disgruntled but provide a foundation for a brilliantly better world. It was the faith in that, the vision of it, that would serve as the moral compass of the whole endeavor. She didn't know what to expect inside these concrete bunkers in the middle of the North Sea, but she was certain a better future would *not* be birthed here.

Zahara waited at the door for her to catch up. Just inside stood a conspicuously armed guard with intimidating black body armor and an impatient, wind-bedraggled minister.

"Now that we're all here," LeBlanc said to her with a glare then turned to the guard, "you can let us in."

The guard took their names and a scan of their faces. Nitara held her breath, waiting for some AI in the system to recognize her, or realize *Nitara Lakshmi* was neither a real person nor employed at the Canadian Department of Natural Resources, but apparently, the conference organizers didn't care who you brought, as long as you were on the registered list.

And once inside, the door clicked shut behind them. *Locked.* But they hadn't gotten far, just another tiny room made of flimsy plywood and crammed with three more armed men in body armor plus one civilian—not obviously armed, normal business dress. Suddenly, her chip threw off a flurry of errors. LeBlanc and Zahara were also swiping away, trying to clear them out.

"Satellite linkage is blocked inside the conference," said the slim, tall man before her. "My name is Søren Norgaard. I'm the head of Renew Energy's Technology Division in Denmark. You will not be able to make contact with the outside world from now on." His English was impeccable, and although his wide cheekbones, ice-blue eyes, and accent were certainly Danish, the cool smile on his face was atypical of Danes. It *hid* something. Nitara couldn't say what, but she'd spent years honing her instincts about people's orientations toward the use of power, and this man was throwing off a dozen alerts of his own. "You may leave now, if you choose, but there will be no re-entries. If you choose to stay, you must give binding legal consent to the terms and conditions." He flicked a finger, and a message popped up on her chip, which had otherwise gone completely offline. "Take your time reading it, but notice that if you consent, you will remain at the summit for the duration." His tone said he enjoyed wielding this power, but it was also somewhat beneath him.

Nitara pretended to read over the extensive legalese, which LeBlanc was furiously scanning, while downloading a copy to her chip to read later. She wouldn't be bound by anything she signed under false pretenses. Zahara was flicking tentative smiles at the stone-faced security, probably trying to judge the possibility of charming their way in. Nitara assessed that at zero, possibly less—they might get thrown out if Zahara got cute. Søren quickly became impatient, despite his invitation to take their time, but he only pursed his lips and interfaced with his still-functioning chip. Which must be on an internal network, given the block to the satellites.

No communication with the outside world. Why?

A small flutter of fear danced around Nitara's chest. What if she were discovered? Matti and crew had to be freaking out with the sudden drop in comms. Nitara caught Zahara's eye, but the woman just gave a tight smile, obviously waiting for her boss to declare he was done reading the terms of entry. Was there really an option to say no? FV Winter Queen had left, and Nitara hadn't seen any other ships docked. They were sliding in at the last minute, just inside the window of arrival on the invitation. If they didn't get inside, where exactly did Søren expect them to go?

Finally, LeBlanc huffed and spoke his verbal consent. "I agree to the terms and conditions for entry into the exclusive energy summit sponsored by Renew Energy."

Zahara and Nitara quickly did the same.

Søren glared his displeasure at the delay but then strode through a weapons-detection arch against the wall, opened the rough wooden door that was the exit, and waited while the guards ushered each of them through. Nitara had to untether the minister's autobag so they could search it, then reconnected, so it would bumble along behind her again. The other side of the door was another narrow passageway, but this one had concrete walls, floor, and ceiling. The security checkpoint they'd just passed must be a recent add-on. More armed guards stood in pairs under the glare of the bare overhead lights.

Søren flicked a finger at each of them as he walked with determined speed down the hall. "Your chips now have access to the internal network so you can message each other."

LeBlanc scowled at Søren's back, and Zahara lifted an eyebrow in Nitara's direction. *An open internal network?* They might as well broadcast their thoughts through a bullhorn.

"Otherwise," Søren continued, "there will be no communication with the outside world allowed for the duration of the summit. A block is enabled everywhere inside the buildings. This will prevent the leaking of information. All exits will also be locked, for your safety." He paused at a heavy metal door with that enigmatic smile. "You are the representatives of your country now. It is an honor for which you have been carefully selected. I wish you luck in rising to the occasion."

LeBlanc leaned back, seemingly out of surprise more than making room as Søren opened the door, and Nitara felt the chill of the words as well. *Carefully selected?* Based on what? As far as Nitara could tell, the Minister of Natural Resources was a fairly low-ranking member of the Canadian government, at least for deciding on world-changing energy technology. And Søren's criteria couldn't be too selective if Nitara had managed to sneak in.

Something was off about all of this.

On the other side of the door was an auditorium-sized room with hundreds of folding chairs on the bare concrete floor. Dozens of people milled around, few actually sitting. A dozen more guards were dispersed around the room, warily watching the attendees. A lectern up front perched on a rough wooden stage, which was backdropped by a row of industrial batteries, the kind Nitara would have expected to see filling bunkers on an island windfarm. The room smelled of electricity and sawdust with an underlying stench of unwashed bodies.

"The auction will take place here." Søren's hard-soled shoes rapped the dull gray floor. "The main battery room has been cleared for this purpose. There are ten other battery rooms on the island, plus Renew has recently expanded capacity, anticipating our special role in the summit." They were garnering looks as Søren hustled them through the room and toward another metal door. "You may travel freely between the main room and any other rooms connected by the island's enclosed walkways, but any attempt to breach locked doors is cause for expulsion. I'll show you the cafeteria and your lodging spaces, but you will want to return here shortly. The main presentation will begin soon. The demonstration will be conducted at three."

"Demonstration?" LeBlanc asked as Søren opened the door and stepped through.

"You will learn everything you need at the presentation beforehand." He slid a look to LeBlanc. "I do not recommend missing it." They passed through an enclosed walkway between the two buildings. The storm clouds overhead splattered the transparent domed walls with droplets. Then they were inside again. "This is the cafeteria."

It was a similarly cleared-out concrete room with pairs of armed guards at each of the two entrances. Instead of a stage and residual batteries, this room had an entire wall stacked with one-foot-cubed brown boxes. An open one displayed the contents on one of several wooden picnic tables that seemed as hastily constructed as the rest. Zahara dashed a look to her, and Nitara shook her head. The last time she'd seen rations like this was in the Pandemic Corps. They had to be ready-to-eat. There was no sign of cookware or even paper plates. A bored guard stood near the food.

"You've got to be kidding." LeBlanc was staring in horror at the display. The only other people in the room were a trio huddled near the table, talking quietly among themselves, not eating. Tall and dark-skinned, possibly representatives from an African nation, although Nitara couldn't hear them well enough to place their language. They were dressed rugged for sea-travel, like their trio supposedly representing Canada, with no identifying insignia. What kind of summit was this supposed to be when you couldn't even tell who the players were?

Maybe that was the point.

Søren smirked. "Help yourselves. You have just a few

minutes until the presentation begins." Then he swept his hand through the air, sending something to their chips. Coordinates popped up. "This is where you'll find your accommodations. Again, the external doors are locked. Anyone who leaves will not be allowed to return." Then the man turned on his heel and strode back toward the main conference room.

LeBlanc swiped away the coordinates on his display and vaguely waved at her. "You—what's your name?"

"Nitara." She kept her face neutral but made a mental note about the minister's lack of attention to detail in personnel serving him.

LeBlanc turned to Zahara. "Give her your things. She can set up our room while we attend this presentation. Let's go." He didn't wait for a response, just turned and hurried back the way they came. Zahara shrugged off her backpack and handed it to Nitara.

"LeBlanc will posture his way up front," she said in a whisper. "Look for us there."

Nitara nodded. "I need a bit of privacy anyway."

Zahara lifted an eyebrow but didn't ask, just gripped the briefcase and hustled after the minister, who was already blustering at the guards by the door to move faster. Nitara pulled up the coordinates for their accommodations, but her normal locator was offline. She stifled her curse, wondering if this was some power trip on Søren's part, but tapping through the message brought up a local positioning system that took the coordinates and set up a guide. She heaved Zahara's backpack on top of her own, and with the autobag on her heels, she followed the guide. It took her through four more battery rooms, each linked by interconnected outdoor tunnels, before dumping her into the middle of a room twice the size of the others. Each was more crowded than the last, filled with rows of identical military-style cots and dozens of people talking in small groups. A steady flow of humanity moved toward the larger main room. Nitara had to work her way past them, her digital guide finally bringing her to the coordinates, which pointed to a trio of empty cots in the middle of the room.

It took her a moment.

Then she snort-laughed, imagining LeBlanc's face when he realized the nature of their "accommodations." She flung the backpacks on the bunks and de-tethered the auto-bag, shoving it under the center cot. Despite the armed guards at the perimeter of the room there was zero chance their belongings would be secure. It would serve LeBlanc right to have his belongings riffled through, but she could use a bit of privacy for a minute. That no one was paying attention to her would have to suffice.

Her earring cam fed a live audio/video stream that Matti was supposed to be recording over their secure link. But with that cut off, Nitara had lost her best way to document the summit and spy on its attendees. Her base station had limited storage, but it would have to do. The cam had shut down as soon as their secure link was cut, so she needed to trigger it again and reroute it to store on her base station without accidentally sending a signal through the local network. She took the earring out, used the pin from the other one to reset it, and while it rebooted, she quickly swiped up the feed and captured it to her local storage.

Her peripheral vision sent up an alarm. *People were moving toward her.*

She flicked a quick look, but they were simply heading *en masse* toward the door. A red pop-up alarm from the local network said the presentation was about to begin. Nitara double-checked the cam feed had recorded properly, shut it off, and enabled a thought-command sequence to easily trigger it when needed. Then she joined the river of humanity flowing toward the main conference room.

The energy of the crowd was tight, and she recognized that kind of tension. It was the same as every other international conference with high stakes. Everyone knew the basics, why they were in the middle of the North Sea and that there were machinations at work, but no one knew what secret negotiations were slipping by them. Information was always incomplete, the players weren't always known, and the advantages were seldom obvious until after the fact. Did all these low-level government attachés truly understand the world-changing technology Miller was set to auction? *Did she?* What was Miller's end game? The average attendee had to know less than she did, and she didn't have much. As they shuffled through bottlenecks in the tunnels, she calculated the size of the conference. If the cots were representative, maybe two or three hundred. CarbonCon had well over two thousand attendees. Each of the 197 member counties would send a staff of up to a dozen. Here, there appeared to be at least three representatives per country, judging by the small groupings, but that would mean six hundred attendees, not two or three.

Who was left out?

As the crowd dumped into the main conference room, it became clear the overall complexion of the room was much lighter than the global average. There were representatives of every skin tone on Earth, but not in proportion to their population. Or even their country number.

Miller had excluded a whole swath of humanity.

There was a time when the Global South had been routinely excluded from powerful conferences, and even more so from the rooms where things were truly decided.

But that had dramatically changed with the formation of the Climate Club, where the importance of universal representation was finally seen as a necessity—and was obtained by the structure, intent, and not least, threat of tariffs. No one wanted to be excluded and no one was allowed to be.

This conference seemed a throwback to an earlier time, when the colonial past still had ghostly fingers clenching the reins of power. As her brain wrestled with the implications of that, a gruff, amplified voice called for their attention. Up front, on the makeshift stage, a huge screen had been erected, and in front of it stood an older white man with a slightly disheveled fluff of white hair.

"My name is Dr. James Ellis." He cleared his throat. "And you are the luckiest people on Earth."

SIX

It was five minutes into Ellis's meandering discussion of physics before Nitara remembered to start her recording. She flicked a look at Minister LeBlanc to see if he noticed. He was scowling at the presentation, as if the complexities of mathematics were a personal insult, despite elbowing his way to the front, as Zahara had predicted. For her part, Zahara was passing notes and having silent conversations with at least three different people, assistants to their country representatives like herself, making connections that hopefully would reveal crucial information. It took a moment to bubble up into Nitara's conscious awareness but... *they were all women.* The assistants were women, whereas the stiff-backed official representatives, the ones ostensibly wielding power, were men.

Just like their trio representing Canada.

Coincidence? Nitara glanced around the crowd. It was impossible to tell which were in charge like LeBlanc, and which were along for support, but just as the overall complexion of the crowd was decidedly lighter than the global average, there were far more men than the population average of ~50%. Probably less than 25% female, and if their small sampling was representative, even fewer of those held positions of power.

That had been the norm when Nitara started her career. International conferences of the past were comprised of men from the Global North telling men from the Global South why they were reneging on their aid money for climate mitigation. Meanwhile, the women at the conferences did all the hard work of negotiating agreements, pushing forward compromises, and trying to repair rifts from the failure to live up to prior promises. That was how it worked while the world pretended the climate wasn't changing, the Great Extinction wasn't happening, and they could continue to merrily pump CO_2 into the air. But over the three decades since she'd joined the Pandemic Corps, and eventually, the IEC, a lot had changed—mostly, the people at the table. When the ones in power, the people negotiating the terms and penalties of the agreements, represented the full range of people affected by the outcomes: progress happened.

Carefully selected. Søren's comment about who was allowed into this room held more weight now, and the implications of that settled heavily at the bottom of Nitara's stomach.

"All this will, of course, be available for your further inspection." Ellis's words commanded her attention again. Nitara turned so her earring cam would get a good shot of the mountain of math he'd sketched out for his tense audience. "I understand you are not mathematicians, much less physicists," Ellis went on, waving a hand at the screen to banish the equations, then letting his clasped hands drop in front of him, fully in professor mode. "I will explain it simply, so you can grasp the potential." He paused for dramatic effect. "I call it the Ellis Vacuum Energy Generator, or EVEG. You will, perhaps, allow a small bit of hubris for a world-changing technology."

Small wasn't the adjective Nitara would choose, but men who styled themselves as geniuses weren't known for their humility.

"A single EVEG device is capable of generating twenty gigawatts of power." Ellis's smile was full of pride. Twenty gigawatts still seemed absurdly large, even though Akemi's stolen data had shown as much. A gigawatt was a thousand megawatts. Utility scale power generation ran from 100 to 1000 megawatts, depending on the size of the facility. Ellis was claiming to generate 20 times peak utility scale power with his one egg-shaped device. He was confirming data she already had, but the rest of the conference had to be skeptical.

When the response from the crowd was a mere scattering of whispers, Ellis's smile faded into a scowl. "To make it even *simpler,*" he grumbled, "five of my EVEG devices produce enough energy to power the entire Los Angeles Metro area, even under peak demand."

That brought gasps of appreciation.

Ellis nodded like this was his due. "The beauty of the EVEG is sublime. The device is quite simple, although it must be exquisitely tuned, both in the formation of the quasiparticles and the actual geometry. The physical structure does much of the work—there is very little power required to create the quasiparticles and activate the zero-point energy pump. As I have shown the EVEG induces a space of lowered zero-point energy density. The quasiparticles then function as a one-way filter, disturbing the quantum electromagnetic vacuum and further reducing the energy density in that small, localized space until the potential, the difference between the device and the vacuum of the universe, is so large that energy has no choice but to flow. It is a bolt of lightning from the emptiness of space! The EVEG creates the storm, the quasiparticles churning the clouds of virtual particles, building the potential until it releases, a vast discharge in a very short period of time. We capture the universe's energy gift and conduct it into the waiting storage. This analogy is, of course, terribly flawed. It captures nothing of the magnificence of the device nor how it breaks open the nothingness of space and allows us to scoop out the raw substance of the universe." Ellis was beaming now.

Nitara scanned the crowd with her earring cam, catching the looks of skepticism and outright disbelief. Some expressions were more horror or confused concern. No one was talking, not even Zahara with her note-sharing comrades, who were staring gap-mouthed at Ellis.

He wagged a finger at his audience. "I have my theories about this energy. Its source. What it means. It is wonderfully counter-intuitive, this quasiparticle pump, increasing the order of the universe—*negative* entropy—so that it may, ultimately with our device, dissipate energy faster. Of course, we do this all the time, making order out of chaos. And what is any kind of order, any organization the universe has constructed—planets, galaxies, the human mind—but a negative entropy engine? This energy is connected to that grand mystery: the dark energy by which the universe organizes itself so it may dissipate entropy more efficiently. Now that we know it can be extracted and tapped, for any purpose the mind can imagine..." His gaze unfocused, and he looked over the heads of the crowd to a seemingly infinite distance. "We are Prometheus, using a hollow reed to steal fire from the gods."

Zahara leaned close. "What is this guy *on?*"

"Power," Nitara whispered back. "Apparently a lot of it." She sincerely hoped this wasn't as... *crazy? dangerous?...* as Ellis made it sound. She'd read all of Dr. Sato's conjectures about the capabilities of the ZPE reactor—she resolved to never call it the EVEG—but hearing it straight from Ellis made it more real.

The man came back from whatever fantasy he was having on stage and beckoned someone from the side curtained-off area. Two assistants wheeled out a large, black egg-shaped device, the height of Ellis, trailing an umbilical of electrical cabling. A thin blond woman pushed an instrumentation cart attached to the cable. Nitara recognized her —Astra Olsen—from Akemi's spy video, and the device was identical to the one in Ellis's secret lab. A duplicate or the same one? Last she heard, they were still pulling data from the spy bug, so it seemed likely this was a second device. On the video, the ZPE reactor had seemed flat, more like a strange sculpture than a power-generating device, despite the evidence of operation. On stage, in person, it had a whole different feel. The surface glistened darkly, catching light and reflecting it in ever-shifting ways. The bulging size was unexpectedly menacing, a dark potential waiting to be born, yet it was already alive with a slight hum from its bundled umbilical of power.

The murmurings of the crowd had fallen silent again. The wheels of the cart squeaked as it rolled to a stop next to Ellis.

"And now, a demonstration!" Ellis quickly shooed away the two assistants, who retreated to the side of the stage. He checked a few connections then joined Astra at the controls. She stepped back, nearly tripping over another thick cord that ran back to the curtained area.

Zahara flashed Nitara a look. "Are they really...?"

She nodded, her heart rate picking up as she remembered the images of people sliced in half in Palm Springs. She wet her lips, glanced behind her, and had a sudden, very sincere wish that Minister LeBlanc's ego hadn't demanded they stand so close to the front.

Zahara grew alarmed when she saw Nitara looking for a way out, so Nitara squared her shoulders, gave Zahara a small affirming nod, and trained her gaze on the stage. There wasn't anywhere to go, and she had no idea the actual level of risk. Killing the audience didn't seem like the best sales tactic. *No need for panic.*

Still, her heart thrummed along with the machine as it wound up, the sudden electrical whine filling the room as everyone's attention fixed on the large black egg on stage. Nitara knew what to expect—she'd watched it on the spy videos—but when the whining sound reached a peak and released a loud *crack,* she jumped like everyone else. The device buzzed and shook for about ten seconds, emitted another *crack,* and then started to wind down.

Astra was tapping furiously at a virtual display, while Ellis peered over her shoulder. When the whining had dropped enough to speak, a chatter rose in the room.

No one appeared to have been killed.

"What the hell was—" Zahara whispered, but then Ellis cut her off.

"Our brief demonstration," he said, his hands raised, signaling the demo wasn't anywhere near complete, "was just to familiarize you to the performance of the EVEG. It is, of course, possible to operate continuously, but that is too much energy for such a small demonstration." He glanced to the side of the stage, where one assistant was giving him a thumbs up while clearly monitoring something on their display. To the audience, Ellis said, "Please check your chips. You should have received a notification about a small virtual display where you can monitor the experiment yourselves."

Indeed, there was. A hundred hands flicked as they swiped up the notification. Nitara thought-commanded hers to install and display. Since everyone was momentarily distracted, she took that opportunity to quickly layer in the device monitor over the feed from her earring cam. She already had the data from Ellis's lab device. If she could capture the data from this one, Dr. Sato should be able to verify whether this was real. She had to be the only one in the room with access to such information. She couldn't imagine what the rest were thinking—Ellis could easily falsify all of this. It was a simple display: time, input energy, generated power.

"And now..." Ellis drew her attention again. "During this second demonstration, you will see exactly the capability of the Ellis Vacuum Energy Generator!" The man seemed like he had lived his whole life to utter those words. He stood, triumphant, arms spread wide in front of his machine as the electric whine spun up again. The input energy jumped and slowly climbed, but it was only a few kilowatts, apparently fed by the larger umbilical that lay on the stage and led to the curtained-off area. This time, the crowd knew what to expect and most seemed enthralled by the display of the monitor. The *generated power* number was still pegged at zero. When the *crack* came, it still made her jolt. The amount of generated power leaped, a blur of numbers that changed almost too quickly to follow. Two, then three, then four digits, it counted up like a time-accelerated stopwatch, freezing when the second crack signaled the energy generation phase had passed.

Elapsed time: *10 seconds*

Generated Power: *21,230,801 kilowatts (peak)*

If you could take it at face value, it was astonishing. And Ellis's comments about continuous power generation and having to limit the run time in order to not generate too much power seemed like something that needed a lot more explanation.

As the device wound down, Minister LeBlanc muttered, "This is meaningless." But he was shooting looks to Zahara for confirmation.

She shrugged. "There's an attached white paper with all the math. I downloaded it, but I'd need a physicist to decipher it."

"How does he expect us to believe—"

"How about a round of applause for our Nobel-prize-winning genius!" Miller had suddenly appeared on stage next to Ellis, and he was all smiles. Amid a smattering of uncertain applause, Miller shook Ellis's hand, emphatically, then turned to the crowd. "I know you're wondering whether this can possibly be real, but I'd like to remind everyone that both Renew Energy and the Environmental Ministry of Denmark are sponsoring this demonstration." He gestured to someone in the crowd, but Nitara couldn't make out who. "I'd like to thank the Danish Minister of the Environment for their belief in this project and their support. As well, a representative from America's Defense Advanced Research Projects Agency is here on behalf of the United States." *DARPA.* Miller again pointed out someone in the crowd, this time closer. Nitara craned her neck to get a shot of the DARPA official and his assistants on camera with her earring cam. They did *not* look happy. Which answered one of her questions: Exactly how pissed were the Americans that Miller was selling his technology to bidders from around the world? *Very.*

Miller continued as if he were simply thanking them for bringing the cocktail napkins. "Dr. Ellis and myself sincerely appreciate the early support both these agencies—and Renew Energy—provided in the development of the EVEG. They have well-earned the perks coming their way, which I'll be discussing shortly. But for everyone else, I ask you to take that support as evidence that this technology is truly world changing."

He paused to pull something up on his personal display and flick it out to the crowd. "I've sent you the full terms and conditions of the auction, which I will review in detail momentarily. But I'd like to remind you that you've all been *very* carefully selected for this opportunity. Before the demonstration, Dr. Ellis said you were the luckiest people on Earth." He threw a smirk to Ellis, who was standing back with Astra, next to the ZPE reactor. "With apologies to the brilliant physicist..." Miller swept a slow look over the crowd. "You are not lucky. *You are chosen.* You, as representatives of your respective countries, along with my newly formed company, *Eternal Energy,* are going to be the re-makers of the world. As we've clearly demonstrated—and again, you will have a chance for your experts to confirm the tech details at a later date—the EVEG taps unlimited energy from the universe. *Unlimited,* my friends. And there's no limit to where all our fortunes will go with such a device."

The murmurs had ramped up enough that Miller had to raise his hands. "I know you have a thousand questions, so please—permit me to give you the answers you're seeking. Namely, how do you get your hands on this device and what are the terms?" He paused for a moment, his eyes alight, and Nitara guessed this was the moment *Miller* had been dreaming of. How long had he been working on this? Over a decade, if the timeline the Governor brought to her was correct. The clench in Nitara's stomach said this was the crux. What would be Miller's price?

"You must first understand the precipice of history on which you stand." Miller's whole body was enlivened now, hands gesturing to punctuate his words. "There was a time when people like yourselves would have been the natural leaders. When your intelligence and acumen, your foresight and ambition, would have been rewarded by placing you at the pinnacle of society. But we've changed the way the world works, and not for the better. This is a chance to start again. To empower those who understand there's a natural order to things, and those most *capable* should be at the top." He swept a hand back to Ellis. "A brilliant physicist's research was prematurely cut off. Those of lesser intellect, of shorter vision, saw no use for his ground-breaking find-ings. But Dr. Ellis knew—as did I—that it had the potential to change everything." He smiled wide. "And here we are today. *Fortune favors the bold,* my friends, and you will have your chance, right here, today, to demonstrate that boldness. This is not a sales pitch. This isn't some gadget that will produce a marginal change in energy production. *This is a revolution.* And *you* will be the princes of the new guard. You are here today because, of all the possible representa-tives of your country, I saw a spark of *greatness* inside you. You're the kind of men who, if the world worked as it should, would already be at the highest levels of power. This world-changing technology doesn't just generate gigawatts, my friends. In the right hands, it creates *power.* The power to disrupt markets, manufacture possibilities, and change the calculus of the entire world. Everything from geopolitics to military capability to resource valuation will be reconfigured. This is the kind of power that will remake the world. You won't just win the race for net zero and rescue the planet from the ravages of excess carbon. You will be the rightful kings restoring the natural order once again." Miller took on an air like it was time for serious business. "With that, let us review a couple key details about the auction itself..."

What the fuck? Zahara was mouthing to her, and the alarm tripping through Nitara had set her every nerve on end. She knew what this was. It went by a lot of names. *Ecofascism. PureGreens. Lifeboaters.* They were all flavors of the same extremist ideology that believed the answer to the climate crisis was eliminating people. Certain kinds of people, and always *other* people. This kind of rhetoric had been discredited long ago by the success of the Climate Club, along with dozens of other initiatives which showed the climate crisis could be fought by unprecedented levels of cooperation, not competition or exclusion, much less genocide. There were no boundaries to pollution. No national borders to the world's ecosystems. The D-10 and the Climate Club had succeeded in organizing the world-wide cooperation necessary, but even authoritarian govern-ments eventually recognized the benefits of making the race to net zero a cooperative venture. Wars and the climate crisis could be fought simultaneously, but at a basic level, if nations spent their talent and treasure bulking up their mili-tary, there would be fewer resources for tackling the climate crisis. But Keynes was right: *Anything we can actually do, we can afford.* Money was never the primary obstacle: *it was always cooperation.* And peace was the necessary precondi-tion for the worldwide, all-hands-on-deck, cooperative effort required to reach net zero before it literally destroyed the thin biome upon which all living species depended. Especially that resource-hungry one, Homo sapiens.

Not that every nation was a paragon of freedom—China continued engage in human rights abuses, even now—but every country had been brought into the Climate Club for two simple reasons: 1) everyone needed to control their carbon to have any chance of getting to net zero, and 2) it was economically disastrous not to be in the Club. That lesson had been learned by Russia even before the Climate Club was formed. Their ill-fated attempt at empire restoration with the invasion of Ukraine had resulted in economic devastation. For a generation, Russia was the object lesson of the cost of authoritarianism in the 21st Century. The world was too interconnected. Standing alone was death. Even creating a polar world, authoritarian vs. democratic, was insufficient to survival. The planet was a singular biome, and it was madness to think otherwise.

That didn't stop strongmen everywhere of dreaming of illiberal power.

It *did* stop them from posing any appreciable risk as nations scrambled to *not* be the target of the collective outrage of not only the world's most financially powerful countries, but the citizens and corporations who wielded their own financial might in favor of stability and peace. Even China, with their decidedly undemocratic governance, understood there was no path forward in economic isolation: their prosperity depended on peace and a rules-based international order as much as any country, regardless of how they ran things inside their borders.

Yet Miller was resurrecting the idea of kings and "natural order"? That was the language of autocrats, not to mention racism, patriarchy, and colonialism. There were wannabe fascists in every country, and their movements were always agitating to gain power, especially feeding off any setback in the race for net zero. But after flirtations with autocracy early in the century, the majority of the world's people considered "strong men" too dangerous to be allowed any measure of power. And yet, with this short speech, Miller had already sparked ambition in the hearts of his audience. Nitara could see it in the rapt attention of Minister LeBlanc and the others around them. Men who Miller had *carefully chosen,* and now she could see why: they harbored an unspoken resentment. Perhaps their ambitions were higher than their station. Perhaps they were secret members of their country's authoritarian movement, always fomenting unrest and trying to drag their countries backward. These people were *already* in significant positions of power within their respective countries, yet Miller was feeding their sense of grievance, that even *more* was due to them.

He would make them modern-day kings.

Every authoritarian's sizzling hot dream.

The chill in Nitara's stomach was the cold fear of realizing you're in a room full of sociopaths. Sociopaths who would soon have access to unlimited energy.

"So, you can see..." Miller was still going over the fine print of the terms and conditions for the auction. "It's fairly straight-forward. You'll have until midnight to discuss amongst yourselves. As I mentioned, zero contact with the outside world. You'll have time for verification later, and if the technology is not to your liking, you can certainly opt out." He gave a small, cold laugh. "I doubt any of you will make that choice. But for now, this choice is yours alone. Are you to be the leaders of this new world order? Then step up now. *Be bold.* And carefully consider your bids. What your country can reasonably muster. But bear in mind the $1 billion table stakes. Only the countries which could afford to sit at the table were invited here today."

Nitara scowled as the nature of the group became even more clear: the richest countries, the ones who could buy their way into the new era of unlimited free energy. Zahara was seething but keeping her lips tightly pressed. LeBlanc's eyes kept getting wider, his mouth dropping open. If he salivated over this opportunity any more literally, drool would drip to the floor.

"As I said, it will be a closed bid." Miller was winding this up. "There will be three tiers in the end. Well, a fourth tier for anyone who fails to bid at least table stakes. Renew Energy will be handling the contracts, distribution, and maintenance. America and Denmark, in appreciation for their early contributions, will automatically be first tier, along with the top third of bidders. Those countries will get the first round of production models for the device and a lower *fixed* licensing rate *in perpetuity*. Including any future upgrades on the technology. The ROI on that is substantial, so consider your bids carefully. Second and third tiers will have to wait their turn, with licensing rates that start higher and adjust over time. Again, the details are all in the terms and conditions."

He paused for a breath, and a smile spread across his face. "You have until midnight to submit your bids. There will be no outside contact until after the bidding is closed. In the meantime, you can caucus, strategize, inspect the EVEG—whatever you like. Starting..." He swiped up a timer and flicked it out to the crowd. "*Now.*"

The countdown clock showed up on Nitara's display, angry and red.

The crowd broke out into mayhem.

SEVEN

If CarbonCon had an evil twin in a mirror universe... it would be Miller's auction.

It was almost impossible to be heard over the chaos. People were panicked, yelling, gesturing wildly. LeBlanc had pulled Zahara and Nitara in close, so he could exuberantly shout his demands in their faces.

"Can he really do this?" LeBlanc directed that at Zahara.

Her shoulders hunched up. "He seems to think so."

LeBlanc flung his hand toward the stage. "This could be complete bullshit! How do we know this thing even works?" He was shouting in her face, but Zahara was focused on her display, scrolling through something, probably Ellis's white paper or Miller's terms and conditions.

"Well, if it *doesn't* work, it's not like he can hold you to your bid." Zahara stopped swiping. "Here. It says, *Bids due upon verification of the EVEG by an independent validation team of the bidder's choosing.*" She met LeBlanc's wild-eyed look. "That's your out. If it's all smoke and mirrors, it's just the cost of verification and, well, the embarrassment of being taken for a ride."

His jaw set. "Why would he make fools of us all? What's in it for him?"

"Nothing that I can see." But Zahara's face pinched in, and she slipped a glance to Nitara.

LeBlanc scowled but kept directing his ire at Zahara. "What are the details on this? There has to be something in the details... some catch..." He seemed... *confused.* Like he didn't even know where to start.

Nitara drew back slightly. Miller had *carefully chosen* men whose egos he thought he could manipulate. Men who had some grievance that would play into Miller's larger plan to re-establish the hierarchies of the past, with them at the top. Which was an obviously heinous idea and rolled back decades of progress. But it had been so long since that was the way of the world, she'd forgotten one reason it was so dysfunctional: the world *needed* people of competence in positions of power. The complexity of the world was insane. The problems immense, truly difficult problems with hard decisions, even for the most brilliant and good-hearted leaders. Restricting the people allowed at the table, as Miller had, by definition meant you weren't getting the best humanity had to offer.

Minister LeBlanc was *way* out of his depth.

Nitara glanced at the near mob frenzy around her. None of these people were the kind with the foresight, brainpower, and competence to forge a new path forward into a world with access to unlimited energy. They were driven by ego, not competence. *That's why they were chosen.*

Her earring cam was still recording, and she let it run.

Then she thought-commanded open a chat channel to

Zahara, who was intensely scanning her display, probably reading the terms and conditions in detail. LeBlanc was fuming and rubbing his face. Did the man not read?

Nitara sent a message to Zahara. *Your boss is an idiot.*

Zahara's scrolling was interrupted by a sideswipe to open Nitara's message. She checked to see if LeBlanc was watching, flashed a smirk at Nitara, then went back to looking at her display. She must have thought-enabled commands in her chip because Nitara didn't see her air-typing, yet a message came back. *Who do you think does all the work?*

All of this is a nightmare, Nitara replied.

Copy that. "From what I can see here," Zahara said, pulling LeBlanc out of his dark staring contest with the floor, "you can change your bid anytime up until the closing at midnight, after which point, it's locked in. Countries that bid high enough to be in the first tier pay per device delivered, and there's a separate contract for maintenance and upgrades, but the main perk is that you get fixed licensing fees forever. Well, indexed to in-country inflation rates, but otherwise, not adjustable."

"How much?" LeBlanc demanded.

"It's per-capita, but for Canada's 49 million people..." She tapped quickly, then looked to LeBlanc. "$10 billion Canadian per year."

"*What?*"

She hiked up her shoulders again. "It's less than Canada pays for energy now. And it's unlimited."

"But this is supposedly *free* energy!"

Zahara pressed her lips together, holding back.

LeBlanc snorted his disgust then rubbed the back of his neck. "It's not impossible. What else does it say?"

Zahara went back to her display.

Nitara was still doing the math on the "table stakes." At least $1B from the 100 richest nations—and she could see now it would be *much* higher from most, that was the whole point of the auction—and Miller's new company, Eternal Energy, would likely mint as an instant trillion-dollar enterprise. And that was just to get started. Licensing? Royalties? The total energy sector of the planet was only $5 trillion. But Miller was disrupting that, wasn't he? Creating free energy yet monetizing it to become the richest man on Earth. *In perpetuity.* Because there never would be a better deal than "free"—even if you had to pay a fee to get in on the deal.

How did you fight that? This "auction" was happening at midnight, which was less than eight hours away. Was it even *possible* to stop this?

Should they?

LeBlanc isn't wrong, Nitara messaged Zahara. *This is all messed up. The people. The cost. This isn't even Miller's IP.*

Zahara froze, dashed a look at Nitara, then dragged her gaze back to the document on her screen. *What do you fucking mean by that?*

Nitara hadn't read her in on everything. Obviously. *Ellis's research—his initial discoveries were all on Energy Island. It's IEC intellectual property.*

You mean every country in the world owns a piece of this?? Zahara gave up pretending to read and turned to Nitara with an incredulous look that said, *Why didn't you say so?* without bothering to message.

"Zahara!" LeBlanc was radically disturbed that she wasn't on-task. Or worse, that she might share with Nitara first. "What did you find?" he demanded.

Zahara gritted her teeth and turned back to him.

"There's a lot to look through. I was just splitting it up with Nitara."

"Oh." He leaned back a little. "All right. Be quick about it. We need to figure out how much to bid." He swiped up the display and appeared to look at the document for the first time.

"Yes, sir." Zahara's expression said she was restraining herself from violence. Given her history in the Corps, Nitara was sure LeBlanc would be out cold before he knew what hit him.

Instead, Zahara sent her a message. *What are we going to do?*

No idea. But we can't let this go forward.

It's a fucking disaster, Zahara agreed. *Miller's got these low-level bureaucrats thinking they'll be the next titans of the universe.*

And did you notice who's not here? Which countries are left out?

Global South? Maybe?

Table stakes are $1B. That means no small, struggling, or impoverished countries. Often the ones without major industries, which means they may only have strategic logistics or mineral resources.

That's Miller's fourth tier.

Exactly. His licensing scheme puts them in last place, assuring the rich countries will get richer, leaving the developing ones even more vulnerable to exploitation. He's reconstructing hierarchies we've spent decades deconstructing. We leveled the field precisely so we could all work together to get to net zero. He's undoing everything even as he promises to leap-frog to the end.

Zahara paused the fake scrolling and looked to her with wide eyes. *With unlimited energy... there's no more race.*

No more need for cooperation.

"Holy shit," Zahara let slip out. It was so quiet, it didn't attract LeBlanc's notice over the noise of the crowd, which was getting louder instead of quieting down.

Nitara nodded. Then thought-messaged, *Decades of peace and security. Energy independence for nearly every nation. The climate has ravaged everything, created hundreds of millions of refugees, been a boat anchor on every economy on Earth... and yet we've reaped the peace dividend of working together. The IEC and Climate Club accomplished that. Miller's scheme will undo it all.*

He's dragging us back to... I don't know what. But I do not want to live in a world where these guys are running the show.

Agreed. Nitara pressed her lips together and swiped up the document again. They paused their chat while they both scanned the thing in earnest.

This hierarchy of rich nations dictating terms to the poorer ones—the climate crisis had forced hard choices on the powerful. They had to beat back the nativist elements, those who wanted to subjugate people as well as the planet. That simply wouldn't work anymore. The Global North had to make good on monetary assistance to the Global South—it was necessary for them to modernize with only a fraction of the pollution the Global North had pumped into the sky during *their* modernization. Meanwhile, the Global North was shrinking—pandemics, wildfires, heat domes that wiped out people by the thousands, sometimes millions. Birth rate had cratered. The Global North needed *people,* and refugees from the soon-to-be-unlivable parts of the Earth needed homes. The only way the rich could sustain their standard of living—which largely depended on the poor being able to simply *live*—was to open the door to allow everyone into the Club. That guarantee of life, and a ticket to the benefits of modern living, was the only way to get the developing nations on board with emissions reduction. The Carbon Tax, a whole lot of forgivable loans, and a dozen other policies all orbited around that central premise.

And it worked. It was her life's work, facilitating this.

But Miller, Ellis, and their giant black egg of "free" energy were about to upend it all.

Yet for all the success in coming together, they were still losing the race. It hadn't been *fast enough.* Bringing the world's highly impoverished people up to a decent standard of living, the agreed-upon Global Standard that meant access to food, housing, healthcare, education, while simultaneously pulling back on fossil fuel usage had made the planet more energy-hungry every year. Clean energy build-outs barely kept pace. They'd achieved extraordinary things, but it hadn't been enough, not yet. And because of that, one tipping point after another had been reached, and the catastrophes were spreading wildly, unpredictably, more every year.

The world *needed* this ZPE device.

Was a return to human misery the price they would have to pay? Nitara refused to accept that. Miller's fever dreams of controlling the world's energy supply could *not* be the only way.

LeBlanc roused from his pained inspection of the terms document. "What's to keep people from just copying this egg thing?"

The question was pointed at Zahara, but Nitara answered. "International copyright law." At least, that was what Miller and Ellis would no doubt claim.

LeBlanc made a face, and she couldn't be sure if it was

her answer or simply the fact that she spoke. "That would stop literally no one."

Sadly, he was probably right. Besides, Miller had no actual claim to ownership, no matter what he said. But more than a legal claim, there was a moral claim. All that technology belonged to the citizens of the world, given that's who paid for it. Miller *shouldn't* be able to claim copyright, but even if he did, others would reverse engineer the technology. The stakes were simply too large.

"Miller's got safeguards built in." Zahara had delayed answering, apparently scouring the text, but she must have found what she was looking for.

"Like what?" LeBlanc seemed relieved he could ignore Nitara.

Zahara waved her hand, clipping a part of the document and sending it to them both. "This says the construction is fairly simple, but two things are highly proprietary: the calibration and the generation of the quasiparticles. Which, I only barely understand what that is, but the two of those things combined—the geometry and the particles—is the basic "engine" that pumps the thing down until it pops and makes a bunch of energy."

Zahara shrugged one shoulder, but it was a more cogent explanation than what Dr. Ellis had given. "Miller's also put in a kill switch," she said. "So, this super delicate geometry that has to be precisely calibrated? If you try to take it apart, it basically self-destructs. And Miller has a remote control where he can trigger the whole thing to melt. Which sounds super dangerous, but whatever. It's also run on some code that DARPA helped quantum encrypt, and any attempt to tamper with that *also* triggers the self-destruct. So, it's kind of a bomb. Plus, every year, you gotta pay your licensing fees to get the encryption key from Eternal Energy. If all that doesn't dissuade the hackers and pirates, Miller says any evidence of tampering invalidates your contract—which means no free energy for your entire country. He locks you out and burns your devices. *And* you'll be barred from ever having the upgraded versions, which, to be honest... if this is their first-to-market attempt, it's already damn impressive." She shook her head. "With access to all that energy at stake, are countries going to mess with reverse engineering? The payments aren't *that* high. I don't think even China would take that risk. Maybe one of the fourth-tier countries, since they're screwed anyway."

LeBlanc scowled at that. Nitara couldn't tell if he thought Canada would end up fourth tier, or he simply didn't like being reminded there were *losers* in Miller's scheme.

Zahara ignored him. "My guess is most countries will just pay the licensing fees—"

Shouts punctuated the general roar of the room. All three turned, as did the rest of the nearby representatives, to look at the commotion between them and the stage. Two men were going at it, their words escalating quickly to fists. Others backed away, clearing room for the fight. Two of Miller's private security pushed their way through the crowd, with more backups running from the periphery of the room. LeBlanc and Zahara were close enough that as the crowd thinned, they had front-row seats, with Nitara standing behind them.

One of the security goons pulled out a slap-tap. *What?* Nitara had seen some thuggish police use those against demonstrators, especially in her time working with desperate crowds of refugees. It was a shock weapon, and not a nice one. Military grade, not the kind you used on civilians who had actual rights against assault.

The guard flicked the slap-tap to extend it, then shoved it in the back of the closest combatant. He grunted and seized up, then fell twitching to the floor. The guard didn't even try to break the man's fall. The other man involved in the fight lurched back, eyes wide, away from the convulsing man. Nitara set her teeth and kept her objections locked down. *A taste of Miller's new world order,* was all she could think. The entire crowd immediately settled, appalled and unsure.

Miller strode into the empty space that had formed around the fallen man. The disgust on his face was clear but momentary. "Take him away." He waved at his security pair, as if the now-inert man—he'd stopped twitching—were trash to be taken out. Was the man even alive? Slap-taps were specifically banned by several international treaties for use with civilian crowd control, precisely because the shock was severe enough to kill in many cases.

Miller glared at the increasingly shocked crowd that simply watched as two of Miller's security men grabbed the man's arms and dragged him away.

To the crowd, which had belatedly started to voice its objections, Miller said, loudly, "Your invitation here is a *privilege.*" He almost spat the words. "You have a chance to make history, right here, *today.*" His eyes narrowed as he swept his gaze across the crowd. "If you can't handle it, you might as well leave right now. And as I've said before—" He stopped cold when his gaze fell on Nitara.

Oh, shit.

Miller's eyes trained on her like a missile lock. He continued, "Once you leave, there are no re-entries to the summit."

Nitara's heart lurched. She waited for Miller to resume whatever bombastic speech he had prepared, but his eyes just narrowed further.

"Excuse us!" Zahara said, her voice falsetto, breaking Miller's line of sight and shoving Nitara toward the back of the crowd.

"Where are you going?" LeBlanc demanded.

"Ladies room!" Zahara sang then kept hustling Nitara away.

"Thank you," she whispered as Zahara shoved a pathway through the crowd. She didn't know Zahara's plan, but whatever it was, Nitara had to disappear and lay low until this was over. She glanced at her display: midnight was still *hours* away.

They broke free of the crowd at the back of the room, but the security team at the door stepped in front of it, blocking them.

"Look," Zahara said, a little breathless. "Urgent ladies room business here, guys—"

"Director Nitara Desai of the International Energy Consortium's Office of International Agreements!" Miller's voice behind them was triumphant and terrifying.

Nitara turned to face him. "I'm afraid you've mistaken me for—"

He gave her a very unimpressed look.

LeBlanc came up behind Miller. "What is all this?" His eyes were wide, fearful.

Miller arched an eyebrow. "You didn't know? No, of course you didn't." He shook his head, dismissing LeBlanc.

"I had no idea!" LeBlanc said anyway. Nitara wasn't even sure if he even understood what he was disavowing.

Miller gestured to one of his security men to give him something. It took a moment for the man to comply, but he came up with a metal ring, too big to be a handcuff and glittering with electronic indicators.

Miller's smile came back. "I supposed it's flattering to have the Director of CarbonCon herself infiltrate my summit." He leaned in to false-whisper. "I'd want to be where the real action was, too." He eased back. "Can't let you stay, of course. And I can't exactly let you go. Not while the auction's underway." He held up the metal ring, and now that it was closer, Nitara recognized it: an ankle cuff, the kind you used for house arrest. Usually had a built-in damper to block chip function.

Miller smirked and handed her the cuff. "I'll let you do the honors."

She bit back her impulse to tell him to fuck off and do it himself. Instead, she bought herself some time by fussing with the cuff, heavy and cold in her hands, its electronic prison not yet enabled. As she bent down, she thought-commanded her earring cam to stop and filed the recording in her encrypted folder. With any luck, that would protect it from the cuff's interference. By the time she stood up again, Miller had activated it.

His expression had gone cold. "You can't stop this, Nitara. So don't bother to try."

"Why would I want to do that?" She met his stare. "You've certainly got everything under control." She smiled.

His eyes blazed. "Put her outside." When his thugs didn't instantly move, he wrenched away from his staring contest with her. "Do it!" he growled.

Their hands were on her, practically lifting her from the floor. Zahara's face was full of alarm, but she said nothing and made no move to stop them. LeBlanc seemed lost, per usual.

Nitara offered the security men no resistance.

But, by the time they shoved her out into the darkening storm, wind howling around the concrete bunkers of Miller's floating island...

She almost wished she had.

EIGHT

She was freezing to death.

Huddled against the concrete wall, sheltered slightly from the wind, her arms pulled inside her jacket to conserve body heat. Still, she was going to die from the North Sea's bitter nighttime cold. It didn't seem possible—it was *July*—but the wind extracted heat from her body and swept it out into the darkness. She heard the torrent, waves crashing. She felt the dampness soak her, spray flying in her face and seeping through her clothes. But she couldn't see any features in the ocean's vast seething blackness. Stars marked where the sky began, the Milky Way standing on end, a vertical slash across the night, but the invisible waves of the sea swallowed all reflections, even the red beacon atop the floating island's comm tower.

Nitara resisted the urge to power-on her chip just to check the time. It had been hours, and it didn't matter. She needed to conserve energy in her base station. If nothing else, she wanted that recording of Miller's summit to be recovered along with her body. Who knew how he would present that monstrous gathering to the world, but his own words in that room were damning. He wouldn't want that revealed.

That's why he'd sent her out to die.

A full-body shiver rattled her brain and shook loose that train of thought. She could feel it leaving her to tumble down into the sea. She blinked, forgetting why she should care. *Mental confusion.* It was a sign of hypothermia. She untucked her hands from their safe harbor in her armpits and snaked them out of her jacket to vigorously rub her cheeks. The cold nipped at her fingers, but her face was numb and damp. She fumbled with the jacket again, tucking her face into its warmth.

How many more hours did she have? At midnight, with the bidding complete, would the doors be thrown open? Would Miller allow her back in? Or would the delegates, all high on their visions of power and wealth, retire to their bunks, waiting until the morning to venture out into the world with their great news?

By morning, she would be dead.

She went over what she knew, just to keep alert. She'd already checked for any waiting ships at the dock, craft of any kind that might spell escape. But they were gone, of course. Next, she'd scoured the outside of the concrete compound for any shelter or accessible structures—even a tool shed left unlocked—but there was nothing. It had a certain logic: why keep things outside the concrete bunker when the North Sea would just snatch them away? She reminded herself she had settled on this spot on the leeward side of the island, near the entrance, because it was as sheltered as any, and if someone *did* come looking for her, she wanted them to find her. Soon. Preferably now. Second choice: before she died. Third choice: after she died but before the North Sea swept up and claimed her.

Every minute that ticked by seemed to say, *You blew it.*

You waited too long. You should have told Matti how you felt, you should have made it legal, and you should have quit the unwinnable race while you were behind.

She physically shook herself inside her barely warm cocoon, breathing warmish air across her clasped hands. She didn't want her last thoughts to be so ridiculously self-pitying. She had done the best she could. She was here now because that seemed the only way to stop a catastrophe. That's what she did, all day, every day. Stop disasters before they happened, so the world's people could reap that peace dividend, living their lives, loving their loved ones, and bringing their talents into the world. That was *her* talent. Negotiating agreements, easing points of conflict, using international treaties to reduce suffering.

She couldn't regret doing the only thing she'd ever been good at.

The air inside her jacket was getting stuffy, suffocating her with her own CO_2. But the outside was so bitingly cold, and her face was still numb. She stayed buried in the warmth. Matti would laugh if she saw Nitara all tucked up, trying to survive. Well, first, she would parachute out of a helicopter into the storm to save her and *then* she would laugh that Nitara had got herself tossed out of the only shelter for 50 miles. Her father would frown in that way he always did. *Did you not think about the shoelaces?* His voice was hazy, thick with that Mumbai accent he held onto, but the pain from that long-ago rebuke was still sharp—not from tripping but from the indictment for not planning ahead. Even at eight, she should have foreseen the possible disaster of untied laces. It was the way he thought, and she learned early to think the same, if only to avoid that frown. Her mother would come to her defense, in that brightly modern way, always up on the latest slang. *Chillax, Pranav! She'll figure it out.* Nitara did. She always double-checked her laces after that, especially in the Pandemic Corps. The world had moved on to Velcro, but not the services. Shoelaces were durable, military-grade, unlikely to fail if you tied them right. Reliable. Nitara appreciated that in a thing. And a person. The kind of person she tried to be, if only to avoid the pain of failure clawing her from the inside. Failure got others hurt. It tasted of smoke and chemicals. It sounded like the crackle of fire and screams. *When did you understand there was a problem with the sourcing of the solar tents?* Dress uniforms in the heat, sticky and stiff, demanding an answer. But they already knew as well as she. *Too late, too late, too late... Matti.* She was too late for Matti. Couldn't stop. Couldn't save. Couldn't say the words that mattered. They were thick in her mouth and her throat. Choking her because she never let them get spoken. *So hard to breathe—*

"Nitara!"

Her body twitched, a reflex, jostling the jacket from her face. The blast of cold pinched it, her eyes slitting against the wind and light. Why was there a blinding whiteness hovering over her?

"Holy shit," the light said, then it went out.

Then a shroud fell over her, blocking the unblinking stars. Nitara jerked back, but only managed to bang her head against the concrete wall. Her arms were trapped inside her jacket, her whole body too stiff and numb to do anything.

"I got here as fast as I could. *Christ*, it's cold out here. When the fuck did that happen?"

She heard the words, but they were detached from meaning. The voice was close, under the shroud, exhaling warm air on Nitara's face as she slowly blinked her way back to comprehension. Everything was shaking: her teeth, shivers running races around her body, her hands cramped and rattling against each other under her jacket.

She didn't try to speak.

Hands rubbed her arms, over her jacket, and it hurt, every nerve stabbing her, but she didn't protest. A tiny voice in the back of her mind said, *This is help.*

She let it happen.

After a short time, the rubbing stopped and the light came back, this time pointed down, so the reflection bounced all around the blanket she was now huddled under.

With Zahara.

Nitara blinked. Several times.

"Let me take a look at you." Zahara pressed warm fingers to Nitara's cheek. It hurt, even more than the rubbing on her arms, but she leaned into it, eyes falling half mask. "Hey, no sleeping!"

Nitara snapped her eyes open again.

"*Shit.* You're so cold. I took too long. *Fuck.* I was waiting for the bids to be submitted. I figured they'd open the doors or lower the gateway block or something, but then they didn't, and I had to scramble to get a few things and find a way to—" She cut off, her brows furrowing. "Are you okay?"

Zahara's words floated in a soup Nitara could only poke at. She nodded, but that made her dizzy. She suddenly plowed face-first into Zahara.

"Whoa!" Zahara grabbed her and held her upright, steady.

Nitara shook her head, but in a small motion, enough to clear the dizziness without pitching her over. "Mmm'k."

"The hell you are." Zahara cursed again then peeled off her jacket. It was a struggle to get Nitara's off—everything hurt—but they did, then Zahara spooned up behind her, a buffer against the concrete wall, her bare arms now in skin-to-skin contact. With the jackets layered on top and the blanket draped over that, warmth finally infused Nitara's body.

Her mind started to clear, even if her body was still shaking. "It's-s good."

"This fucking *sucks.*" Zahara folded their collective four arms across Nitara's chest, slowly rubbing life back into the length of them, down to her hands. "I should have broken out sooner."

"Soon enough." Before she froze to death. Hard to come back from that. Anything else is a win. "Tell m-me." She'd have to leave the talking to Zahara for a minute.

"I had to find someone with survival gear." Zahara's tone was calmer now, maybe because she could feel the heat building as well. "Not easy, but some boy scout from Brazil was using his head and had packed a military-grade field blanket. Made of a synthetic material that's rated for Antarctic conditions. I think he was freaked about coming to the North Sea. Anyway, I traded for it and then—"

"What?"

"What do you mean, *what?* I'm telling the story here—"

"What did you trade?" Her teeth had stopped chattering.

"That's for me to know, and you to mind your business."

She shifted to feel Nitara's legs, which were folded on the concrete. "How are your feet? Frostbite?"

"Don't think so."

"Let's get the blanket underneath."

That was an awkward twenty seconds of shifting around, letting in more of the cold and damp, but then they settled, a layer of thermal blanket between them and the ground. Zahara talked her into taking off a boot to check her feet, but Nitara's fingers were still useless. Zahara managed to unlace it and pull her foot out. Her hands were painfully warm on Nitara's bare feet, but after a moment, Zahara declared her frostbite-free.

"Good thing I got out here when I did." Zahara slid her sock back on. "That was too damn close."

Nitara took over getting her foot back into her boot. Her hands weren't as stiff anymore. "You stayed for the bids? How did that go?"

"I thought Miller would announce the winners right away, but he blasted some bullshit about having to inspect the bids to make sure they were valid. I think he's doing some back-room negotiations to drive the bids up. You know each of the delegates, like LeBlanc, are the official signatories? Like *they* are written into the contract with Renew and Eternal Energy."

"What?" Her foot finally popped back into the boot. She tried to lace it but gave up. Not there yet.

"I know, right? Crazy. But it's all part of Miller's plan. LeBlanc makes the bid, but he's also explicitly written into the contract: if Canada accepts, then he's appointed the EVEG Czar of Canada, or whatever. *And he gets a share.* Guaranteed income for life. He gets to appoint the next czar, and so on. Miller's creating a dynasty inside every country that wants access to his free energy technology.

Canada either accepts the terms to get into whatever tier LeBlanc's bid lands in—first, second, or third—or they reject it, because what the fuck kind of contract is that? And then they automatically get remanded to fourth tier. And no one wants to be fourth-tier because it's not clear whether fourth-tier countries will *ever* get the tech."

Nitara twisted to look over her shoulder. "Why would he do that?"

"Artificial scarcity?" Even in the low light from Zahara's base station, Nitara could see she was livid. "This is all about creating hierarchies and wealth for the men in that room."

"Miller at the top."

"There's no way he won't be a trillionaire. *Mega* trillionaire. Probably overnight." Zahara growled. "I don't know how he thinks he's going to get around the exclusion."

Nitara nodded, weary, but some of her strength was coming back. "He's been planning this for years." Miller must have some scheme, but she couldn't imagine what. Enforcement of the exclusion was tight. The 2023 Global Minimum Tax kept profits from moving to avoid taxation. Then various dark money laws were passed in previously lax countries—US, UK, and even Switzerland—followed by a growing anti-monopoly movement. Next came the Trillionaire Exclusion Tax in the 30s, a worldwide revolt at the arrival of the first trillionaire. By then, *Billionaires Acting Badly* had become a worldwide meme. It wasn't just the mega-yachts, joy rides to space, and transparent charity-washing. The billionaire class had started openly siding with ecofascist movements that allowed them to operate above the law, while rolling back human rights for most people and burning a hundred times more carbon than average.

The world simply had enough. And the Climate Club had shown the power of coordinated action, which they used in 2033 to declare a global 99% tax rate on individual wealth over a trillion dollars. Effectively confiscating that level of wealth—and not indexed for inflation, which was the type of wonkery Nitara truly appreciated—billionaires soon realized there was a finish line. *Congratulations, you won capitalism! Now, for the safety of everyone, you need to be constrained against turning into a sociopath with unlimited power.* The wealthy still jockeyed to stay right under the line—or intentionally went over it and made dramatic speeches about their "donations" to the betterment of humanity through taxation—but mostly, it ended the society-destroying upward spiral of wealth accumulation. And funded an unprecedented alleviation of poverty and investment in human education and empowerment the world over.

Miller's scheme was a transparent violation of that upper limit.

Your nation can have unlimited energy... just sign here to allow a single man to shatter the monetary-power limit that keeps the world in balance.

She couldn't imagine a man like Miller going to all this trouble just to trigger the exclusion and lose everything above the cap.

Nitara was warm enough now, she felt she could untangle from Zahara and the gift of her body heat. "Did Miller say anything about the exclusion?" She scooted around so she was facing Zahara under their shroud against the elements.

"No mention of it," Zahara said. "You feeling better?"

She nodded. "What's our plan?"

"Well, now that you're not *dying* on me..." Zahara

fussed with the jacket draped over her head and pulled a tool from a pocket. It glinted silver. "Let's get that ankle cuff off."

Nitara leaned back as Zahara bent over her leg with the metal ring that was blocking her connection to the rest of the world. *Including Matti.* Zahara dug at the cuff with the tool. Nitara braced for some cutting action.

"How are you—" But her view was suddenly swarmed with error messages, the kind chips threw off when trying to reboot. Nitara hastily swiped, trying to clear them out to get a real signal.

"Excellent." Zahara grinned. "My hacking skills are rusty but apparently functional." She dug around at her own ankle cuff next.

The string of messages from Matti was *hundreds* long. Nitara quickly scrolled to the end.

Goddamn it, Nitara, I'll send them in, if you don't respond.

Wait, what?

She scrolled back.

"Yes!" cheered Zahara, apparently disabling her own cuff. She swiped at the air while Nitara tried to rapid skim the messages from Matti. One stopped her cold.

FV Winter Queen ETA 1 am local time.

"What time is it?" Nitara asked, then remembered she could look, now that her chip was connected again. *1:15 am*

"Holy shit."

"What—"

Nitara clawed her way out of the jacket and the field blanket draped over her head. The darkness swallowed everything, and the concrete building blocked her view of the dock. She scrambled up, her untied boot slipping around her foot and tangling with the blanket below her. She nearly went down. *Shoelaces.* Goddammit.

"What the fuck? Nitara!" Zahara clutched the blanket to keep it from blowing away.

Slow down. Think. "There's a boat coming. For us." She needed to do five things at once, but missing that boat was not an option. And having Matti send in a squad of Pandemic Corps buddies—or worse, IEC security—would be a diplomatic disaster. An unnecessary point of conflict in a situation already spinning out of control.

She flicked open a channel to Matti. "Are you there—"

"Oh My God, where have you *been?*" Matti's fear and fury sliced her with guilt.

Nitara tossed that useless emotion into the wind-swept sea. "Matti. Listen. Did you send anyone in after me?" She'd managed to work her way to standing, boots firmly rooted to the concrete, the cold of the wind sluicing away what little warmth her body had acquired.

"No. I haven't." Matti's tone had matched Nitara's serious one, the panic parked on a shelf like any good member of the Corps knew how to do in an emergency.

"Good. Keep everyone on board. I'll be right there."

"Copy that." The debriefing about this entire situation and all that had transpired would come later. Matti knew better than to ask right now.

Nitara knelt down to lace up her boot. "I'm going to dump a video file to our secure folder. Right now. That has to get off this island, even before I do. Understood?"

"Copy that." Matti's voice had a new string of tension in it.

Nitara stood, swiped up the file that recorded all of Miller's secretive conference, and started the upload. Zahara handed her the jacket she'd recklessly tossed aside and waited for her to fight the wind to put it on. It wasn't much to fend off the cold, but she only had to make it a hundred yards to the dock. Assuming Fishing Vessel Winter Queen had actually returned for them. She tilted her head for Zahara to follow.

"I've been meaning to tell you," Nitara said lightly, not to Zahara, but to Matti on the open channel, "how much I sincerely appreciate your utter conviction that I would screw this up and need rescuing."

"Do you want to know what I had to do to get the Winter Queen to come back for you?" Matti wasn't pissed, but there was a warning in that.

"Not yet."

Nitara rounded the corner and blinked fast against the wind... but FV Winter Queen was there, gangplank lowered, at least a dozen dark-clothed figures hunkered on the dock. Even from the building, Nitara could see the bulky outline of their body armor and the long guns slung over their shoulders. "Holy shit, Matti."

"I wasn't the only one concerned." Matti's defensiveness made Nitara smile.

"That is *not* Pandemic Corps," Zahara said, worry in her voice. "Are we sure these are friendlies?"

"We're sure." Nitara pressed forward against the wind, watching her step, not entirely trusting her body, which was still waking up from nearly freezing to death.

They were halfway down the dock when a splash of light lit up the Winter Queen. Behind them, the door to Miller's conference had swung open and several of his security team spilled out. Miller was a half-step behind.

He pointed at them and shouted something snatched away by the wind.

"No time for slow." Zahara locked arms with Nitara and

dragged her toward the boat. Nitara was afraid they'd both go down. Matti's troops went on high alert and started toward them.

"Stand down!" Nitara shouted, not to them, but to Matti. "Tell them *no shooting*, Matti!" She didn't respond, and the troops kept coming, enveloping her and Zahara in a brigade of bodies before Miller's men could reach them.

They hustled them up the ramp to the boat.

Nitara caught one last glimpse of the island.

Miller stood at the door, staring death at her.

NINE

"How much longer is this going to take?" Nitara shouldn't harass the doctor, especially given Dr. Yousif was a highly regarded Sudanese physician doing her a favor by serving as the concierge doctor during CarbonCon. Delegates liked to think they were receiving premium healthcare services, especially when they traveled halfway across the world to attend.

Which she had just done, completing a harrowing 72-hour round-trip to Miller's floating conference in the North Sea. Her head had no concept of time, her stomach was in full rebellion at the thought of food, and her extremities felt like they couldn't get entirely warm. The electrodes Dr. Yousif had placed on her chest felt strangely cool, like they were sucking heat out of her. She repressed a shiver.

"I understand you have important work to return to," the good doctor said, but he was patronizing her as he monitored the EKG scan while tapping her blood samples into several different analyzers. "But I am under strict orders not to release you until I've completed my examination." He waggled a long finger without looking at her. "And only if you are recovered from your ordeal."

"Orders?" Nitara gave him a pinched look.

"Yes." His beard was neatly trimmed, dark curls on deeply brown skin. "The highest authority. One you would be wise not to question." A smile tugged at the corner of his mouth as he assiduously avoided her pointed gaze.

"It's Matti, isn't it?"

"Yes." His smile broke out as he turned to her. "She was insistent."

Nitara sighed. Matti had arranged a doctor in Denmark for when the FV Winter Queen had arrived in the dead of night. Then she'd insisted Nitara sleep on the flight back, despite the urgency of the entire situation. Nitara fought that but then succumbed to her own fatigue. The moment she hit the ground in LA, she was ready to meet with the team and strategize their plan. Instead, Matti had her driver deliver her straight to Dr. Yousif's medical suite inside CarbonCon's quarantine perimeter. She could hardly object. The WSO's Level Two alert was still in effect. Dr. Yousif had administered a battery of viral-detection tests, and those were necessary to clear her to enter the building, but that didn't explain the thorough head-to-toes exam, in addition to what seemed like dozens of other tests.

This was all Matti's doing.

Nitara *was* exhausted, but she was also *fine.* And she had a Category 5 political storm to fight. She needed five cups of coffee, her best staffers, and a moment to think when she wasn't hustling across the globe or being prodded by Dr. Yousif's strong-but-cold fingers. He seemed especially concerned about the lymph nodes in her neck.

"No symptoms you want to tell me about?" He lifted her chin with one finger and peered seriously into her eyes.

"No headaches, confusion, memory loss? Low energy? Unexplained shivering?"

"My symptoms are impatience and general surliness. But I think that's explained by not yet being cleared to work." She felt desiccated and achy, but that was normal jet lag.

His smile returned. "Your friend said you would be a difficult patient."

"That's not a medical diagnosis."

"You might be surprised." But he was teasing, and she was irrationally annoyed by it.

Your friend. It bothered her more than it should, the looseness of that term. Dr. Yousif said it in a way that allowed any kind of relationship under that umbrella, opening the door for her to explain, which she absolutely was not inclined to do. She just wanted to get to work. And to *see* Matti. Somehow, in the chaos, she had to make time, and privacy, to talk about where they stood. Exactly what was under the umbrella.

"You don't have any presenting infections."

"So, I can go?"

He was peering over his instruments now. "You can remove the electrodes. I'm waiting for a few more results."

"*Dr. Yousif.*"

He held up a finger to her, tapping at the displays with his other hand.

She let out a long low breath that she reined in just short of a growl. *Fine.* She could work from here. But as soon as she swiped up her display, a news feed blared out the worst was already happening. And her messages were on fire.

Breaking News: Energy entrepreneur announces revolutionary new energy source! Miller's picture showed a handsome man with intelligent eyes, youthful-looking but with enough seriousness to plausibly be a "revolutionary energy entrepreneur" in the public's eye. The image showed him speaking… somewhere. Not the clandestine conference. It was a staged photo designed to not appear staged and attractive enough for the press. It was everywhere, all over the news, along with Ellis and his crazy hair, playing the part of the mad scientist in the background.

Top Secret conference reveals world-changing energy technology!

Is Zero-Point Energy Real: Inside the Mad Science and the Man Who Made It Work

Will ZPE Save the World?

D-10 has no comment on whether the race for net zero can be won with ZPE.

"Oh, no." A quick scan of her messages showed one from her boss, the IEC's Deputy Executive Director for International Agreements. *What the hell? Nitara! I need you in my office as soon as you're cleared.* "Shit shit shit."

"What is it?" Dr. Yousif's attention was pulled from his test results.

She swiped her messages away. "I've changed my mind. I'm going to need a least a few more hours of rest. Doctor-mandated. Can you do that for me?" Her chest was tight. She tried not to obviously labor at breathing.

Dr. Yousif arched an eyebrow. "You are not going to rest."

"No." She slid off the exam table. The aches in her body filed a complaint, which she dismissed. "But I really need a chance to meet with my team before my boss hauls me into his office and murders me."

He shook his head but swiped up his own display. "You're dehydrated, cortisol high, blood pressure far above baseline, even for your medical history, and I suspect that isn't coming down anytime soon. But your cardiac function is normal, kidneys and liver check out. I can prescribe some electrolytes and a mandatory two-hour rest period for observation before return to normal duties."

"Thank you."

He held up that solitary finger again. *"If* you promise to return to this office in precisely two hours. If your blood pressure does not come down, Ms. Desai, we will need to take some precautionary steps. You're going to give yourself a stroke. Or a heart attack. I want to see you in two hours. No more. Agreed?"

"Two hours. Promise."

"All right. I will make a note in your conference passport—"

But she was already heading out the door.

As she rushed through security, flicking her passport credentials at them without even slowing down, she thought-commanded a message to Matti. *Gather everyone. My office. Five minutes.*

She had to go through CarbonCon to reach her office, and it was a frenzied gauntlet. Everything was in chaos, the meeting rooms were an unruly mess with people huddled, sharing displays and either whispering or shouting. She hoped her rumpled travel clothes would let her slip through unnoticed, but several people whipped their heads her way as she passed, two calling out her name.

She kept her gaze down and didn't stop. Any faster and she'd be running, and that would only attract more attention. Plus, her coordination was shit. Her pulse pounded in her temples as she broke free of the conference crowds and lurched into a run to the elevator.

She had a moment to catch her breath while waiting for it to arrive.

She was head of the conference, but her actual job—Director of IEC's Office of Multilateral Funds and International Agreements—was 100% why the Deputy Exec wanted to see her. The IEC was a UN specialized agency, like the WSO, but instead of being chartered to bring all the science together to combat climate-fueled pandemics and vaccines, coordinating the world's response to the endless parade of viruses and pathogens, the IEC was the mini-UN of energy. The Executive Director reported straight to the UN General Assembly, but the IEC Directors were powerful in their own right. The two Deputy Executive Directors oversaw the two major divisions, one focused on operations and technology, the other on legal matters. Matti was in the Office of Energy Technology, so any new energy tech would seem to fall under operations, but in reality, the world ran on money and the law, and that was Nitara's division. She literally ran the Office of Multilateral Funds (money) and International Agreements (the law).

Which was why Nitara's boss was losing his mind over Miller's announcement.

Matti had given Nitara a heads-up on the way back. When her communications had cut out, Matti had been forced to go to *both* their bosses to formulate a rescue plan. Then the Deputy Execs had brought in the Exec Director himself to commandeer some special-ops IEC security stationed in Denmark. Matti said they'd been pulled from standby on a mission to extricate a high-level refugee from Russia.

Nitara had left her boss, Matti's boss, *and* the Exec Director of the IEC twisting in the wind with no information, forced to call up special forces to rescue her from a world-changing energy conference *they knew nothing about...* and which shook the world news cycle less than 12 hours later.

It was hard to screw up at that level, but Nitara had managed it. She might be looking for a new job by the end of day.

For the moment, she had to solve the problem. The Deputy Execs would forgive everything if she had a plan. *Forgive* might be too strong a word. She might avoid getting fired. More importantly, they could focus on the actual crisis, which was almost too large to fully comprehend—and she was sure they didn't—and the recriminations and fallout could wait until after they'd averted disaster.

That's all she cared about, anyway.

She needed to have a plan *hours* ago, but as she barreled into her office, she was starting at zero. Which would have to do. *Always start where you are.* Her dad's quippy quotes applied more often than she liked.

Her office was jammed with bodies.

At least a dozen: Governor Kipo'mo, Dr. Akemi Sato, Sherri-the-intern, Matti and two of her staff, Milly and Umberto, plus a half dozen people Nitara didn't know, several huddled and syncing displays. Zahara had stayed behind in Denmark in case a return to Miller's North Sea wind farm island was necessary. Nitara's assistant Ian had been out on paternity leave for a few months now, and Matti had kept the need-to-know list small.

Except everything was splashed on the news now.

Matti interrupted herself, mid-gesture to the group, and turned to Nitara as she closed the door. "I'm assuming Dr. Yousif cleared you?" There was an entire conversation in that question, half berating comments about Nitara diving back into work after the near-miss death-by-North-Sea and half pressure-cooker-level stress about the fallout just getting started.

The unspoken concern melted some of the tension in Nitara's shoulders. "I bribed him to let me go."

Several awkward glances zipped around the room.

"That's *not* coming out of OET's budget." The Office of Energy Technology, where Matti and her staff worked.

"You're over budget anyway." Nitara smiled. "IEC security doesn't come cheap."

The tension diffused a bit as everyone caught that they were joking.

Nitara worked her way into the room, to her desk, where Matti stood, and briefly embraced her. Matti hugged her hard, the way she usually did, then almost roughly pushed back. "You *owe* me." She waved her hand, encompassing all of Nitara's person, bedraggled sea-faring clothes and all. "And I'm not okay with any of this. For the record."

"Noted." It was so good to see her.

But the tension was back, everyone holding their breath while she and Matti worked this out. Although this was nowhere near the conversation they needed to have. *Later.*

Nitara pulled in a *Let's Get to Work* breath. "All right, bring me in." She scanned the room again. The unknowns were no-doubt safe, from a security standpoint, which they would still need—whatever plan they conjured, Miller needed to be caught unaware.

"You know most of the team." Matti gestured to a striking young Latina woman. "This is Lucía Ramirez, power engineer at Power Island One, currently on loan to us from USEC. She's also the first to uncover Miller's work on the ZPE."

Nitara recognized her from Akemi's data drive. The answer to stopping Miller might still be buried there.

"This is Gwen, on loan from USEC data operations," Matti continued, nodding to a slim white woman with an *Angry Hats* t-shirt. (Band? Brand? Hard to tell.) "She helped lock Miller out when he was hacking the LA Basin grid, but more relevant to our pressing problem today, she's been helping Dr. Sato gather data on Ellis's experiments with the ZPE device."

"How much do we know about how it works?" Nitara vaguely addressed that to everyone in the room, then keyed in on Sato. "Akemi, can you build one?"

His eyebrows shot up, and he cleared his throat. "No."

Nitara tried to trap her impatience in her chest. "No, as in you'd need some funds and a tech crew, or no, it's technically not possible."

"We have schematics," Akemi explained. "Not impossible, but not even close to simple."

"Our bad guys are paranoid but also arrogant," the woman named Gwen spoke up. "They air gapped their prototype lab, thinking that would keep the data secure, and they take the data drive with them daily, but they're not encrypting. Which means our bug has grabbed everything. Still running, by the way. Whatever they have, we have."

"So, the device at the conference was a duplicate. Or at least a convincing facsimile." Nitara's head was pounding again. If they'd already built two, how fast could they build more? "Do they know we're spying on them?"

"Not yet." Gwen flicked a look to Akemi.

"I've reviewed your video of the demo," Akemi said. "The ZPE machine at the conference does appear to be a functioning duplicate of the one we're monitoring. We have drawings for everything, including specifications for the manifolds, which appear to be critical for creating the local disturbance in the quantum equilibrium. That's how Ellis's quasiparticles tap into the zero-point energy: a local suppression of ZPE that cracks open the universe and extracts energy."

"If we have the drawings, why can't we just build it?" Nitara assumed there was a good reason, she was just prompting for the rest of Akemi's doubts.

"Even with the drawings," he said, "you would need a team of engineers and physicists and an unknown amount of time to make it actually work. Ellis spent a decade developing this, and he has a sophisticated understanding of the underlying physics, which we only have guesses about, at present. As far as we can tell, he just recently had his breakthrough. It appears the fine-tuning on this is extremely difficult. In addition, there's the auto-destruct built in, although it's unclear exactly how."

Nitara rubbed her temple, trying to ease the throbbing. "The kill switch." She looked to Matti. Everyone should have copies of the terms and conditions for the auction and everything else she uploaded. "Zahara said the self-destruct was tied to some DARPA-created, quantum-encrypted code." To Akemi, she asked, "Do you have copies of that?"

"Yes," he replied, "but that's the one thing that's encrypted. Physical keys required."

"Okay." Nitara folded her arms to keep from rubbing at her head. "If we can't stop him with the tech, then maybe money or the law."

"He'll try to circumvent the trillionaire exclusion," Matti said. "I've got someone working on how to stop that."

"Do we have a copy of Miller's actual contract?" Nitara asked.

"Zahara's working on that." Matti shook her head. "Her

status is unclear. LeBlanc put her on some kind of unofficial suspension for leaving the island with us, but it turns out he can't do his job without her."

Nitara almost laughed, but her head was hurting too much. "Definitely keep working that. Maybe there's something in there we can use against Miller. These contracts can't possibly be legal, although I doubt that will stop countries from signing on, if they think it will benefit them. The problem is there's nothing to stop them. No penalty."

"*No penalty?*" Gwen was aghast. "You mean other than bringing back the era when billionaires ruled everything? He's going to undo every scrap of progress from the last thirty years, all in pursuit of being the Richest Asshole on the Planet, no matter who gets ground into the dirt. *Fuck that.*"

Lucía put a hand on Gwen's arm, but she shrugged it off. To Nitara, Lucía said, "Whatever bad thing you think will happen by stopping Miller, it will be ten times worse if we don't stop him. You don't know him like we do."

"The man put me outside to die, so I have a good handle on the possibilities." She meant it as a joke, but it didn't land. Everyone was too tense, including her. She softened it by unlocking her arms and putting up her hands. "Don't worry, I know his *type*. We're fighting this, all the way to the end. We can't afford to go back to men like Miller running the world. We just have to figure out how to stop him. That's why I have you smart people."

Gwen and Lucía seemed mollified but didn't add anything.

"We're going to work every angle," Matti affirmed. "On your video of the conference, Miller says Ellis was 'shut down' on Energy Island. That no one saw the future of his technology. We can use that recording in international court to show the IEC has copyright claim on the ZPE. It belongs to the world, not Miller, no matter what he thinks."

"You're right about the law," Nitara said, even if they would still need political buy-in for countries to abide by the court's decision. But Energy Island wasn't created only as a technology incubator—universal access was the entire point. "The spirit and the letter of the Energy Island agreements are meant to circumvent this exact problem: some individual or corporation having a lock on world-changing energy solutions. Miller thinks he's done an end-run by keeping this secret for a decade and developing the technology with private funds."

"And stealing energy from the grid!" Gwen was still pissed.

"And destroying home batteries," Lucía added. "Also: he tried to kill us."

Nitara didn't want to brush that aside, but it wasn't helping them in this moment. "And yet none of that will matter if we can't enforce copyright."

"Why don't you just use the power of the IEC?" Governor Kipo'mo asked, blunt as usual. "That's why we brought this to you. Get the D-10 involved."

"They're already involved, unfortunately." Nitara grimaced. She needed something solid to take to her boss and this was not coming together. "Miller is an absolute bastard, but he understands international politics. That's why he held the conference. *In secret.* Before revealing the ZPE to the world. He's already hooked every D-10 country —and a whole lot more—with a contract for unlimited energy, putting the worst power-hungry, second-rate wannabe politicians directly in charge and personally benefitting from this massive transfer of wealth." She leaned against her desk, which was reassuringly solid under her. She wasn't dizzy—it was unsettling as hell to think about the dark future unfurling in front of them. "The IEC has a strong position with regard to copyright on the technology breakthrough, but that quickly gets into a gray area with the device itself. It's specific enough to be plausible for copyright separate from the initial physics experiments, that is if you ignore all established precedent and intent with technology coming out of the Power Islands. However, the fact that Miller is already writing contracts when he hasn't filed for copyright on the device..." Nitara looked to Matti for confirmation, and she nodded. "...means he doesn't want us digging up the past. So that's still an option. But they've *effectively* got copyright because, if we can't build one *even with the drawings*, no one else has a hope of reverse engineering it." To Akemi, she said, "Keep working on that. See if you can find a way around the kill switch."

He didn't look too excited about that.

Nitara sighed. "The way Miller is setting this up will destabilize international energy markets. Which is to say, he's destabilizing the entire world." A wave of hopelessness surged up and tempted her. That was a luxury she couldn't afford. But was it even possible to convince the world *not* to access world-saving technology? Did that even make sense? There was zero chance at this point of constructing something like the Climate Club, wielding the weapon of financial power to keep countries from agreeing to Miller's terms. It was too attractive. Even as it destabilized the entire world order. Even if she could convince the D-10 it was in their best interests to resist Miller's tempting offer and enforce penalties against those who signed onto his contracts, it would be a return to the petrostate wars—famine, inflation—and no one would sign up for that. "I need ideas, people.

DARPA is involved. The U.S. is in this somehow. Maybe we can use them."

"Renew Energy is a multinational corporation," Governor Kipo'mo said. "Maybe we can shame them about this. They're Miller's connection to power, literal and figurative."

"They're all-in, as far as I can tell." Nitara's head swam a little. Maybe she was a little dizzy. *Dehydrated.* She motioned for one of Matti's people to hand her some water from the corner dispenser.

"We need to get our hands on those contracts," Matti said. "I'll nudge Zahara again."

Nitara nodded between sips. "That would definitely help."

"Is this thing even safe?" Lucía's question riveted the entire group. "It sliced my turtle-bot in half. Dismembered a massive underwater power structure. And killed at least two people in Palm Springs. How do we know this thing won't just randomly kill people?"

No one said anything for a moment.

Akemi cleared his throat. "We also don't know the long-term — or even short-term — consequences of extracting what's likely dark energy from the background levels of the universe."

"Okay, this is good." Nitara gestured with her glass to both of them. "I need documentation about the dangers. Not sure how we'll use it, but get me data." An angry red alert buzzed on Nitara's display. She'd muted everything except the Deputy Exec's office. Nitara swiped it up, to make sure. *GET YOUR ASS IN MY OFFICE.* Nitara would not have bet Deputy Executive Director Romero could even swear, much less in official communications.

"Okay, I've got to wrap this up—" Nitara stopped at the

horrified looks on people's faces. Everyone had taken the moment to check their own displays, but the expression on Matti's face made her heart jump. "What?"

Matti flicked a stream to her. The headlines scrolled on Nitara's display.

IEC Scandal Erupts as ZPE Rocks the World

Where is the IEC when the world needs them? Mired in scandal!

Video Surfaces Connecting IEC Director Desai to Deadly Refugee Fire

Oh... shit.

"This is character assassination." Governor Kipo'mo's voice was a growl. "Miller's targeting you."

But it was much worse than that.

He was targeting Matti.

TEN

Nitara ordered everyone out of the room.

She barely waited until the door closed to blurt out, "I'll fix this."

"You can't." Matti was blinking, rapidly, and that surged terror through Nitara's body. It had taken Matti a year to work through the PTSD after the fire. Dozens had died at the refugee camp, even more had been horribly disfigured by burns, including Matti...

Nitara lurched over and took Matti's hands in hers. The scars were still there, but you wouldn't know. The tattoo artist had disguised them with a peace dove, swirling ribbon, and a red cross. The ink was camouflage, so Matti could choose which story to tell—the one where the tattoos signaled her commitment to the Pandemic Corps or the one where they hid the reason she had to leave.

And now, years later, Miller was dredging it all up again. "This is bullshit." Nitara's head was swimming. "The investigation cleared us both. Miller can't have anything more because there's nothing more to have."

Matti's blinking had slowed, like she was coming out of

the shock, but that only made Nitara's heart race more. What if this drove her away? She was already one foot out the door, marrying Anthony, maybe moving to New York—

"That was before." Matti's gaze slowly found Nitara's face. "Before you were an IEC Director. And a threat to the soon-to-be most powerful man in the world."

"*Fuck* Miller." Nitara's voice quavered. "I cannot say that strongly enough."

Matti nodded, but it seemed lost. "Go see Romero." She peered into Nitara's eyes. "My boss wants me in there, too, but I'll... I'll stay here. Let you handle it. Okay?"

"*Yes.*" Relief coursed like cold water in her veins. "I'll handle it. You sit tight. Make a plan for how we combat this. Work with the team. I'll settle the Deputy Execs and be right back." She hugged Matti, fiercely, then fled her office, hauling ass through the hallways of the IEC to get to Deputy Executive Director Antonio Romero's office before her tardiness made things any worse.

Flashes from the past bombarded her brain, like a speed run through the tragedy that matched her pace through the halls. That long-ago refugee camp, trapped under a heat wave that was deadly and inescapable. Matti had worked in procurement, but it was Nitara's first tour as director of an entire camp. Neither of them realized the supply chain had been compromised, that the solar tents, which were supposed to generate their own cooling, had failed the safety checks, if there had ever been inspections at all. Even then, no one could have known how quickly the entire camp would become a conflagration—synthetic materials, inescapable heat, burning bodies and belongings and supplies... Matti saved a few children, but it was like beating back the apocalypse with her bare hands. The smoke alone killed dozens.

Nitara hadn't even been there.

But her name was on the paperwork.

She had arrived at her boss's office, but she stood frozen in front of the door, unable to catch her breath, throat thick with remembered pain and the taste of bitterness. *Fucking Miller,* bringing all this back. Splashing Matti's decades-old trauma across the news. The need to make him *pay* for this burned hot inside her. That was what held her in check. *Breathe. Focus.* A screaming need for revenge would only cause her to screw this up. And she had no room for error.

Nitara knocked lightly at the door but didn't wait to go in.

Inside stood both her boss, Romero, and Matti's boss's boss, Deputy Exec Oceane Dubois. *International Agreements* and *Operations,* the two divisions of the IEC. At least the round Spaniard and the slim French woman were alone —the Exec Director himself wasn't in attendance.

The two Deputy Execs' faces looked like they'd already attended her funeral.

Nitara swallowed and closed the door behind her.

"Nitara, please have a seat." Romero indicated a chair in front of his desk. He stood to the side with Dubois, next to his expansive windows which had a sparkling view of the city.

"I can explain—"

"Just take a—"

"Let her stand," Dubois interrupted, but she wasn't doing Nitara any favors. "I want her to explain why she's compromised one of my best employees with this ill-advised extracurricular activity."

"None of this is Matti's fault," Nitara rushed out.

Dubois narrowed her eyes. "I'm aware of that."

Nitara took a tentative step forward, hands up. "I

should have brought you in, before I went to Miller's conference—"

"*Brought us in?*" Romero's voice suddenly went rough. "You mean, you should have gotten *approval*—"

"I apologize. I'm sorry. Yes, of course." She resisted the urge to rub the pounding at her temple. "The urgency of the situation, the unknown nature of Miller's plans, I miscalculated—"

"Like at the refugee camp?" Dubois's expression was ice cold.

This was spiraling away from her. "That was... there was an official inquiry..." Panic was stealing her breath and scrambling her thoughts. She pulled in air and let it out slow, blocking the glares from the Deputy Execs as she stared at a point on the fashionably textured carpet, letting them go on with their dressing-down. *Collect your thoughts before you dispense them.* Her father's words, always on tap, for better and worse, even through the pounding in her head.

"The Office of Technology should have been included from the start!"

"That's not relevant now. Besides, this is entirely a legal matter going forward."

"Revolutionary free energy is an entirely *legal* matter?"

"*Yes.* Obviously."

She let them harangue each other for a moment then interrupted. "We announce the IEC is claiming copyright. Expose Ellis's connection to Power Island One. Force the conversation away from finalizing agreements and back to fundamentals. *Who owns this technology?* I've got a team working on this—"

"Nitara." Romero's expression was grave again. "I can't protect you. Not anymore."

"I don't need *protection*—"

"It's you or Matti." Dubois's glare was bitter. "And I think she's suffered enough, don't you?"

"I... what?" The dizziness rushed back. Nitara gripped the back of the chair she had declined to sit in.

"The Exec Director wants this refugee scandal cleaned up immediately." Dubois's patience was gone, and now the words were aimed to cut. "You made this mess—then and now, I don't care what the inquiry found—and Matti shouldn't have to suffer for it. Again."

Nitara's brain scrambled through the haze to catch up. The Exec Director wanted heads to roll—at least one—to bury the scandal and move on. Reclaim the news cycle as fast as possible. So the IEC could address the massive, sudden crisis that Miller and the ZPE technology represented. Which made perfect political sense. Except it meant Nitara was losing her job. Or Matti. And the thought of either was shorting out Nitara's brain.

"I heard Matti's getting married." Romero's voice was softer now.

Nitara's gaze snapped to him.

"I always thought you two were together." He said it like a condolence.

"We're not... it's not like that..." The utter *last* thing she wanted was to explain her relationship with Matti. It was no one's business but hers. And Matti's. "So, it's Matti or me?" She needed this confirmed explicitly as possible. "The Executive Director wants a sacrifice to the scandal, so the IEC can move on, and it's one of us. There's no chance of fighting back against this—"

"Not after your adventure in the North Sea."

Nitara's shoulders sagged. The shock buzzing her body was the only thing holding her up. "Then it's me."

Dubois gestured *See?* to Romero, but he was busy giving Nitara looks of pity.

The glint of the city drew her gaze, the towers of solar-absorbing windows still reflective in the high LA sun. Where would she go? What would she do? Her entire life was the IEC and had been since she'd left the Corps decades ago. She couldn't begin to process what life looked like without her work. Maybe that was the problem. Maybe that had *always* been the problem. She'd had work and Matti, and that was all she needed—through Matti's breakdown, her first husband passing, Nitara helping raise the kids—but somehow, it had never been the right time to define what they had. Make it formal. The IEC and Matti had always been her *everything.*

And now she was losing them both.

"What?" Dubois' outrage wasn't directed at Nitara, but it snapped her attention back. Dubois swung her anger from whatever she was reading on her display to Nitara. "What did you *say* to her?"

"To who?" Her brain was still drifting in the now-nebulous future.

"Matti's packing up her office!" she accused.

Oh no. Nitara turned... and *ran.* She tore open her boss's door and sprinted down the hall. The only thing worse than Nitara losing her job would be Matti thinking Nitara had gotten her fired. Nitara thought-commanded a call as she raced to the elevator. "Pick up! Pick up!" she muttered, gathering stares. She quickly abandoned the elevator and ran for the stairs. Matti's office was two floors and half the expansive IEC building away. Nitara was gasping for breath by the time she stumbled into the Office of Technology and careened past the cubicles toward Matti's office. She'd just gotten a promotion out of the bullpen a year ago, finally landing an office with a window and a view of LA.

Matti's office was empty.

Her personal photo display was gone. The certificates of training were missing from the wall. Even Frank, the potted fern that graced her hard-earned window... *gone.*

Nitara gripped the door jamb, chest heaving, her heart refusing to slow down.

Matti wasn't accepting her calls. Not answering her messages. But she couldn't physically have gone far. Nitara just had to catch up, explain, and stop Matti before she did... *something.* Nitara couldn't even picture what, but an incredible dread seized her and held her on the threshold of the door. She wrenched herself away, stumbling back through the cubicles. The CarbonCon quarantine was still in effect. There was only one entrance/exit, even for staff. Matti would have to go through there, but once out of the building...

Nitara ran, ignoring her laboring breath and the rising squeeze on her chest. She could fix *everything* if she could only reach Matti. A hard grip on the stairwell railing kept her from losing her footing. Everything seemed loose and uncoordinated. Her body had reached some exhaustion threshold—she was moving on willpower alone. When she finally reached the bottom floor and lumbered toward the security at the entrance, she glimpsed Frank's leafy fronds slipping through the double doors to the outside...

Where a mob of press waited.

"No." Nitara kept lurching forward, but it was too late. Reporters swallowed up Matti, pressing mics and cameras into her face. Nitara couldn't see anything through the glassed entrance but the back of Matti's head and Frank's shivering limbs above. There was zero chance of rescuing

her, pulling her back inside the safety of the building, telling her that Nitara was going to quit—*she had already quit*—that Matti didn't have to take the fall for her.

Not again.

But she couldn't do anything. Whatever had kept her going drained out.

Her foot caught on something, and she went down, splayed on the cold granite of the IEC entrance, in front of all the security and weapons-detection arches and decontamination pass-throughs.

She stayed down.

Panting at the floor, heart exploding from her chest, so dizzy she couldn't think, much less move her liquified limbs.

The buzz in her head drowned out the voices of concern. People were trying to help, but no one could prevent this catastrophe.

It was already done.

ELEVEN

Dr. Yousif sent her home with meds for her
blood pressure and strict orders to rest.

What else could she do?

Nitara's collapse at the entrance of the IEC hadn't
exactly gone unnoticed. Romero had her escorted out
before she could even file her official resignation. The city
was under Level Two alert from the WSO, which meant
public transportation was vastly reduced. Non-essential
personnel had been sent home. CarbonCon was still going,
under an official waiver from the governor, who was also
inside the quarantine perimeter, ostensibly working with
the team—*her ex-team*—on combating the ZPE crisis, but
Nitara?

She'd never been more non-essential in her life.

Her 20th-floor apartment was dark, the windows automatically shutting out the sun in her absence, and she didn't
bother dialing them up. On her way home, she'd caught as
much of the news as she could stand, watching Matti take
responsibility for the scandal while getting destroyed by a
ravenous media. Nitara had lost track of when the wedding

was supposed to happen, but Matti still wasn't answering her calls or messages, so maybe she'd already left town. She was newly unemployed, with the kids out of the house and a new marriage in the works... she could be halfway to New York by now.

Nitara's body ached from her full-contact assault on the granite entranceway. Her brain was stuck in a static mode that buzzed instead of forming coherent thoughts. Maybe it was Dr. Yousif's drugs. She couldn't even think clearly enough to know if that made sense. She felt her way to her bed and simply collapsed.

Time stretched and emptied itself of meaning.

The pieces of her didn't fit anymore. *IEC Director. Matti's anchor and partner.* Energy agreements expert. Director of CarbonCon, the world's most powerful expression of energy policy and the teetering mechanism which kept a fragile, heavily negotiated worldwide peace.

Those things *defined* her.

But it had all blown up, and now she was just jagged parts.

Turns out, those things were merely placeholders, spaces in the world that could be filled by anyone. She was replaceable. Not just replaceable, she was being replaced.

What was left if she was no longer *that?*

Nitara blinked at the ceiling. The solid darkness slowly gave way to ghostly gray. The sun must have gone down. Her windows automatically dialed clear at night, admitting the low lights of the city. They were dim, to conserve energy, and downward facing to reduce light pollution and protect migratory birds, which passed over the city on ancient routes. They intuitively knew, through DNA and an almost mystical sense of direction, how to find their way. Like every bird before them, they had a path, a song, a duty to live, procreate, fly and fly and fly, and then repeat the cycle again. Until they were done.

Maybe she was done.

Was this all she had accomplished? To end up in her apartment, alone, staring at the ceiling and envying the birds? It felt pathetic. And lonely. And if there were any reason at all to get out of bed, she would shake it off and get back to work.

She studied the ceiling a little more intently, looking for that reason.

Plenty of people didn't make it through the dark times— and there were always dark times to be had, around every corner. The ever-present plagues, each new alert from the WSO a reminder of the forever war between virus and human. The constant flow of climate refugees obscuring that each person was beloved by someone, driven from their home by drought or flood or fire. The endless race for net zero with a finish line always just out of reach.

Maybe Miller *should* win. Maybe the price for quenching the fire of a burning planet was to allow one man untold wealth and power. Humanity had always craved their kings and despots, their autocrats and strongmen. They had always wanted *someone else* to bear the responsibility, lift the burden, be the solution.

A chill ran the length of Nitara's body, a shiver that started on the arches of her feet and swept up to raise the hair on her head.

It was wrong.

Further, it was a *lie*.

Nitara had spent her entire life rebutting that lie. Her whole existence was an embodiment of cooperative power. *International Agreements* was simply a bureaucratic term for *working together*. She brokered those agreements. She coordinated the efforts, built the teams, and directed the conferences. Endless meetings and plans and work and more work. She had held Matti through the worst of her recovery, attended her wedding, her births, the funeral of her first husband. Helped raise those three kids, who now were on their own joy-filled and complex journeys. They called her Auntie, and if Nitara had never managed to cement the relationship with Matti any further, it was because there had been no need.

Nitara had simply shown up.

Everyone had losses. Some didn't survive them because, at the end of the day, *who they were* also became lost. It wasn't a tragedy to spend a minute in bed, envying the birds and trying to re-anchor herself. The tragedy would come if she were too afraid to look in the mirror for fear of what she might see.

Nitara wasn't afraid of mirrors.

She feared the catastrophes she couldn't prevent, despite all her efforts.

She couldn't, *wouldn't*, regret being who she was. She'd lived every day stitching an unraveling world back together. If she could no longer do that as an IEC Director—if the scandal and a new marriage meant Matti had to move on— then Nitara would find another way to live that life. To fly and fly and fly until she was done.

Tomorrow is another day. Her father and his endless quips.

She should call him. See what shenanigans he and her mother were up to in Canada. Maybe she would finally move north to join them. Her hot photographer boyfriend was officially out of the picture. He'd sent a note while she was in the North Sea saying they should take some time apart, and given they barely had time *together,* she hadn't even bothered to respond.

Nitara pulled in a breath and sat up, swinging her legs over the side of the bed. The movement made her momentarily dizzy, so she paused, breathing deep to let her head clear.

She had no idea what she would do next, but she wasn't ready to retire. Rest, maybe. Collect herself. Remember who she was. Bring down her blood pressure, so she didn't stroke out before her time. But she'd spent her entire life working for a better world than the one men like Miller had built on the impoverishment and suffering of others, all for their own gain. That wasn't a fight she would quit just because it got hard. Not because she was tough—because she knew resilience was built from equal measures rest and determination.

When her head cleared and she felt steady, she ambled to the kitchen and put on the flash kettle. A few moments later, her tea was steeping in the hand-painted ceramic pot she'd picked up in India during her time in the Corps. Matti had dragged her to the markets, negotiating the press of humanity on their day off when Nitara had wanted to sleep in. The thick glaze on the pot had lost its luster over the decades, but the colorful parade of Hindu gods danced as brightly around it as when Matti first snatched it up from a stall and proclaimed it perfect. And it was. They'd always been like that, from the start, knowing each other as well as they knew themselves. The perfume of her favorite chai blend felt like a hug across time, a vaporous anchor to who she had always been.

She was pouring the cup when a rapid-fire knock sounded at the door.

Nitara hesitated. Had the press hunted her down? Her

address should still be protected, even if she was ex-IEC. She unmuted her display to show who was outside.

Matti.

The tea slopped scalding on her hand as she rushed to set it down and hurry to the door.

As soon as it was open, Matti burst out, "Oh, my God! Are you okay?"

"I'm f-fine." Nitara's voice cracked from lack of use. "Why are you—"

Matti grabbed her into a hug. It took a moment for Nitara to hug her back.

"You collapsed! In the lobby! *What the hell?*" Matti shook loose of the hug but still had her by the shoulders. "I had to find that out from *Dubois?* Why didn't you tell me?"

Nitara was genuinely confused. "I tried to message you—"

"You didn't say you were hurt!"

"I wasn't hurt."

"I could *murder* you!" she steamed. "Can I come in?" She tossed an angry hand at the apartment behind the door.

Nitara was in trouble. And yet, she couldn't keep the smile from her face. "I'm not in the habit of letting murderers in for tea." Then she quickly realized how that could be taken the wrong way. "I don't mean—"

"Oh, *shut up* and let me in." Her eyes were watery in a way that moved Nitara instantly out of the way, ushering Matti inside.

"I didn't mean to worry you."

"Well, you did. Thanks for that." But she was bustling into Nitara's kitchen, pulling out the giant red mug she always used and setting more water to boil. Nitara quietly closed the front door and eased into the kitchen. Matti was busying herself with making tea, a strong Early Grey blend

Nitara kept just for her. It wasn't until it was steeping that Matti balled up a fist and quietly pressed it into the countertop. "*Goddamit,* Nitara. Why do you always have to go it alone?"

"What?"

Matti glared at the counter, her fist still mashing into it. "You're not some kind of superhero. You don't have to rescue everyone, all the time." She slowly turned to face Nitara, and there was pain in her eyes. "I thought we were in this together."

Nitara's mouth opened but she couldn't speak.

Matti waited. She had a much stronger command of herself, her emotions, her reactions than Nitara. Ever since the fire. Ever since the year in which she'd been broken down by the world and had to rebuild her life from scratch. Nitara had held her and made space for her and did everything she could to give Matti the resources to put the pieces back together, but Matti had done all the truly hard work, from the inside out.

And so, she was waiting for Nitara to say something, anything, in response this crazy idea that somehow *Nitara* was the one walking away. But all she could manage was, "You're getting married."

The pain morphed to horror. "Is *that* what this is about? You're *jealous?*"

"I... no, I just..." The dizziness rushed back, so she braced herself against the counter and closed her eyes to gather herself.

"Oh, God, you're not okay."

Nitara shook her head. "I'm fine."

"Go sit on the couch. I'll bring the tea." Then, when Nitara didn't move, she added, "*Now.* Before you fall down. *Again.*"

"Okay, I'm moving." In truth, her legs were unsteady. A strange sort of unmooring had taken hold of her, like the world didn't make sense anymore, and even gravity could not be counted on. She braced herself along the kitchen counter and then the wall until she could navigate to the couch, then shakily eased into it. Matti had hovered the entire way, like she didn't trust Nitara not to collapse, then scurried back to get both their tea mugs and bring them to the couch.

"Are you all right?" she asked, worry squinting her eyes.

"I'm okay." Nitara reached for her mug and cradled it, to show she could.

Matti was angrily choking her own mug in a two-handed grip. "You are incredibly frustrating."

"I'm sorry. What for, exactly?" The dizziness cleared, but the sense of being unmoored left her feeling like any small wave might drag her under. She had no idea what was happening, but she needed Matti to cast her a tether back to reality.

"You're stubborn. You're bent on being a hero. You won't let other people help, *including me,* which is beyond the fucking pale. And apparently, you're *jealous* of my new husband, which I do not understand. Anthony *worships* you. Far more than you deserve."

"You got married." Her throat was tight. "I missed the wedding. Oh, God, Matti—"

"You didn't miss it—it's only Thursday. And besides, we postponed! You were trapped in the fucking North Sea! Nitara, do you even hear yourself?"

Nitara stared at her tea, slowly shaking her head. A vast misery was washing over her. "I don't want to lose you." Her throat was so tight, her voice was barely a whisper. "Not everything and you too. I'll do anything. Just tell me." She looked up, but Matti's face was a blur through the tears. "I could move to New York with you and Anthony. Just let me be around. That's all I ask."

"*What?*" Matti was aghast.

Nitara felt the word stab deep into her chest, and the pain of it made the tears crest. She had to look away because it felt like humiliation. What was she doing?

Matti took the mug from her, which Nitara didn't understand but could hardly fight at this point, then Matti clasped her warm hands onto Nitara's cold ones. "Look at me."

Nitara forced herself.

Matti held her gaze, tight, and it was the lifeline she needed. Just that look and the touch of her hands. She wasn't throwing Nitara and everything they'd had away. She'd let her stay.

"First, I love you," Matti said, still locking that empathy-hold with her eyes. "You're my family. I'm not going anywhere, and neither are you. We'll talk in a moment about what a tremendous pain in the ass you legitimately are, but I need you to know, above all else, right now, that I love you as much as anyone on this planet."

Nitara could only nod. And cry more silent tears.

"Second, we're going to fight this fucker Miller. We're going to do it together, with the rest of the team, and we're going to take his ass down and fix the world and do all the things you always think you can only do by your-self, but it's not true, Nitara. It's never been true. *You know that,* but I think, at some level you don't really believe it."

That anchored something for her, a hard grounded truth. She wanted to wipe away her tears, but Matti still held her hands, and nothing could make her let go first. She blinked the tears away instead. "What don't I believe, not really?" Because she needed to understand.

Matti nodded, like Nitara was finally asking the right question. "All right, good. Let's get a few things straight." She released Nitara's hands. "You're not a goddamn superhero. You need me. You need the team. You need support from everyone, including your bosses, but you most especially *need me.*"

"I know that." Because *obviously.* Nitara was having a complete breakdown at the idea of losing Matti and had been from that first message about the wedding.

"Do you?" The hard squint was back. "Is that why I had to orchestrate my own resignation without you? I knew you wouldn't listen, that you'd try to stop me, to *protect* me, because you didn't think I could handle this, and rather than letting me take the fall for this stupid fucking smear campaign Miller's launched—because strategically, that makes a hell of a lot more sense than letting him decapitate our best weapon against him, *namely you*—I had to lie to you, shove you out the door, put on a show by running the press gauntlet, and I had to do all that without your support. And then you go and try to resign *yourself,* fucking up everything. And if that weren't bad enough, you worked yourself up to collapsing at the entrance of the IEC. If I didn't love you so damn much, I would be absolutely kicking your ass right now."

"This feels strangely like getting my ass kicked."

Matti arched her eyebrows high. "This is where you shut up and listen."

"Right." She pressed her lips together and repressed the manic urge to smile.

"It is *bad enough* that you forced me to do all that without your support," Matti said, and that killed her smile for real. "That was frustrating as hell. But it was *terrifying* to think you'd driven yourself into a state of collapse. Don't fucking do that to me. I need you to be smarter than that. And I need you to stop being the damn hero, thinking the responsibility of the entire world rests on your shoulders alone, terrified that if you slack off for even a single minute, then everything will implode. It's not healthy, it locks me and everyone else out, and that's how you end up with a heart attack or some damn thing. That's how I lose you. And that is not okay with me, do you understand?"

"I'm sorry." And she actually meant it this time.

"You should be." But Matti took a moment to breathe, deep, drawing in those resources that she'd mastered years ago. Somehow Nitara had forgotten how *strong* her Matti was. *"You need me,"* Matti repeated. "I need to hear you say that you understand. For real."

"I need you." It was easy to say. But she understood for the first time, perhaps in her entire life, that this *needing someone* went both ways. All along, she'd been focused on her part: being there for Matti, at any moment, day or night, through literal fire and death and anything else the world might throw at them. But there was another half: letting Matti be there for her. And Nitara hadn't done that, North Sea rescues notwithstanding. She hadn't let herself *lean* on Matti. Be vulnerable, not when it really hurt. Maybe that's why she'd never made it formal. Never took the legal vows which spelled that out quite explicitly. Some part of her didn't want to lose the illusion that, with sufficient effort and self-sacrifice and running herself ragged, she could stop the catastrophes from happening, including anything that might happen to the people she loved. Including the ones that might happen to *her.*

Resilience wasn't built only from rest and determination. A safety net wasn't comprised of the strength of the rope alone, but the *connections* that spread the load. Nitara *knew* that, in a hundred different ways, at every structural level... save the one deeply embedded in her own life.

Everyone needed rest. *Except her.*

Everyone needed compassion. *Except her.*

Everyone needed to rely on others for support and love and resilience in hard times. And yet, somehow, because part of her was a complete idiot, she thought she was an exception to that, too. But she wasn't. Not even close.

Matti looked exhausted. No doubt from everything Nitara had put her through.

Nitara reached for her hand and the warmth of Matti's was like an infusion of love. "I need you so much, the mere glimmer of the possibility of losing you—because you were getting married, maybe moving on without me—absolutely undid me. It threatened me at an atomic level I couldn't even perceive, much less understand. I couldn't deal with it, so I ran off to the North Sea and... I'm sorry, Matti. I'm so sorry. I fucked this all up."

Relief relaxed Matti's shoulders. "You could have just talked to me."

"I know. I should have. I was... terrified." It helped to say it out loud.

"And I'm marrying Anthony because he's this stupidly romantic person who wants the ceremony and rings and everything."

The tears threatened to come back. "He wants to make it legal. That's not stupid."

"No, it's not." Matti squeezed her hand and released her. "Tell me you're really okay. Dr. Yousif waived patient confidentiality at me and wouldn't tell me anything."

Nitara took a deep breath, and miraculously, the dizziness was gone. "I thought I might be losing you. And the stress of that overloaded my system. I can take a lot, but that was... too much."

"I understand that feeling."

"No more of that," Nitara promised.

"Agreed." Matti sucked in a breath again, but Nitara recognized it as her *Okay, we're done with that! Moving on,* signal. "I'm glad you're making sense again because Miller is still out there fucking up the world, and we need you back in the seat."

"I messed that up pretty good, didn't I?" Her brain was swimming in the endorphins that came with realizing things were okay again. Matti was getting married, but they were good. It didn't mean the end of anything, just the beginning of something deeper between her and Anthony. Which was perfectly fine. Nitara *wasn't* jealous—not as long as there was still a place for her in Matti's life. And now she knew there was with a certainty nothing could erase. *Her and Matti.* Whatever else the world threw at them, they were woven together in ways nothing could ever unravel.

"Oh, I checked with Romero," Matti said. "He didn't let you resign. Maybe you noticed?"

Nitara frowned, but of course, she was right. "I figured it was just paperwork."

"Yeah, well, he's not accepting any of that from you." Matti raised her eyebrows. "Unless you need to go out on a medical leave?"

"No." Nitara shook her head for emphasis and picked up her tea again.

"Good, because I did the song and dance. Now, we need you to smack back at Miller to show he can't fuck with the IEC."

A slow smile took hold of Nitara. "You had this all planned out, didn't you?"

"Glad to see you're catching up."

Nitara laughed, lightly, and sipped her chai. It had gone cold. "So, what's our next step?"

"*You* need to rest up. This can wait until morning. Then the team needs you back in the office, making a statement, showing Miller you're not intimidated in the slightest. They're working on the counter-attack strategy as we speak."

"And you?" It was a strangely pleasant sensation, letting Matti take the reins.

"I'm staying here tonight, making sure you're ready to resume duties. Then I'll be remoting in. After all, I kind of dramatically quit. Can't let the press get wind that I'm still involved."

Nitara nodded then sipped her tea. "But you *are* involved. Unofficially."

"You're gonna need me."

Nitara's smile spread wide. "I already do."

TWELVE

CARBONCON, HER STAID CARBON PRICING conference, was in complete disarray.

Would ZPE nullify the need for a price on carbon? Nobody knew. But Miller's staggeringly mediocre picks to be the new Czars of Energy were making power grabs back home while delegates were stuck in CarbonCon's quarantine. Some had already abandoned the conference and managed transport out of the Level Two zone. Most had stayed, brawling over the best spot to set up their crisis centers.

Yet Nitara's corner of the chaos felt like a well-managed disaster response: everyone knew their part and worked with focused haste, mindful of the crisis but not drowning in it. She'd commandeered the largest room and ordered the delegate table disassembled and piled up against the wall, like a barricade against the screens of ongoing news coverage. It could be called a "war room," but Nitara loathed analogies of destruction. Her teams were civilization-building, or at least constructing a highly coordinated defense against forces trying to unravel it.

The room was abuzz, with her flitting from team to team, but it was the kind of energy that went with getting things done.

"You doing all right?" Matti's voice was a constant presence in her ear, coming over the open comms while she worked from home. She'd been asking every hour, at least.

Nitara paused to fill another glass from the Sani-Water station, per doctor's orders for excessive hydration. "How about if we just assume I'm good, and I'll let you know otherwise?"

"I'm sorry, but you've haven't earned that," Matti said, crisply. "I'll be on nag duty for days to come."

"Copy that." Nitara smiled. In truth, she was energized. No pounding pulse at her temple, no free-floating tension messing with her blood pressure. Even the floor felt steadier under her feet. She was anchored right where she should be, doing the work she did best.

Matti had been right about Deputy Exec Romero not accepting her resignation, and Dubois was mollified mainly by Matti's insistence that she would still be covertly involved. Now that Nitara had officially returned—and with a plan—Romero and Dubois had put her in charge of the effort to stop Miller while they flew to join the Exec Director at the UN. An emergency session was being convened to address Miller's ploy to essentially annex the entire world energy market, but it was well understood by all involved at the IEC—including the two Deputy Execs and the Exec Director himself—that the real work would get done here in LA.

Nitara finished her water, then eased up to a group of six in a circle of chairs, including some of Matti's staff in the Office of Energy Technology and several of Nitara's staff from International Agreements.

"How's are those stays of execution looking?" Nitara asked, directing that question to whoever could spare a moment to look past their displays and give her an update.

Umberto swiped something away and glanced around the group before taking the lead to answer. "We've filed challenges to Miller's energy contracts in the D-10, which are all first-tier countries in Miller's ranked system. We're now working on the rest of the first tier, since those are the countries which will be getting the technology first."

"Any idea about the timeline on production?" Nitara couldn't be certain Miller didn't already have a thousand of these ZPE devices ready to ship.

Milly spoke up. "Miller is promising the moon. The first hundred units are supposed to roll off a production line in an unnamed location within a month. We don't know if he can make good on that, but he's setting expectations high."

"We can't let it get to that point," Nitara said, stating the obvious.

Nods went around the group. They all understood the momentum Miller was attempting to create. Contracts were already signed. If they stood up to legal challenge, especially in the powerful D-10 countries, and he could get units into the hands of politicians hungry for power—both kilowatts and the political kind—it would be nearly impossible to claw back. Miller was counting on that.

"We should have the rest of the first-tier stays filed by noon." Umberto made the promise, but the others were already back to work.

"Let me know as soon as you start getting movement on the filings." Nitara expected the legal systems of D-10 countries to proceed quickly under the tremendous political pressure attached to these contracts. "A few successful stays might throw cold water on this *free energy* mania." And the opposite, especially if the courts moved fast to affirm the validity of the contracts, would be a devastating setback, but she didn't need to voice that. Everyone knew.

Umberto nodded, and Nitara swept her gaze over the room, deciding to check on Governor Kipo'mo's team next.

"I think Miller's full of shit." Matti's voice whispered in her ear. "Specifically, about the production units."

"He's got two devices that we know of. If he rolls out even a few more, it's going to build momentum." Nitara kept her voice low as she walked. "How's the WSO petition going?"

While Matti was officially "on leave," she was secretly coordinating the Office of Energy Technology's effort to petition the World Science Organization, laying claim to copyright on the ZPE. She'd filed Nitara's secret video from Miller's conference as evidence, as well as their extensive paper trail documenting the effort to erase the connection between the ZPE technology and Power Island One. The WSO office promised to keep things confidential, but there was some risk. Nitara's press conference this morning had made the overall pitch public: the IEC's mission was universal investment in the Power Islands in exchange for universal access to the technology. With Ellis having developed the ZPE on Power Island One—not just originally but continuing in secret on the Island for the last ten years—Miller was obviously abrogating the spirit of that agreement, and the IEC argued the law as well. That reveal, plus Nitara clearly being back in the game despite the scandal, should keep the press occupied and put pressure on Miller.

But none of that would matter unless they could get the law on their side.

"We've got the WSO petition filed," Matti said, "but most of the D-10 is moving to bury it in subcommittee."

Nitara winced. "What about the U.S.?"

"They're quiet on this. I think they're still pissed about Miller screwing them."

"We can work with that."

"I'm shaking my contacts at DARPA. Trying to track down who those DARPA reps were at Miller's conference. *Discreetly*, of course." Matti needed to be careful if they were to keep up the ruse she was no longer conducting IEC business.

"Let me know if I need to approach the American delegation here at CarbonCon." It was handy to have representatives of the world's countries down the hall —if not CarbonCon reps then the normal IEC country liaisons— but she needed to not step on Matti's backdoor efforts.

"Understood."

Nitara had hung back from Governor Kipo'mo's group, but now caught Dr. Sato's eye, and he waved her in. "What's your latest theory?" Nitara asked.

"About the dangers of the ZPE or whether we can build one from our stolen schematics?"

"Yes."

Akemi rubbed the bridge of his nose, and the entire group looked tired. The physicist and commissioner was the oldest of the group, and his expression the most grim. The young power engineer, Lucía Ramirez from Power Island One, had the bright-eyed energy you got from several pots of coffee. The governor was inscrutable and quiet, flicking through her display and ignoring Nitara's arrival. Only Gwen, the coder from USEC, seemed calm and immersed in whatever she was doing, hands flying through the air and tapping wildly on a virtual keyboard. Everyone's clothes were rumpled, and a debris field of coffee cups and trays from the CarbonCon cafeteria surrounded them.

Nitara thought-commanded a message to housekeeping to come attend to the mess.

Akemi sighed. "It's unclear whether Miller discovered our spy bot or whether they just decided to move the prototype ZPE out of the basement of Renew Energy's facility in Palm Springs."

"My money's on them using the two prototypes as a fake production models," Gwen said, hands still flying. "You know, wow the press with bullshit until they can get production rolling. Meanwhile, I'm 100% going to crack this encryption."

"Really?" Nitara lifted her eyebrows to Akemi. The United States had particular grounds for anger with Miller, given they helped build his kill-switch and DARPA wrote the encrypted code that controlled it. Nitara was no expert in quantum cryptography, but she would have guessed that was unbreakable. Miller certainly acted as though he could treat the United States like any other customer in his empire.

Akemi scowled. "Gwen thinks she can reverse-engineer the physical key."

"It's not my worst idea." She was still intent on her display, fingers dancing in air.

"That is correct." His scowl deepened. "Your worst idea was staging an assault on the North Sea facility and stealing the prototype."

Gwen shrugged. "I could still make that happen. I know some people."

Akemi wearily shook his head.

"Miller would come after you with thugs and shock-taps," Lucía grumbled. "Ask me how I know."

"He'd have to catch us first." Gwen didn't even slow down with her virtual efforts.

"I'm looking for technical solutions from this group, not military ones." Nitara kept her tone light, but she hadn't forgotten the attempted murders of both Lucía and USEC Regional Director Zuri Hill-Gray. Akemi Sato's name was in the file she'd handed over to the WSO as well. Miller hadn't tried to kill the commissioner, but he hadn't known about his involvement either. A lot of lives were at risk, but these ones in particular.

"The ZPE operational code, and presumably the kill-switch, uses quantum key distribution," Gwen said, eyes still narrow-focused on her display. "QKD has been standard for securing the power grid for a long-ass time. And it's been bugging me how Miller was able to hack into the LA grid and shut us down. I know he was manipulating the AI through the interface between the subgrids, but there might have been more. All we know is that we locked him out, eventually. It might have been DARPA fucking around."

"I don't understand." Nitara flicked a look at Akemi but he was rubbing his face with both hands. "Are you saying DARPA has developed a way to hack quantum encryption?"

"Oh, *probably...*" Gwen finally paused her hand flurries and gave her attention to Nitara. "They definitely won't tell us if they do. But that's not my point." She massaged her hands, working blood flow to her fingers again. "Miller tapped DARPA for this code. Why? QKD is standard and will generally let you know if you've been hacked. But Miller's not so much worried someone will hack in to turn off the ZPE—he just wants to ensure *he* doesn't get locked out, so he can flip the kill switch when they stop paying. Standard quantum encryption will do that for him. Why get DARPA involved?"

"We think they were the ones to develop the physical

key," Akemi explained. "It's source authentication for the quantum key and the most vulnerable part, security wise, so Miller might have needed something extra secure. It also makes the QKD hardware dependent and hard to update."

"*Intentionally* hard to update," Gwen said. "If someone's ZPE gets hacked and takes them offline, they can't get back on without another physical key from Miller. Which makes it hard to keep the juice on, if Miller wants to cut you off. But it's also a vulnerability." She smirked. "Arrogance and greed. Always gets these guys."

"You're trying to reverse engineer DARPA's physical key design?" Nitara was just barely following. She had no idea how difficult that task was or even if it was possible.

"Yes!" Gwen was back manipulating her display. "No guarantees, but our bug pulled down a ton of information."

"What about building our own ZPE device?" Nitara directed that at Akemi.

"If we had the physical key... maybe." He swiped information to her display and a file popped up in her peripheral vision. "I've been focused on the dangers inherent to the device. Extracting gigawatts of energy from what's likely dark energy is... unprecedented, to say the least. The physics community is in pandemonium over this, but I've been contacting the world's experts—"

"Everyone except Ellis," Lucía interrupted. "You know, the guy who invented it."

Akemi gave her an uncharacteristically irritated glance. "It's too dangerous for you to contact him. We discussed this."

"What are you thinking?" Nitara asked her. She didn't want to endanger anyone, but any diplomatic meeting carried some risk. Nitara was used to judging the relative danger of such contact, and she'd have the entire IEC at her disposal to ensure Lucía's safety.

"I think he likes me." Lucía shrugged. "In a non-creepy way, I mean. Like he just wanted someone to gush over how brilliant he was. I might be able to get some information out of him, especially now that it's not secret anymore. After all, he wants the whole world to know about it. Obviously."

"The man does have an ego," Akemi agreed. "I saw that plain enough when I met him. But he's not going to accidentally let spill the dangers of the device, especially to a non-physicist."

"You never know."

"What *are* the dangers?" Nitara asked.

Akemi's expression grew even darker. "The entire reason Lucía was tipped off was the destruction of her turtle bot. And the people in Palm Springs were killed by a similarly bizarre unleashing of energy. I thought it might be an inherent part of the device—perhaps used intentionally as a weapon—but going public like this means Ellis must have found a way to tune the ZPE to avoid these errant bursts of energy. I've reviewed the technical information Ellis shared at the conference, but there's not enough theoretical detail to establish what he's tapping into. Where the energy actually comes from. It's very possible even he doesn't know."

Nitara gave him a pinched look. "I thought you said it was dark energy."

"That's *my* theory." Akemi shook his head again. "The world's preeminent minds in physics are in an academic brawl over this. There are many competing views."

"I need plausible dangers to present to the UN." Nitara swiped open the document Akemi had sent her. It was a list with far too much technical information. "Boil this down for me, Akemi."

"We're cracking open the universe to steal energy from *somewhere*. Possibly the zero-point energy tucked in the vacuum of space." His voice was solemn. "Maybe this is just opening a tiny tap on an infinite source. Maybe it's as benign as a solar panel soaking up radiation from the free fusion reactor in the sky. Or maybe it's unlocking a chain reaction that will eventually destroy everything, but we cannot detect the unraveling yet because we have no idea what we're doing." His frustration was clear, but that wasn't giving Nitara the specifics she needed. "Even operationally, we've only seen a few tests. What happens if something goes wrong? The ZPE is extracting tremendous amounts of energy in tiny amounts of time. *What if you can't stop it?*"

That pulled the attention of the entire group. Lucía nodding earnestly, Gwen pausing her hacking to squint at Akemi, and even Governor Kipo'mo finally looking past her display to give him a horrified stare.

"What would happen?" the governor asked.

"We can't begin to know." Akemi let out an exasperated sigh.

But this was getting somewhere. Nitara had seen first-hand the massive ramp-up in energy when the device was in action. Being unable to stop that seemed a legit problem. "If you were in charge, what would you do?" Nitara asked Akemi. "What's the scientifically responsible action plan?"

Dr. Sato didn't hesitate. "Stop production. Fund a worldwide research and testing effort under the auspices of the IEC to develop theories about the energy source and the possible impact of its extraction. Then, once we have reasonable theories about what's happening, start ramping up usage, but slowly... and with a quick off-ramp in case something is discovered on the science side or if dangers become apparent during usage as we scale up."

"Sensible," Nitara agreed. "But the pressure would be enormous to move forward before your theories could possibly be proven out. That would take years, right?"

"Then compromise." Akemi held his hands out, gesturing the absurdity of it all. "It's only catastrophic destruction of the universe that might be at stake. One would think that should be given some weight." Again, frustration overwhelmed this man who Nitara had only seen be mild-mannered and thoughtful.

But this was familiar ground for her. Just because many in the world averted their eyes or told themselves lies to deal with the cognitive dissonance of a world barreling toward destruction but unwilling to brake hard enough to stop didn't mean she didn't see the reality of it. Very clearly. Keeping oriented in the face of that dissonance was Situation Normal for her.

"No, this is good, Akemi. I can use this." Nitara swiped away his report. "Draft me a research and testing plan. *Short.* Something the media and the UN can digest without heartburn. That'll give us a counter-narrative to Miller's plan to exploit first, ask questions later. Good work, team. Keep at it."

Akemi nodded, this time with a little more enthusiasm. It was always good to be working a plan rather than grappling with the world gaslighting itself toward oblivion.

"Is this a good time to interrupt?" Matti asked over comms.

Nitara pivoted away from Akemi and the group. "Go ahead."

"Zahara managed to get a copy of the contract from LeBlanc, and we've got a team picking it apart. But she says Miller's company, Eternal Energy, is basically just a holding company. It's not doing any of the actual work. The contract specifies that all the work building and installing the devices will be contracted out to Renew Energy. The Trillionaire Exclusion Act targets individuals *or* their holding companies. Their collective wealth. But Renew wouldn't fall into that category. She thinks Miller's somehow planning to use that as a loophole around the Trillionaire Exclusion Act."

Nitara knew enough about the law to know that wouldn't hold up. "So, Miller's lawyers are incompetent. If he even has any. He seems to rely on his own counsel a lot. Which is definitely to our advantage. Let's let him keep thinking that might work, for now. Although Denmark's clearly planning to profit hugely by being his base of operations. Their courts might fight the international court verdict on this. We'll tackle that when the time comes." Nitara scanned the room, trying to decide who to check in on next. "Who's working on the contract?" Matti's team could be at the IEC or working remote.

"Trisha's staff in legal. They're huddled in the Copyright Division offices. Do you want me to send them your way?"

"No, just get an update for me. And see if they've got something we can use to petition the D-10 for stays as well."

Sherri, her intern, hustled up to her with wide, concerned eyes. "Director Desai. I've got... there's something you should see. I know you don't want to hear more about the scandal." She bit her lip. Nitara had put her on media surveillance so the rest of her teams could focus on their work.

"The press might keep the scandal in rotation for a while." Nitara's press conference earlier should be consuming the media, plus Matti's suspension should have put the scandal to bed, but it might take time for the chattering to die down. "Unless there's something new?" Nitara couldn't imagine what other skeletons Miller could dig up, but the stakes were impossibly high. Pure fabrication was likely at this point, which meant setting up a disinformation counter-effort. Not her specialty, but the media relations department had experts.

"It's not that, specifically." Sherri was wringing her hands.

"Just tell me."

"There was some court ruling in Canada. It didn't go our way. And now the press is saying..." She visibly swallowed. Nitara tried to remember what it was like to be that young and having to tell your high-level boss in a high-stakes situation that something was not going to plan.

"It's all right. Whatever it is, we'll deal with it."

Sherri nodded as she spoke. "They're talking about you, specifically. Not the scandal, but questioning your 'motives' in trying to stop the ZPE." Her expression scrunched up in distress. "They're treating Miller like some kind of hero! They're going on and on about all the carbon draw-down technologies and how fast they can be scaled up with unlimited power. As if Miller's here to save us, get us *beyond* net zero and *solve* the climate crisis, and how that would put you out of a job, and how you're just... *bitter*... saying that it doesn't make sense for you to object to the copyright and try to stand in the way of Miller saving the world."

Nitara rolled her eyes then quickly assured her intern that she was taking this seriously. "I expect them to trash-talk me. Don't worry about that. Tell me more about the ruling..." But her assistant Ian had barreled into the room and was rushing toward her in a way that cut off that line of thought. He'd insisted on coming back from paternity leave to help with the crisis, despite her objections, and he'd been managing the deluge of press and other callers so she could focus on the problem, just like her teams.

He wouldn't be interrupting her if it weren't critical. "What's wrong?" she asked as he hurried up to her, breathless.

"Dr. Ellis called," he rushed out with that slightly British accent, acquired during his time in Oxford even though he was born and raised right here in LA. "Wants to meet with you."

"Ellis *personally* called my office?" Nitara's attention narrowed to scan Ian's earnest expression. "You're sure it was him?"

"I ran the call through the authenticator. 99% probability it's not a digital fake. Had our IT department track the source: *Denmark*. I wouldn't have brought it to you unless I was sure."

Ian was nothing if not extremely thorough.

"What's his stated reason for wanting to meet?" she asked. "And under what conditions?" It went without saying this could be some elaborate setup. To influence the press? Gain some leverage with the public? She had to actively tamp down the speculation racing through her mind just to focus on Ian.

He glanced at Sherri, who was staring at them wide-eyed.

Nitara nodded to indicate it was all right to speak in front of her.

Ian lowered his voice anyway. "He wants to meet in immersive. No recordings. He said he wants to discuss the copyright issue."

A flood of some neurochemical suffused Nitara's brain. It took her prefrontal cortex, the thinking part, a moment to identify the feeling. *Relief.* "He wants his glory. *Untarnished.* And he can't have that if we're fighting him on Intellectual Property."

"I think so." Ian's brow furrowed. "His affect was calm, urgent, reasonably professional, like he was making you an offer you shouldn't refuse in meeting with him, but there was an underlying arrogance and hostility. I read it as him thinking he could talk you out of your position on the IP."

"Thank you, Ian." It really was good to have him back. "Set it up."

He practically fled the room.

"You're not going to give up on the IP, are you?" Sherri's tone said she already knew the answer was no, but she wasn't sure where this was headed. Or if Nitara would tell her.

"No." Nitara swept a look around the room. They could manage without her for a minute. Then she turned back to Sherri. "But if I can bring Ellis in, then Miller's got nothing left to stand on."

Sherri nodded vigorously.

Nitara deputized her to keep watch over the teams, which left her intern looking shell-shocked, but she would recover.

"Are you sure you're ready for this?" Matti sounded worried.

"I'm good." The stakes were sky-high, and there were a million fronts on this effort. Not an army but an orchestra, all playing together, a symphony of strategies to shift the mood of the world, to resist this takeover by Miller. But Nitara's blood pressure was fine. Better than fine.

This was what she did best.

"Then go get 'em." Matti's support was an extra shot of adrenaline.

Nitara smiled as she hurried after Ian and out of the room.

THIRTEEN

Immersive was one of the most secure ways to meet.

Your brain, your chip, and a heavily secured gateway meant very little chance of eavesdropping. Nitara had briefly considered bringing Lucía into the immersive meetup, but Ellis had asked for Nitara personally, and she needed to build trust. Immersive had emotional vulnerability built into it as well—to engage, you had to go full motor-block, which meant your chip dosed you with neurotransmitters that triggered a sleep paralysis while it commandeered all the inputs to your mind. Nitara had the highest non-military-grade chip you could implant, so she had the works: full-body haptic, motor block, control-by-thought. Most people used immersive for entertainment, especially the haptic parts, but it had a place in statecraft as a way to make contacts that went beyond what you could see or hear in standard video. There was a subtlety to human communication that involved full-body non-verbal aspects—voluntary and involuntary—and with a chip wired directly into your brain, those could be rendered even more expressively in immersive than in real life.

It was encouraging that Ellis chose this method to meet.

Nitara settled into her office chair, reclined it for when the motor block would engage, and sent Ian out. He had work to do, and there was no need for him to hover.

"Okay, I'm shutting comms down," she told Matti, ever-present in her ear. Nitara could get used to that constant connection.

"What's your safe word?"

"*Wollstonecraft.*" The 18th Century feminist philosopher was one of her comfort reads, when she needed a retreat from the world and a little fire in her belly. "But you knew that."

"Just making sure *you* remember."

"You're always looking out for me, aren't you?" Nitara smiled at the ceiling, settling further into the reclined chair.

"It's about time you noticed."

"I love you." A pulse of shock ran through her. She hadn't meant to say that. It wasn't the kind of thing they said to one another. A tumbling rush of emotions swelled and washed through her. *Panic. Joy.* A confusing anxiety that maybe she'd made a mistake, not in saying it now, but in not saying it sooner.

Matti's voice turned soft. "You okay?"

"Physically? Yes. But I need to park these emotions because I've got a high-stakes negotiation to conduct." She was filling the anxiety with words and mostly talking to herself. *Get it together, Nitara.*

"I love you, too, you weirdo."

That erupted a half-laugh which released the tension. "Glad we cleared that up."

"You got this."

"I'll check in as soon as I'm done." The silence on the comm line as it disconnected left the world a little emptier.

She needed to discuss all of that with Matti. *Later.*

For now, she popped in the ear plugs and slid on the goggles that helped block out the real world in preparation for the immersive one. Her command-by-thought was always live, so it was easy enough to think-open the invite Ian had sent. At its activation prompt, she spoke aloud the required language. "I consent to a motor block." A half second later, her body lost tension and sunk into the seat, which her conscious mind could only note for a split second before she was mentally whisked to a virtual meeting room.

The disorientation of the transport always threw her, but her brain quickly adjusted. The virtual space was formless white with no sign of Ellis, only the giant black egg that was his invention. Unlike the glittering darkness of the ZPE reactor in reality, here it had a feeling of hyper-realness. The absolute flat blackness felt like it might pull her in. No umbilical, no connection to the real world, just an infinite potentiality, like she was peeking into the dark matter itself. Was this Ellis's rendering of the device or her brain's idea of the void it cracked open?

Maybe Ellis and his pride simply created this contrast of white and black to make his invention stand out to maximum effect. Which was fine. No distractions. The full haptic feedback built into her chip helped anchor her to the room despite the lack of visual cues. The white virtual carpet felt as real under her shoes as her actual office flooring.

Not shoes, *slippers.*

Her virtual attire was the same as her last immersive experience: a Diwali celebration Matti had conjured. That meetup environment had been the extreme opposite of this

—a night-black vista blanketed with stars and a million virtual candles to celebrate the Festival of Lights. Matti had generated an entire troupe of exquisitely dressed AI characters to dance with them. Nitara was still wearing her gold-trimmed orange-satin sari from that night. Matti had designed it in the traditional style of Odissi, a classical prayer dance. It was believed that on the night of Diwali, the goddess Lakshmi blessed her devotees with great wealth, but first, one must worship Ganesha to gain wisdom to avoid the misuse of that wealth. Matti and Nitara had danced a prayer that all with good fortune would possess great wisdom in its use.

Maybe she could convince Ellis to do the same.

Unfortunately, only Matti would appreciate the accidental appropriateness of her attire. Nitara didn't have time to figure out how to change, so hopefully, Ellis wouldn't be too distracted by her glittering orange sari.

She was here to bring him in.

Enough time had ticked by for her to wonder if the now-famous physicist would simply not show. As she contemplated whether to drop back out of immersive and get Ian—maybe strategize where this had gone wrong—Ellis faded into existence in front of her, jolting her attention and causing an involuntary step back.

He flicked a look over her attire, then ignored that and fixed her with a tense stare. "Director Desai, thank you for meeting with me."

"Of course."

"It's incredibly urgent that you cease these inconsequential motions disputing the ownership of the device." The man's intensity was electric in virtual. She felt the crackle as if it were an actual static charge building in the air, awaiting contact to release.

"I don't believe these motions are inconsequential," she replied. Neither did Ellis, or he wouldn't be here objecting, and she was glad to see her intuition confirmed. *It bothered him.* Enough to generate this deadly-earnest intensity in immersive.

"You cannot stop this, Nitara. Please reconsider what you're doing."

The switch to personal appeals was sudden and unexpected. "I'm sure you understand the technical aspects better than I do, Dr. Ellis, but I believe I understand the full societal consequences of the technology better than you." Her pushback on authority, combined with a reversion to titles, might throw him. Mostly, she was buying a minute to judge her own affect: immersive had a way of telegraphing more than a person intended, and she'd forgotten that effect went both ways.

"I doubt that very much." But his voice had softened slightly. He waved a hand at the vast whiteness around them, and it transformed into a dizzying display on all sides and even above. A mad rush of images of pollution and nature, green energy and environmental destruction, all intertwined. "This device has the capacity for tremendous good in the world. We'll win the race for net zero practically overnight. The benefits of that are incalculable." Ellis flicked a hand at the display, and it switched to a different cacophony of silent images, this time of courts and councils, the seats of power rendering decisions. "We have high-powered advocates in every country. All your legal machinations will go nowhere. Your resistance is highly annoying, but it is of no real consequence. You can't possibly win with any of it. You're wasting everyone's time, including your own." His voice went soft again. "Nitara, please. Don't fight this. There's no point."

But this was an ancient argument. "Don't resist? There's no point?" She smiled. "Sounds like someone is *very* concerned about how effective resistance would be." It was the first resort of every tyrant, to convince the people, especially the agitators and malcontents among them, those who are naturally not inclined to submit to tyranny, that all their efforts at resistance would be pointless, and they should simply let the tyrant have his way. Much easier, for everyone. It was also the first rule of safeguarding freedom: don't concede to the tyrant in advance. "Or you could refuse to let your incredible work upend every power structure on the planet, Dr. Ellis. You could not allow your brilliance to be co-opted by Miller's plans for wealth and domination."

Ellis's gaze hardened, but he retreated a little—not physically, not in the body language of his virtual avatar, but his earnest expression faded into a stolid resolve.

It occurred to her, belatedly, that *he* had called this meeting, and he certainly had an agenda of his own. And while her intuition had been correct—he was bothered by the attacks on his ownership of the intellectual property rights for the ZPE—she was wrong to think he was here to offer himself up.

He was here to *stop her*.

She could work with that. She'd spent her entire life fighting the exploitative power Miller was trying to re-entrench. The chances of her *not* fighting were vanishingly small. It shouldn't take much to convince Ellis that resistance wasn't futile, but inevitable. Implacable. Something that would require compromise on *his* part. At least if he wanted to avoid the fallout, which he clearly did—or he wouldn't be here.

Normally, she was an ardent fan of compromise... but at

times, an uncompromising stance was the fastest way to get there.

"James, you truly have invented something wondrous. *World-changing.*" She held her arms open, palms up, a gesture of conciliation even as she brought the terms on which she would never compromise. "It belongs to *the world.* You know we're correct on the law and the merits, but even more, you know it's the right *moral* stance. No one would dispute your brilliance in unlocking this potentially unlimited energy source. But if you let Miller co-opt and control it, *your name* will forever be tied to the regime he's trying to establish. And all its atrocities. Because you know there will be many. There always is."

But his expression only turned calculating. "This *regime* is an orderly way to share an unprecedented gift with humanity. Whatever you have in mind at the IEC, I guarantee you haven't thought through the consequences of just handing out devices. It would be chaos, literally overnight." A flick of his hand changed their silent background of discordant images to scenes of war, oppression, conflict. "But if you are so concerned with EVEG-generated power going to the right people, I could arrange for the IEC to be given a license, *first tier,* full access to the device and the ability to distribute energy to whomever you like. Within reason, of course. But accommodations could be made."

"Accommodations." She'd quickly dropped her open-armed stance. This was a dangerous offer. She knew it instinctively, but her mind was racing to zero in on the catch.

This time Ellis spread his arms wide. "We have no desire to see people suffer. Those without the wealth to buy into the first or second tiers could apply for a needs-based exception. We could develop—*the IEC* could develop, on terms acceptable to you—a process for such exceptions."

Her instinctive disgust stopped flitting around her chest and settled into her stomach. "This technology belongs to the world."

"That's irrelevant—"

"That's *everything*." She let her feelings show on her face. "If you think you can buy my acceptance of your system of scarcity with a few *exceptions*, tightly controlled and monitored by Miller, you've misread me entirely, James." She hated how much Ellis's offer actually tempted her. Do a little evil in the world, or in this case accept the inherent evil newly built into the system, so you can eke out a small amount of good... that wasn't "compromise." That was the justification used by every person who was co-opted into a systemic evil. It was their reason for *not resisting*. Because, of course, there was no point! You couldn't fight the system! When the system couldn't exist without wide-spread acceptance, at some level. This was the kind of corruption—bring your objectors into the fold and make them complicit—that kept even the most egregious systemic evil in place. And which forced reform efforts to become more desperate and often pushed into violence.

It was the kind of thing that erased decades of progress overnight.

"I'm afraid you're misreading the situation, Nitara." A flash of fear in his voice underwrote those words, which was discordant enough to pull her out of her seething anger.

"You're not seeing the possibilities here, *James*." She held her hands out again, slightly less effusive. "What this technology needs is *development*. You have the entire world's attention and resources. You could oversee the most well-funded technology development program the world has ever seen. Your name would be clearly attached to all the accolades that are rightly yours without the stain of Miller re-engineering the world's economy to benefit himself and a small cadre of mediocre bureaucrats. You would go down in history not only as the man who discovered the technology but who shepherded its development into a truly safe and reliable form of unlimited energy... and whose wisdom heralded an era that was true progress, not a rapid backsliding into the very fossil-fuel era politics that nearly destroyed the planet."

He was shaking his head, and the sigh that seemed to ease out of him was unnecessary in immersive, but nevertheless communicated his impatience.

"I don't want it to be like this, Nitara." Again, there was more pain in those words than seemed to fit the situation.

Was he ready to walk away? "I do appreciate you reaching out, Dr. Ellis. I'm sure we can come to an understanding."

"I genuinely hope you're right." Ellis waved away the chaos of images, returning the environment to static white with the black ZPE egg in stark relief. "You're an intelligent person. You have a deep understanding of the law and the issues the world will face in this transition. You have incomparable director-level experience in the largest energy agency in the world."

He took a small step forward and slightly bent his head to look earnestly into her eyes once more. It was excessive flattery, so she girded herself.

"Join us," he said.

"I'm sorry, what?" He couldn't be serious. More than that, he couldn't possibly think *she* would take this seriously, whatever this "offer" was.

"I'll talk Miller into it." His cadence picked up speed,

like he'd gone off-script and was now concocting some scheme on the fly. "He's halfway convinced you should be a natural ally anyway—that you're clearly ambitious but simply misguided in limiting that ambition to the IEC's narrow ideas about morality. He understands the reality of how the world works, Nitara. But he has too many fools in his inner circle. He needs someone like you, someone who can see things clearly and will warn him away from the shoals. Someone who can actually make this work." He waved his hand vaguely at her and her glittering orange sari. "We'll let you write better contracts for the lower tier countries since that's your pet interest. I'm sure with that intellect of yours, you will find even better ways to achieve your aims, whatever you decide they should be, from within the inner circle. You'd sit at the right hand of the most powerful man in the world. With that, anything is possible. Anything you wish. But you cannot afford to pass this up. You have no idea the stakes here. Trust me, this is an offer that will only come once, and you do not want to reject it." He nodded to himself, as if he'd finally said what needed saying.

Nitara just blinked. Twice.

As far as she could tell, the man was absolutely serious with this nonsense.

He should have stayed on script.

As she took a moment to formulate a response—and, she supposed, to give the impression she was actually considering this—it occurred to her that Miller, of course, had written the script. This last part, the personal ambition, the proximity to power, the appeal to toss morality aside, was purely Ellis.

Had the scientist always been this mad? Or had extensive time with Miller corrupted him? Regardless, it was clear that he was Miller's handmaiden and bringing Ellis in was never a real possibility.

She made one last try anyway. "Or you could join *us*, Dr. Ellis. Your fate doesn't have to be conjoined with Miller's."

Ellis let out a deep sigh and took a full step back. "It's unfortunate you're unwilling to see reason." He waved the displays of chaos, war, and oppression back on the walls. The ZPE device faded. "I'm truly sorry, Nitara. I had hoped we could gain your cooperation. But if this is your choice, the consequences are on you."

It was vague and threatening, but that didn't concern her as much as giving him a final message for Miller—since that was where this would go next. "Tell your boss I'm not the kind to give up easily."

"He knows." Then Ellis faded out of existence.

She took a moment to search for any thread of hope regarding Ellis. He seemed utterly convinced of the inevitability of Miller's plans... except somehow Miller needed someone to "guide him away from the shoals" and "actually make this work." That was Ellis, off-script, exposing his doubts in a ham-fisted attempt to gain her cooperation. But it only revealed that things might not be going as well as Miller would like everyone to think.

Nitara thought-commanded her way out of the motor block.

Which should have whisked her awareness back to her office immediately... instead, the displays around her shifted, showing a desert refugee camp. Sun blazing overhead. It could have been any camp, but it wasn't. The solar tents were long outdated, replaced in the real world by a different design after the conflagration that burned Matti and drove her out of the Pandemic Corps.

"Fuck you, Miller!" Nitara shouted, despite there being no one to hear. This flavor of petty seemed low even for him. "Wollstonecraft," she said to hard-boot herself out of immersive.

Instead, the scene shifted... and she was inside it.

What the fuck? She could feel the sun's heat through her sari, scorching her skin.

"Wollstonecraft!" Why was the failsafe not working? The brightness was blinding. She shaded her eyes, but then a blast of heat curled her up, reflexive protection. Screams, the kind made by people in agony, followed the blast. Then something hard knocked her to the ground. The source of the screams—no, just *one* of the screaming people—had blindly run into her. It was a man, now hurtling into the desert. *On fire.* He didn't get far, collapsing to writhe on the ground. Which was also searing burns everywhere her body touched. She lurched to her feet, but her slippers were nothing against the heat. She hopped from foot to foot. The nearest tent was on fire. One next to it burst into flames. Then another. They were no refuge. Just as it had been.

There was nowhere to go.

This isn't real. She stood still, willing her body to endure the heat from all sides. Her *body* wasn't real. None of it was. But she also knew with absolute certainty it didn't matter... her mind believed it. All of it *had been* real. She hadn't witnessed it the first time, but her brain was all too ready to accept this as reality now.

Penance.

Miller had trapped her in a tailor-made immersive to pay it.

"Wollstonecraft," she whispered. Nothing changed.

More screams. A woman tried to beat the flames engulfing her child only to catch fire herself. Heat and flames and more screams and another tent exploding, this time sending fiery material through the air that Nitara had to dodge.

People died in immersive. Literally frightened to death by their own nightmares.

In the real world, Nitara hadn't been there to save Matti. And no one was coming for her now. No one even knew she was trapped, not still negotiating with Ellis. There was no way to signal for help. No way to stop the nightmare.

Penance.

Her mind was accepting it. She didn't even have words to fight it.

Another tent burst into flame. Her skin stretched tight with the blasted heat.

A woman ran out of it, encased in flames, a blind torch running.

Straight at her.

Horror held her in place, even her virtual body no longer responding to her commands.

The woman slammed her to the ground, engulfing Nitara in a burning hulk of human flesh.

She screamed and screamed and screamed.

FOURTEEN

The room was blurry and pale yellow.

Maybe the safe word had finally worked? She couldn't remember getting here.

Where was here?

She squeezed her eyes shut, and the yellowness went away.

"Nitara? Honey? Can you hear me?"

She pried her eyes open again. Everything was still blurred, so she tried blinking rapidly, and after a moment, her brain made sense of the face in front of her.

Matti.

Nitara sighed in relief.

Matti's face lit up. "She's awake!" she cried out to someone then moved away.

No! Nitara pawed after her, sitting up, but her wrists were tangled in plastic spaghetti, which made no sense, but she was desperate to keep Matti within reach.

Was she even real?

The rest of the room was still blurred yellowness.

Matti quickly returned, holding a glass of water with a

straw and adjusting something to support her while she sat up. Then she helped Nitara drink. As the coolness soothed the sandy desert of her mouth, the rest of the room started to sort into shapes and sounds that made sense. The calming yellow of hospital room walls. The faint blips of medical data on a wall-mounted display. An adjustable bed with crisp white sheets and pillowy-soft blankets around her. The tubes attached to her wrists were IVs. *Multiple.* Half-formed questions tumbled over themselves in her mind, but she couldn't quite grab hold before they slipped away.

It wasn't her eyes that weren't working, it was her brain.

A pulse of fear shot through her, ricocheting and lighting up a dozen memory flashes. *The camp. Burning. Screaming.* The echoes retreated, but her body shook.

The straw had fallen from her mouth, but she still held Matti and the glass with both hands. The hospital room was solid again. The nightmare world had faded. But the barrier between them felt as thin as a wisp of ashy acrid smoke.

How long? she tried to say, but it came out as a croak.

"Don't try to talk. And your chip is disabled, so no thought-messaging either."

Nitara couldn't picture how to even try. Her brain could hardly sort the reality in front of her. A realization leaked through her thoughts like an oil spill. *Her brain had shut down.* She couldn't remember the nightmare—didn't want to try—except to know it was there, nearby, but locked away. Miller's immersive had driven her brain into a survival mode that had maybe broken it. Into parts but not completely. She was here. Alive. With Matti still holding a glass of water and peering earnestly into her eyes.

Nitara took another drink and tried again. "How long?" The words were rough but they successfully left her mouth.

"It's been 24 hours since I found you." Matti's voice was

steady, but Nitara saw the glassing of her eyes. "You were completely catatonic. Alive, breathing, but unresponsive." She squeezed Nitara's hand, gently, encouraging her to sip more water. "It's so good to see you... awake." She'd had to watch Nitara lie in a hospital room. *Inert.* For twenty-four hours, and by the haggard shadows under Matti's eyes, she had slept none of it.

Nitara hated that, hated the idea of it, but even that swell of emotion threatened to break the barrier, so she let it go, drift safely away. She focused on drinking more water. And trying to speak again. So Matti would know she was okay. *Was she okay?* She wasn't entirely sure.

"What happened?" she managed.

Matti frowned. "You'd have to tell me... but you don't have to.... the doctor said..." She was struggling, holding something back, then she swiped at her display, annoyed. "You should take it slow. The doctors are coming. But you're awake and talking. They said this would be the best possible outcome. Many who get trapped in immersive..."

She didn't have to finish. Nitara knew. People didn't always wake up.

Nitara reached out a hand, and it was steady. Matti clasped it. Her skin was surprisingly warm. "I'm okay."

"Are you?" Matti scanned her face intently like she could see the scars inside her mind if she looked hard enough. Nitara hoped not. Whatever Miller had done to her with the fabricated reality he shoved into her brain, she'd survived. And she would get better. She felt sure of that, although she couldn't say why. Each moment in this reality made her feel more anchored to it.

"I'm tired." She pulled her hand back, but only so she could rest against the raised bed. "Tell me what happened. While I was out." That's what she needed. Matti's voice.

Something to fill in the blanks. Keep her attached to the here and now.

"Okay. All right." Matti was still hesitating. "But you stop me if it's too much."

Nitara nodded for her to go ahead then sipped more water.

"Once we figured out things had gone wrong, we immediately brought you here. Then we tracked down what we could about what happened. It appears your chip was hacked—and it came through the immersive connection, so we know Ellis is somehow responsible."

"Ellis left." Nitara coughed a little, but the words were coming easier. "Negotiation failed. My safe word failed. Then the nightmares started." The words brought another flash of the fire, smoke, pain... but it quickly faded. *Just a nightmare*, she told herself. Although she knew better. Her brain had experienced it as *real*. She couldn't undo that. Or pretend it hadn't happened. That wouldn't help.

But she was awake now. The barrier solidified, a little stronger, more distant.

Matti's expression pinched in. "You don't have to tell me. We figured... we know it was traumatic. The doctors explained it."

Nitara nodded. There would be a time to talk about it later, maybe, but not until the barrier was stronger. And Matti never needed to know what the nightmares were about.

"I should have..." Nitara paused to clear an almost-cough. "...gotten a Healthcare Power of Attorney." Just one more way she'd waited too long.

Matti gave her a small smile. "Well, yes, that would have helped. But trust me, getting legal authorization to disable the chip of an unresponsive IEC director negotiating world-changing technology? That wasn't the problem." Her expression tightened again. "The problem was you might not have come back to me."

Then a whole battery of medical personnel came flooding into the room, which was disorienting, and Nitara had to focus on answering their questions and letting them take their measurements. Matti stepped back so they could do their jobs. Nitara tried to track what they were telling her, but most of it was just reassurance of one kind or another. Her scans were good. No permanent brain damage. Chip disabled until appropriate mental health care. Could take a long time, maybe months. She should be prepared for flashbacks. But she'd already done the hardest thing: *survived*. And woken up. From here, chances of full recovery were very good. If she took things slow.

By the time they left, Nitara was more tired but also more clear. The fuzziness was receding. She was increasingly aware of every ache in her body. Apparently whatever happened in immersive, the body reacted, even with the motor block, it just didn't show until later. But all of it, even the sore *everything,* was helping to anchor her in reality. *This* reality.

Nitara leaned back on her elevated bed to rest but didn't close her eyes. She couldn't imagine doing that for a while. A long while.

Matti shuffled over from the corner to sit by her bedside again. "How are you doing?"

"I've got this bone-deep tired like I need several hundred naps."

"You're sounding better." There was a cautious relief in her voice.

She reached for Matti's hand and gave it a squeeze. "It

helps to have you here. You're... grounding." She couldn't explain that too much without puncturing the barrier.

"Of course." Matti's eyes were glassing again.

Nitara couldn't worry about that right now. She had to put all her effort into getting from one moment to the next. "My brain is back online. Mostly. As far as I can tell."

"Your medical team seems impressed."

"That is definitely one of my new goals in life."

Matti smiled.

It felt like sunshine in the cool sterility of the hospital room. "I'm a little freaked that Miller hacked my chip," she admitted. Who knew what the real scars of that might be? She'd be finding that out along the way. "But I'm okay. I feel like me. Only beat up."

The tentative relief worked its way onto Matti's face. "Maybe it's time for a nap."

"No sleeping. Not for a while." A small shudder ran through her. She wasn't afraid, not precisely, but she wanted to put that off as long as possible. It would be... challenging. "Distract me. Update me on everything. Please." The normalcy would be good for her. For both of them.

"Okay. But stop me if it's too taxing."

Nitara nodded then reached for more water. It was like she'd been desiccated and couldn't fill up fast enough.

"All of this has captured the press." Matti sighed and settled back in her bedside chair. This wasn't the preferred way to alter the news cycle, but they would take it. "No one's speculating anymore about your motives in wanting to claim copyright for the IEC. Now the headlines are all about who tried to assassinate a sitting IEC director."

Nitara blinked then set her nearly-empty glass on the swing table. "Assassinate." It felt strange, like the word didn't quite fit. *Death by mental torture.* That had clearly been Miller's intent. Or Ellis? He had to know. At least complicit. Anger boiled low in her, but she again let it dissipate. Anything like that felt too raw, too close to the barrier. But thinking it through, with the logical part of her brain, it wasn't a surprise that Miller had tried to kill her. Again. The surprise was that, despite everything, she hadn't seen it coming.

Some catastrophes you can't stop. You can only survive. And she had.

Matti was peering anxiously at her again.

"Sorry, I was just..." Nitara searched for the right words. "Angry. Thinking how Ellis could have warned me. Maybe he tried." His warnings swam in her mind, but that was too close to the barrier, so she let those thoughts drift away too.

"Ellis gets zero passes from me." Matti's anger was hot enough for the both of them. "He was part of this, even if we all know Miller was behind it. I want them in prison, and I'm not the only one. You're a U.S. citizen and a director of the IEC. I can't tell you how many law enforcement agencies are involved in this, but let's just say DARPA is suddenly a lot more cooperative."

That caught her attention. "Has this changed the Americans' stance on the ZPE?" *This* being her almost-murder. Which was still twisting in her mind, a surreal concept hanging out in space that didn't seem like it could attach to her. But she would gladly take any shift in the political landscape in their favor. All of that still mattered, despite landing her in a hospital bed in this... *state.* In fact, it mattered more because of that.

"Nothing's really changed." Matti scowled. "The U.S. is informally reaching out, and that's part of how we were able to trace your chip hack to Denmark, although they still can't link it to Ellis or Miller personally. But officially, the Americans are still proceeding with the ZPE contracts."

Nitara's hopes dashed on the hard truth that energy politics always warped the international order. Wars had been fought over oil. Green energy moved in the other direction, stabilizing the world with local, resilient power, turning petrostates into electrostates, but there was still competition for exotic materials. Fortunately, it was easier to recycle and mine local than wage new wars of extraction. But Miller was counting on creating a new scarcity to warp the world again.

"I will say the U.S. is officially *pissed off*," Matti added. "So that's something."

It was, but not nearly enough.

"We can't keep going this way." Nitara's mind was still in a strange state, but locking away the immersive night-mares in order to survive had *shifted* something. Jarred things loose, connecting ideas in a way she hadn't before.

Matti had gone quiet. "We can talk about this later. You need to rest. I've got the team working every angle—"

"No. I mean we need to do something different."

"Well, no more immersive for you, that's for sure." But Matti was waiting for her to explain.

"We can't do this alone." The ideas were forming almost too fast for her to grab hold, slippery like before, only this time the mini thought-tornado swirled around a central idea. "Technology should be used for the betterment of humanity. Not the enrichment of the few and exploitation of the many."

"Basic IEC philosophy. Continue."

Nitara sat up a little straighter in her bed. The tornado was gathering power. "The IEC wasn't formed by some executive decision in a single country. It wasn't brought into being by a decree from the United Nations, even though technically, those things also happened."

Matti peered at her, like she wasn't sure why Nitara was taking this historical tour, but she was all-in on the ride. "It was the Summer of Plagues."

Nitara nodded. "2028. Third plague in two years."

"The Neanderthal virus from the peat moss," Matti supplied. "Then the cholera outbreaks that were supposed to stay in the Global South but started showing up in the north. And then the outbreak in the camp."

"A climate refugee camp."

Matti was nodding now. "Historic drought in southern Iran. Wildlife and humans living on top of each other. An old variant mutated and made the jump to humans. Wiped out the entire camp."

"And woke up the world." Nitara took a deep breath. The world needed to wake up to what Miller was doing. "The climate fight and the forever war against the viruses— they're the same battle. And we were *losing*. You can't stop a virus with a bullet. Or a hurricane with a wall. People finally understood we needed a new way of thinking."

"That's when the IEC was founded." Matti was right with her now.

"An *International* Energy Consortium. A historic coop-eration between every nation on Earth. And a dozen more sprung into being: WSO, the D-10, the Climate Club, CarbonCon, the Climate Refugee Accords, the radical increase in the size and scope of the Pandemic Corps. All because the world finally said *enough*."

Matti's expression grew thoughtful. "It wasn't the governments. It was the people."

"And they didn't flood the streets—they filled their networks. With stories of sickness and death, of contagion and climate destruction. We couldn't *conquer* nature. We were part of the ecosystem—a dysfunctional part that had to change. It wasn't a new idea, but it had new urgency. The amazing thing about Energy Island wasn't the fusion research or green tech... it was the *cooperation* that made it possible."

"Cooperation Miller wants to unravel." Matti's anger was cold, and that was the entire point. *No one* would sign on to that if there were any other choice. "How do we..." Matti spread her hands, gesturing at this nebulous idea of triggering a second revolution in worldwide cooperation.

"I don't know." Nitara shook her head. "But that's the wrong approach. I don't *have* to know. We just have to give people another choice than what Miller is offering them."

"A choice." But she could see the gears turning in Matti's mind now. "Bring in a hundred stakeholders. Brainstorm. Find another way."

"A *million* other ways."

She frowned. "You're talking about irregulars." A term from the petrostate wars, the non-military types who used open-source intelligence to fight.

But Nitara would take it. "The anonymous hackers and data-scavengers. The social networkers and mutual-aid organizers. Even better, the commons."

The commons weren't a shareable resource like land or water, but a million small communities with shared purpose. They'd multiplied exponentially—quietly, almost without notice—since that summer of plagues: voluntarily formed collectives, an informal worldwide movement that self-organized in the wake of unprecedented international cooperation. Neighborhood group chats, hobby interest groups, care-work groups, found families, communal living, retirement apartments, bowling leagues. They weren't a new idea: this network of invisible care work and community building had long existed, but they gained stature and visibility. Governments, in discovering they had a duty of care for their own people that they neglected at their own peril, also realized the advantage of openly supporting the commons. Because it had become understood that *the commons* were the bright cords that held the world together.

"But that's... everyone." Matti's skepticism warred with a kind of pure bafflement.

"Yes. That's what it will take." The bone-weariness started to lift, a sense of rightness shoving it out of the core of her being. "We need to remind the world it has a choice."

"But... how?" Matti's confusion had won out.

A second wave of medical personnel arrived, interrupting them, but Nitara didn't have an answer anyway, not yet. Matti stepped back, already swiping at her display, probably communicating with the team. Which was exactly the right place to start, but the IEC wasn't going to win this fight alone.

Something much bigger would be required.

FIFTEEN

Nitara had been deep breathing for five minutes.

Someone had brought her a seat.

The steady buzz of the IEC's conference room—the same room they'd been working in all along—had its own soothing effect, anchoring her. Two days ago, she'd woken up in the hospital. Last night, they released her. Everyone in the room today was tiptoeing around, giving her tons of space, which was just what she needed.

She'd managed enough sleep last night, despite the nightmares, to do this.

Matti finally stopped asking if she was okay, because it only increased Nitara's stress, and there was zero chance of her backing out. Despite this being one of the most dangerous things she'd ever done. Well, short of stepping into an immersive with Dr. James Ellis, but she hadn't known that at the time. Today, she knew exactly what she was doing.

She was about to give an unproven, world-changing, unlimited energy-generating technology to the world. *Was this wise?* Not in the slightest. *Was this approved by her boss and her boss's boss?* For once, yes. But Nitara only brought the idea to them because she believed it was the only way to stop an even bigger catastrophe.

There's nothing wrong with failure unless you fail to learn from it. Her father's quips seldom worked above a certain level, at which failure had consequences, often death and suffering at horrific scales. It still surprised her how powerful simple policy could be—for good or evil, thus necessitating the careful crafting of it—to contain the destructive tendencies of human beings. But Miller was ignoring the laws that didn't suit him and rewriting the balance of power in the process. It was an attack on the basic structure that kept the world running. Each of her teams had been engaged on a different front in the scrambling effort to stop him before he could do too much damage. Or at least slow him down until the mechanisms of diplomacy could grind out a containment strategy built on imperfect agreements and understandings. But none of that was enough.

They needed a new way of thinking.

And it would have to involve everyone.

"I'm not going to ask if you're okay," Matti's voice spoke low in her ear, "but I would like to remind you that this doesn't have to be done today. Or even tomorrow. It's not too late to put this off."

Nitara's chip was still disabled, so she wore an ear clip. It had a built-in cam, mic, earphone. Like having an open channel all the time. She liked it.

"Never put off until tomorrow what you can do today." She grinned, even though Matti couldn't see it.

"That's one of your dad quotes, isn't it?"

"He's not wrong." In this case, he was exactly right. Because tomorrow wasn't promised, and she was feeling that keenly today. You had to do your part, when the time came, and it was rarely convenient or comfortable or without risk. For her, that was keeping her blood pressure down, her emotions in check, and the barrier between reality and her quarantined nightmares intact. With that, and Matti in her ear, she could do anything.

"Are you ready, Director Desai?" The most skilled camera person from the IEC's media relations department had perfectly tuned the lights and sound environment. They were waiting on her now.

"Yes."

"Alright." The camera person swiped something on their display, and a small red light lit up on the orb perched on spindly legs. "You're live in three... two..." They finished the countdown with their fingers then pointed to Nitara.

She looked straight into the camera. "Hello. My name is Nitara Desai, and I'm the Director of the International Energy Consortium's Office of Multilateral Funds and International Agreements. You may have seen reports about my being trapped in immersive, unable to wake up, while in a meeting regarding the new Zero Point Energy, or ZPE, technology. I won't tell you what nightmares visited me during that time, but I can tell you that my brain shut down to keep me alive. The doctors tell me I'm lucky to have survived. The IT folks say they've tracked the hack of my chip to a group in Denmark who may have ties to Miller Zendek. He's the man behind the attempts to claim copyright on the ZPE and license it to the world for a very hefty, ongoing fee. Miller certainly had motive to stop me. I have been fighting Miller's corporation on their claim to the copyright to the ZPE. I believe it belongs to the IEC, and hence the world, due to the origins of Dr. Ellis's research on Power Island One. But when I woke up, my thoughts weren't on the technology or the legalities. The knowledge that these people, whoever they were, would rather torture someone to death than give up the money and power that came with owning this new 'unlimited free energy' source chilled me to my core." She paused and wrestled with the slow-rising anger that saying the words out loud was summoning. This was her *personal* danger, and she was very clear about it. But she managed to shunt her outrage into a shudder that ran up her spine and raised the hairs on the back of her neck. Then it dissipated, from her body and her mind, leaving her free to complete her task.

"I've spent my entire career at the IEC making sure technology serves humanity—specifically tech developed on the Power Islands. The world paid for that development, and the fruits of that investment, that leap of faith in unprecedented international cooperation, belong to all of us. The people trying to claim this technology for them-selves... these are the kind of people I've been fighting my entire life. But as I lay in that hospital bed, I had to take a moment to think: is it really worth it?" She paused for a breath, letting it out slow. The anger was still contained, the barrier holding. "I could quit. Or I could keep fighting the largest and most dangerous fight I've ever engaged in. I'm broadcasting this reel to tell you—every one of you, the entire world, and Miller Zendek in particular—two things: one, *I'm not stopping*. And two, I'm releasing the copyright of the ZPE technology, along with detailed drawings and test data, to the world."

She paused to let that sink in. A wide range of viewers were in the audience: media sources, news watchers, ordi-nary people, perhaps even Miller and Ellis. This was live, but word would quickly spread, and the recorded version would, she hoped, be replayed millions of times. So her affect, her every word, had to be precisely delivered and backed up with the release of everything: the entire data trove that Dr. Sato's team had acquired on the operation of the ZPE.

Nitara made a swiping motion, as if uploading from her display, but of course that was shut down. It was actually a signal to her team to release the information onto a famous open-source server. One that would timestamp the upload and verify its origin. All of Dr. Sato's data plus one more legal document, one Nitara had drafted herself. It was a release of all claims of copyright, authorizing anyone to build, test, experiment on, develop, and otherwise use the ZPE for energy production purposes. She carefully crafted the language to make any weapons research a violation of terms, but once the technology was out of their hands, anything could happen.

Gods help them all.

"Miller is trying to monetize a new world-saving technology for himself," she continued. "It's not that the technology itself is evil—it could very well bring all the abundance that's been endlessly discussed—but it could also be dangerous. We need to be cautious about the use of it. But Miller, in his hurry to secure world-destabilizing wealth for himself, has rushed this out without any kind of safety testing plan. And this hack of my chip... let's just say that *safety* isn't the top priority for people like him. I'm taking a risk in releasing the plans to the general public. I urge you to use caution. Help find whatever risks there might be. Even if the tech itself is safe, we still need to proceed carefully in its use. The last time we thought energy was infinite in supply with no negative consequences, we unleashed world-changing consequences we're still trying to unravel. But Miller's scheme to enrich himself with the rapid rollout of the technology leaves me no choice... no choice but to release it to the world and ask for your help."

She looked away from the camera and signaled for her team to move into frame. Gwen, Akemi, Umberto, Ian, even her intern Sherri, filed in to stand behind her. Lucía needed to stay off camera, given she'd already been targeted by Miller. The rest would represent all the people involved in the IEC's effort to stop Miller. She introduced them, one by one, and then said, "This is my commons. These are my people. They're the ones who've been working behind the scenes to pull everything together and make it available for you. All the plans, all the theories, all the data you'll see uploaded and now open source for anyone to access. I'm old enough to remember the days when a few powerful men controlled everything. I remember the petrostate wars and the summer of plagues and how we decided to do things differently. We decided, collectively, to work together to change all of it. *And we did.* Not just teams like this, but local commons everywhere. You worked with your people, and you demanded change. And now we need your help to make this release of the ZPE serve humanity, not just one man." She glanced back at her team then to the camera for one last pitch. "The IEC exists to serve the world. We've done all we can. We're at a pivotal point: we need your help to ensure the ZPE is used to make the world better... and not to drag us back to a worldwide system of inequality and exploitation. Every one of us has a stake in making this work. Every one of us has a part to play in this. Thank you, in advance, for doing your part." With that, she nodded to the camera person, and they shut down the feed.

"All good," they said, eyes on the stream via their display.

"Far better than good." Matti's voice was almost as clear as Nitara's chip would have been, even as the chatter swelled up throughout the conference room. "Miller is right now regretting his life choices, especially in coming after you."

Nitara allowed herself a small, secret smile. "We'll see about that." Everyone wanted to shake her hand, but she needed a moment to calm her pounding heart, so she closed her eyes, still perched on the stool, and let the sounds and people flow around her. "We've denied Miller the one thing he really needs," she whispered, for Matti.

"Control of the ZPE knowledge," Matti said, but it was tentative, like she wasn't sure where Nitara was going with this.

"No." Nitara's shoulders were slowly relaxing as the adrenaline waned. "Cooperation. Until now, he's used coercion and greed to get it from the world. Now he'll have to earn it. And that's one thing his kind has never been able to do."

"Not when people see behind the veil. See what he's actually up to."

"Exactly."

Nitara opened her eyes and prepared to face the fallout.

———

"Did she just... did she say what I think she said?" Yang Do-yun stabbed the air with his chopsticks, which only paused the reel and threatened to drop his noodles on the floor.

His roommate, Luis, sitting at his desk with his back to Do-yun in their cramped Brown University dorm, said nothing. He must have his ear plugs set to silent.

Do-yun set down his bowl, ate the noodles off his chopsticks, swiped the reel to keep playing then tossed his chop-sticks at Luis. They didn't smack his head, just sailed past and clattered on Luis's desk, but it made his roommate jolt so badly, Do-yun couldn't help the laugh.

Luis tapped his ear and turned a murderous look to him. "The *hell?* Studying here."

"You have *got* to watch this," he said around the noodles then flicked a share copy of the reel to his roommate's chip.

Luis sighed and glanced at his display. "Is this that ZPE tech again? You're way too wrapped up in that drama."

"It's *world-changing* technology!" Do-yun sputtered. "And the IEC just put it in the public domain!"

"Wait, what?" Luis's gaze sharpened up. He was pre-law, which meant almost nothing, given they were both rising Sophomores still taking basic classes even during summer, but even he had to know this was huge. "You're kidding."

"I am very much not kidding." Do-yun watched the tail-end of the IEC director's reel. *Every one of us has a part to play in this.* It finished with instructions on how to access all the data the agency was apparently releasing. "And neither is she. Holy shit."

"This is crazy." But Luis was already swiping through to check out the site.

"I need to call my brother." The idea made his noodles threaten to come back up.

Luis looked past his display to squint. "The one at CERN? I thought you two were on the outs?"

Do-yun talked too much, and Luis knew all about his family problems. His brother Jae-sung wasn't just the respected oldest of three brothers—whereas Do-yun was the ridiculous "baby" who never did a serious thing in his life—Jae was also the runaway family favorite. Everyone loved the brilliant scientist breaking physics with all the best minds in the field, doing Very Serious Things at one of the most well-known physics research labs in the world. That Do-yun *also* wanted to go into physics had been seen as some kind of mockery—never mind he was interested in quantum gravity, and Jae was building his career in particle physics. *Totally* different fields. But it had soured what was left of his relationship with the eldest Yang son, along with the rest of the family.

"This is more important," Do-yun said quietly, mostly to convince himself.

Luis was back to watching the clip replay. "This sounds... dangerous." He looked to Do-yun.

"Exactly." He took a deep breath and sent off a call request to his brother.

———

A newscast director had to constantly make hectic calls on what to post, what to hold for further review, and what to drop-kick into the recycle bin to be forever forgotten... until she needed it in the next news cycle. Myla Odanye knew this when she took the position with London's premier newscast station, the Daily Record, but she radically under-estimated the toll the constant adrenaline would take on her sleep schedule. Or how her required caffeine supply would play vicious havoc as well.

Still, this was no time to turn down coffee.

Her assistant news director, Michael, returned with her steaming refilled mug just as the reel from IEC Director Desai finished playing for the second time, giving everyone a chance to fully digest what the hell just happened. Her team had already finished up today's rundown of news stories, dispatching field crews and sending the writers off to run scripts, but this was breaking news, so all that would get scrapped. Or at least half. They could still gather some B-roll, run a few topicals on big events, but this was *the* story, and they needed to decide how to cover it in the next five minutes. The anchors had already bumped the day's wholesome-interest story on the new penguin chicks at the London aquarium to air the IEC's press release directly.

Katerina, the show producer, Oliver, their top onscreen talent and a decent reporter, and Michael started talking over each other as soon as the clip ended.

"She's what? One day out of a coma?" Katerina objected. "And they're letting her decide to go public with the free-energy machine? Something's not right about that."

"She's not rogue." Oliver had gotten a fresh coffee from Michael too, and he sipped it calmly, the least visibly amped of the team. "This is approved from the top. But why? Do a deep dive on skullduggery at the UN and IEC."

"It's an obvious smack-back at Miller." Michael swiped away something on his display, hopefully keeping on top of the news elsewhere.

"He tried to murder her in immersive." Katerina was obviously salivating over that part of the story. "You could do a whole series on that."

Obviously missing the entire point, Myla thought. "What's the coverage look like so far?"

"Nothing yet," Michael said. "Just Breaking News and a few hot takes. What are you thinking?"

She was thinking this was much bigger. "She released the copyright."

"Is that even legal?" Katerina lifted her chin to Oliver. "That's the whole question, right? She can't just release it and—"

"She already did," Myla said. "It's out there. Legal or not."

"Which is a hell of a power move," Oliver commented. "What is she getting out of this?"

"I don't think that's the right question." Myla's tone had everyone's attention. She wanted to gulp the entire mug of coffee, but it was too hot. She set it down. "This isn't about Nitara Desai at all. The story is: what are *we* going to do now?"

"We?" Michael gave her a look. "The Daily Record?"

"No." She scrubbed her face, willing the pieces of this to assemble in her mind. "What are *all of us* going to do? That's what she's actually put out there. A call to action. This is Organizing 101 only... different. She's leveraging her personal story to toss this to the public, saying *Here, you take the ball.* When she's a director at the fucking IEC. It's wild. But *she* isn't the story. Not anymore. The people's reaction to this will be."

They were all nodding. And that was all the consent she required. "Okay, we need to find the people 'doing their part' on this. What are they doing? Who are they? Why were they inspired by Director Desai to take action? What impact is it having? I guarantee you no one else is running with that story out of the gate. They'll be gathering their experts and their pundits and pestering the powerful for reactions and statements. I want us scouring the nets for reaction stories from people. Get me at least one really good one before the evening cast. *Two,* and I'll get you each a pound of your favorite fair-trade roast for the coffee room." She didn't need to incentivize them. They were already swiping at their displays, chasing the story.

Which was good because she'd lied to Michael.

This *was* about what they would do at the Daily Record.

And this was *her* part.

———

"Director Desai, buenos días. Thank you for taking our call." The reporter from Televisa—Nitara hadn't caught her name but knew she was calling from a newscast station in Mexico City—wore an excessively colorful trim on her solid-black sweater.

Nitara struggled to focus. "Buenos días." Was it still morning? In which time zone? Nitara had lost count of the interviews she'd done since the announcement. Dozens, and they kept coming. She would keep it up until Matti forced her on break again.

"I will get straight to the point, Director. What do you say about those who have accused the IEC of abandoning its responsibilities during this time of great uncertainty?"

Nitara nodded to acknowledge this was, of course, reasonable to ask. "We are doing our jobs here at the IEC, which among other things, is safeguarding the world's right to access technology that was developed on the Power Islands."

"Normally, *safeguarding* would mean keeping it safe, not releasing the drawings and technical specifications for anyone to use."

"We are not in normal times." A brief surge of longing washed over Nitara. What she would give for normal times. Boring CarbonCon meetings where the most dramatic thing happening was an intemperate translator trying to keep up with a flustered delegate. But there were times when the world had to fundamentally shift... and then, if you were terribly lucky, you might have boring conferences once again.

The reporter was unimpressed with her short answer. "Are you aware that people all over the world, at this moment, are actually attempting to build the ZPE devices?"

"Yes." She hadn't been, actually. Her latest updates from her team mostly included nasty demands for attention from the world's most powerful people—people who she was purposely ignoring in order to work the media circuit and speak directly to the world's people. But it was good to hear. Time had lost all meaning, but it had hardly been a minute in the scheme of things. That people were already attempting to build the device was a wonder to her. That sharpened up her focus on the lovely reporter from Mexico City.

Milena Sanchez, she finally remembered. "Ms. Sanchez, I understand that people look to leadership to keep the world running smoothly. That is completely reasonable and very much the job of leadership. But in reality, it is not the IEC, and never has been national or international leadership, which has kept the world on course. It is entirely the collective actions of the people. Almost definitionally, *you* are what makes things work." She was speaking now directly to Sanchez's audience. "There is a deep relationality, an invisible connection, between every one we encounter every day: our families and friends, coworkers and casual acquaintances. The shopkeeper who's always open at six in the morning. The teacher who gathers up her students every morning at nine. We trust these people to show up and do their part, every day. As they, in turn, trust us to do our part. This trust, these connections— this assumption of cooperation—is how the world moves forward, minute by minute, day by day. Over the years, the informal commons, formed in addition to all those existing connections, have strengthened that unspoken cooperation even more, especially in parts of the world where we had become too disconnected, too fractious, too suspicious of one another. We were never meant to fly alone. That was part of what had come to ail the world. The commons are what have saved us. *We* got us here. All I have done is put this revolutionary technology in the hands it truly belongs to."

"But, Director Desai—"

"I'm sorry, but I must go to my next appointment." She should have let the reporter ask more questions, but Matti was already insistently flagging that her next interviewer was waiting. With an additional note for a mandatory rest break after that. Nitara allowed herself two deep breaths between her interview with Televisa and the next one: the Australian Broadcasting Corporation.

Meanwhile, people had already begun the real work.

It threatened to put a smile on her face.

———

For three days, Chizua Amaechi studied with great attention the plans that were to make the Zero Point Energy device, but she had to admit: she was no engineer. For two years, she had worked to install solar microgrids in all parts of Taraba State, but she was not the electrician connecting the power lines or the construction worker who assembled the panels. Her function was to coordinate funding and fix the problems. She could do nothing with these drawings or this testing data.

But she knew the man who could: her brother, Ndukwe.

She also knew he would not do anything on such a project unless she could convince him there was no other option for Taraba. For all of Nigeria. For all the years she had worked with the grants organizations to build a power infrastructure for rural villages, Taraba was still the state with the lowest electrification and most outages, especially outside of Jalingo and the more populated cities. And diesel was far too expensive now to use for backup. Many people still did not have power every day. Which cut off students from their lessons. And stopped the small businesses from pumping water or running their machines, all the commerce needed to pull her rural cousins out of the terrible poverty from which they suffered.

It was a trap that snapped shut whenever the power went off. This ZPE could change everything for her people.

She sent a message on her phone to Ndukwe, then left her small office and hurried to find him and speak directly to him. He would either be in the solar field north of the village, working on those maintenance requests, or he would be in the manufacturing shop he rented behind the market.

Of course, he was in the shop that he loved.

Chizua couldn't argue, at the moment. "Kedu, Nduk-we!" she said brightly. They were from Igboland, in the city, different from Taraba in every way. They used English to encourage the villagers to learn more than their native Hausa, but maybe their native language would soften Ndukwe up. She slipped past the worktables busy with machinery. The grants had provided many machining tools, and Ndukwe was always finding more or repurposing some old motor to run in his shop.

"I'm busy, Chizua." Ndukwe was being excessively rude. He must be busy, but this couldn't wait.

"*Ndu,*" she admonished as she got closer. "Am I no

longer your sister? I could be dying here, and you have not even looked up to notice."

He lifted his gaze from his jumble of wires and parts. "Are you dying?"

"Not yet." She smiled wide, but it got nothing from him.

"Perhaps you could *not die* somewhere else."

"I need to talk to you about the ZPE."

That got her brother's attention. "Did you see that IEC lady, huh? She just put it in the public domain. Can you believe something like that?"

"I want you to build one."

Ndukwe only blinked. "You are serious."

"Think what it could do—"

"*Chizzy.*" His face contorted like she'd presented him with a dead rat. "We are doing good work here, but I don't want to live in the villages forever."

"What do you mean—"

"I am teaching myself robotics so I will have a career when we are done with this project. A career *in Lagos.*"

"If you built a ZPE here in Taraba, think of what it would do for the village."

"I'm thinking what this nonsense will do to my career."

She held herself straight. "You want to do well for yourself. Good for you."

"Don't be that way." His expression melted. "This is something for the government to do—"

"The politicians are afraid. They don't want to upset this man Miller. They think they must beg from him for the chance to buy his machine. But he has already locked out Nigeria. We don't have the money to play his game. But now we don't have to wait for him to give us this machine. We can build it ourselves!"

He gestured to his shop. "Here? With these tools?"

"I believe so. The forums say it's possible."

"The forums." But he was listening to her now.

"We fight for this or we will be left behind. I can go on and tell you what all the people online are saying... or you can get started right now. I have money for materials. Extra for technological development. It's the fund I've using to buy your tools all along."

He frowned and glanced at the half-built thing on his workbench. "Do you honestly believe it can be done?"

"I believe we will never have a better chance to change Nigeria."

"All right." He sighed. "But if it works, I want to move to Lagos."

She beamed. "If it works, Lagos will come to us."

SIXTEEN

"Dr. Lavigne, Past President Lavigne, thank you for taking my call." Benicio Suárez was accustomed to the confidence that came from running his own lab at the University of Buenos Aires, not to mention working with Nobel-prize-winning physicists from all around the world, but the role of President of the IUPAP—International Union of Pure and Applied Physics—still felt like hiking boots not yet broken in. De verdad, he'd only been in office a month, and now this.

"*Benicio*," Annette chastised him. "How long have we been friends?"

"Since I interned in your lab for a semester and tormented you with my unbearably awful French."

"Sí." She chuckled softly. Her hair had turned gray, but the warmth of her smile was the same as always. She had been a constant guide for him, and it surprised him to need that even more now, so much further in their careers. "Please call me Annette before I begin to think this is not a friendly call."

"It is not. Well, it is, but..." The stress of this was piling up in his brain. Too many nights without sleep. He needed to fix that, but there was no respite in sight.

"You're calling about the student protests, no?"

"Yes." He held his breath, not sure how she felt about all this.

"And I am no longer the president of IUPAP. That devastating duty belongs to you now. So this *must* be a friendly call."

"Annette, I'm facing the Executive Council in less than a half hour." He scrubbed his face and let the fatigue show. "They'll want to take a vote on whether to bring this to the General Assembly. You know them all. I could use a consultation on... I'm just not sure it's advisable to..." Dios mío, he should just resign. "Would you perhaps like the job back?"

"Not on your life." But she was smiling broadly now. "I'm sorry, Benicio, I shouldn't tease. I will help in any way that I can."

"*Merci.*" His held breath escaped, audibly. Embarrassingly. "The student protests keep growing." It had started with a young undergrad, Yang Do-yun at Brown University, but had quickly spread to the entire American Society of Physics Students, and now the International Association of Physics Students had joined in. Which meant every lab in the world had students, graduate and undergraduate, engaged in a massive pressure campaign on every organization of physics, national and international, to sign on to their demands. *Protocols,* as they called them. But the threat was hardly idle. His own lab had ground to a standstill, and the strike hadn't officially started.

"I've been watching the news." Annette's humor had faded. "And I may be Emeritus Faculty now, but I'm not unaware of what's happening at Université."

"So your students are threatening a work stoppage as well?"

"Bien sûr. Not all of the physics students are French, but the solidarité is quite strong. Even outside of France, if there's a lab left in the world that hasn't joined the protest, I would be surprised."

Of course. And to be fair, it was the most exciting—and terrifying—time to be in physics. He only wished the "interesting times" could have occurred on someone else's watch.

"I've reviewed the protocols the students are demanding we adopt," he said. "They're well-constructed. Not a surprise given Dr. Yang at CERN was instrumental in crafting the safety guidelines and testing research plan."

"I understand the entire staff at CERN, including the Director-General, have co-signed the protocols at this point." That was announced yesterday—only a week since the IEC released the ZPE drawings and test data into the public domain—but Benicio would not have been surprised if Annette herself was involved in the crafting of the protocols. She had many close ties with CERN. With the entire world of physics, really. That came from being President of IUPAP—connections he would likewise have developed, if he'd had more than a month on the job.

"It's not the protocols that are controversial." Even he could see where this was headed. "It is entirely reasonable to formulate safety protocols and a research plan to explore this unproven technology. In any normal circumstance—"

"But this is not a normal time, is it?" Her pale blue eyes were unblinking on his display.

"No." It was time to state this bluntly. "The Executive Council will not want to lend their imprimatur to these protocols because of what the students will demand next."

He left unspoken that *he* would be the one to defend this to the press... and the world's governments.

"And what will they demand?" Her tone said she knew but would make him say it.

Fine. "Once the international associations of physics—the world's preeminent physicists—establish a protocol for the ZPE, declaring the world's most accomplished minds in physics think this technology must be safely researched and developed before any implementation, then... then the students—and let's be honest, Annette, not just students but organizations all over the world—will use that to pressure the world's politicians to adhere to the protocols."

"But of course." She gave a small smile. "That is why they have been written."

"I'm not a politician, Annette," he protested. "You should know that better than anyone."

"And yet you did not object when I nominated you for this position."

"That is not true. I did very much object."

"Not too strongly." Her smile grew.

Benicio's chest shrank. How to explain that his father was ailing, and that attaining this position gave him bragging rights with his father's friends while watching fútbol? That Benicio had always had more than admiration for her, a feeling that would have bordered on unseemly if they hadn't kept it entirely professional, partly but not solely due to the restrictions of power imbalances and age. How to explain, most of all, that he was unbearably *flattered* when she thought him worthy of this? But, perhaps, she was wrong. He was not actually worthy.

Her smile waned as he struggled to respond.

"Benicio, my friend—"

"Is this a friendly call?" Never mind that he initiated it.

He was starting to wonder if she hadn't known all along that he would turn to her. Was this a test? Was he already failing?

A gentle frown creased her brow. And she paused before answering.

He felt a hundred doubts blossom in that pause.

"Do you know what they call themselves?" she asked, and he was thrown. Was she changing the subject, or was this the only thing that mattered? "*The Physiverse.* It is quite clever, this new commons they have formed, nearly overnight, driven by youthful passion for science and justice and liberté. I would never have expected such a thing, but I should not have been surprised. The youth are almost always better than we are. At least, one hopes."

She was probably their leader. He should have known. "You think I should tell the Council to approve."

"I do. But more importantly, Benicio, I want you to understand this is the moment when you can stop doubting yourself."

"I don't—what are you saying?" His heart hammered, and he desperately wished he could travel through time and make his feelings known for her *or* had summoned the strength to walk away from her friendship, professional or otherwise. Either would be preferable to living through this moment.

"You are a brilliant physicist, Benicio." Her smile was warm again, and it melted some of the terror from his body. "Your mind grasps the full gravity of this moment, whether you want to acknowledge that or not. What we decide here, today, is not the only determinant of the future, but it is our part. Our chance. *Your* chance, Benicio. I am so pleased you are the one to make this decision. Your great mind and great heart have always been apparent to me, from that first day in my lab, when you were this young thing from Argentina, full of math and irrepressible energy. But you could never see yourself. You had no mirror. I've tried to be your mirror all these years, my friend, but *this moment* is your mirror now. Look into it and see that you are ready to lead us all into the future."

He laughed out of sheer anxious release and pretended there weren't tears gathering at the corners of his eyes. "Did you practice that speech? Is it the one you gave the *Physiverse* students?"

She smiled wide. "You never did want to hear me, Benicio."

"All right, all right." He pulled in a breath and found it surprisingly steady. "Are you ready for this future? Because I may need someone to write beautiful words for the Assembly motion."

She shrugged an innocence that she never had. "I am retired now."

He shook his head. "Then you will have time to entertain me when I come to France for a visit." He didn't know where that was going, and he would be horribly occupied through the fallout from this vote he was about to take, but he decided in that moment he would at least pay her a long-overdue visit. Soon.

"For you, always," she said.

And he wondered if that, too, had been her intent all along.

"I don't know about these people with that free-energy machine." That's Imani Johnson, Rashe's Wednesday regular, getting her two-strand twist out. They'd gotten through washing and detangling with just the regular chit-chat, but now halfway through the sections she'd clipped up so she could twist, Imani was going off on the ZPE.

Rashe wasn't sure her client's thoughts, and her hair salon was a safe space, so she just said, "Mm hm."

"I mean, if they were really here to save the world, would they need to assassinate the director of the IEC to do it? I don't think so." Imani shook her head, a small motion, so it didn't mess with Rashe's rhythm, but she took that moment to get some more cream to add to the ends, then wound them up in a flexi-rod to finish the curl.

Rashe let the silence sit for minute while she pulled out a new section to twist. Imani had been going natural for a while, but there was still some damage from the relaxers she'd been using before, so Rashe wanted to be careful. Plus, she prided herself on being professional to her clients, which not every stylist in Athens could say. Rashe respected her clientele and expected that respect in return. She'd been a shop baby, grew up in her mama's salon—now passed, God rest her soul—and Dominque Brown didn't put up with no nonsense from no one.

However, this ZPE business had been on Rashe's mind a lot. For reasons.

"You remember that cousin I told you about?" she said, starting up the new twist. "The one who went to Georgia Tech?" Atlanta was only an hour away, but it was a whole different place from Athens. It was good for Jael to go, with that big smart brain of his—the world needed his talents, and he needed to be out in that world—but *Lordt* she missed her baby cousin. And now he was wrapped up in this.

"Oh, yeah!" Imani adjusted her cape and met Rashe's gaze in the mirror. "Of course, I do. I know you wanted him to stay here in Athens. Nothing wrong with UGA, right here. But you get that scholarship, I guess you gotta go. How's he doing?"

"He's doing real good." And Rashe was glad that was true. If Jael had any trouble there, she would've driven out to get him herself. But he was a whole year in and doing fine. Didn't even come back to Athens for the summer. "Got himself a research position, so he's staying at Tech for the summer."

"What's he studying again?"

"Physics."

Imani's eyes went a little wide and met hers in the mirror again. "Is he one of those students doing the protests?"

Rashe had to make a choice: either let this go or bring it home. But she shouldn't have brought it up if she didn't think following through was the right thing to do. Just like her baby cousin.

"Yes, he is." Rashe finished off that curl but didn't start another. "And let me tell you, sis, I sure am proud of him. I can say that."

"Well, sure."

"In fact, I'm heading up there tomorrow."

"Yeah?"

"For the protests."

Imani was quiet a moment. And Rashe couldn't tell if she was being respectful or just not sure what to say. Rashe busied herself unclipping another section to twist.

After a moment, Imani said, "What exactly are they asking for, in those protests?"

Rashe nodded but kept her smile tucked in her chest. "The students have gotten together with scientists around the world and come up with these *protocols* about how to use the ZPE safely. They want the President to cancel that contract to license it from those people—the ones that tried to kill the IEC director?—and sign up to follow the protocols instead."

"The President of Georgia Tech?" Sister was confused.

"No, *the* President. Of the country." She finished off the twist and let her hand rest on Imani's shoulder, dropping her voice and pulling close. "They're already starting to build some of those reactors. You know how they've got all those smart folks at Tech? Well, they're building one and testing it, and they're saying countries have to sign onto these protocols or else they won't share any of their knowledge about how to do all that."

Imani gave her a pinched look, and Rashe wasn't sure if she understood. She barely followed it herself.

"Do you think it will work?" Imani asked.

"The protests? I don't know." She straightened up again. "All I know is Jael's one of the best souls on this planet, and if he thinks it's the right thing, then I'm gonna show up with my support."

Imani nodded because that much was easy to understand. You showed up for the folks you loved. And for the people doing the right thing. That's how anything worth doing got done.

"Well, then, maybe I'll get some of the girls, and we'll all make a trip into Atlanta."

Rashe let her smile loose. "Jael would appreciate that."

And she kept going with this twist-out, making sure to get it just right for one of her new favorite clients.

———

Saanvi dialed her earplugs to total block—she wanted to hear The Daily Aarav, not Crunch's incessant snacking.

Today's audio offense was kabuli chana, but not the good kind—she doubted he even knew how to make a decent fried chickpea—but instead, some nasty pre-packaged thing in a bag.

Saanvi turned up the volume and focused on Aarav's words as she waited for her latest, and probably pointless, SQL injection attack on a public-facing site to come back. "The value of money is not the value of life. The theory that says everything has a market price cannot tell you of the importance of clean air. Or the benefit of the vaporous beauty of Dudhsagar Falls in the monsoon season."

She wanted to go there, someday. If she could ever get through her studies and out of Bangalore. Remote work, a chip implant, and a satellite connection, and she could go anywhere.

If there was any beauty left to see.

"We are all connected," Aarav's voice in her ear continued, "not merely on this planet, but to the larger reality, the larger universe. We have an obligation to that as well. For many years now, we have rejected the idea of being human locusts on the planet. Or even locusts in the wide openness of space. The universe does not exist merely for us to spread out, colonize, and exploit. That is how we arrived at the edge of the cliff—"

Something poked her shoulder. *Gah.* She tapped her screen to stop the guru's words. *"What?"* She directed an unmistakable look of irritation at Crunch. She knew him only by his hacker name, but they often ended up together in this tiny space above an innocent-looking retail tea stall in the tech district. He should know better by now than to mess with her.

"Hey, chill," he objected. "Just thought you might want to see this."

"See what?" But she wrestled her annoyance into submission. They were on the same side, and it wasn't Crunch's fault that he was loud, and she was short on sleep.

Okay, maybe the loud part.

He tipped his screen toward her. Neither of them had chips or any kind of implants—that was also in the *someday* category—besides, the security on that was shit for the work they did. Part hacktivists. Part threat hunters. One hundred percent working on ancient computers to proactively defend climate workers and their non-profit activist organizations against the real threat actors... and sometimes crossing the line into offense.

Like her efforts today to trick America's DARPA into revealing their secrets.

Crunch's screen showed an encrypted message from one of their cells in Ukraine. *Made contact with irregulars working clandestine in maker spaces. One has a mod on the design to remove the kill switch.*

"Do you think it's real?" Saanvi asked. Even though their normal work—part-time around their actual jobs, hers being school and working normie IT—was defending eco-warriors and their IT infrastructure, everyone had redeployed their resources to hacking the ZPE. The encrypted code, trialing out the design specs, and for her, going straight to the source: DARPA. But this was a solid win, if it was real.

"Ivanov is as much a maker as a hacker," Crunch said. "I've known them for years. They don't oversell. If they say they can build a ZPE reactor without a kill switch, I believe them. And I've heard other chatter that someone's close to making power in Ukraine. Probably them."

"Still need the code, though."

"Still need the code," Crunch agreed and resumed

snacking. But his attention remained on her screen. "Any luck?"

Her SQL attack had bombed out. She queued up her next idea. "I found a third-party with possible access. You know how Renew Energy is deep into this, funding Miller for who knows how long?"

"You think you can get into Renew?" Crunch seemed skeptical.

"Not Renew, but that new company Miller founded? Eternal Energy? Turns out it's not so new." She brought up some listings she'd found buried in Denmark's registration system. It'd been two weeks since the IEC made everything public, and it had taken her most of that time to hunt this down. Then a frenzy of coding over the weekend. "Used to be called Giant Balls Enterprises."

Crunch choked on his kabuli chana. "Oh, come on."

"I know, right? So gross. Anyway..." She swiped that away and brought up an archive of the original company's public-facing site. "Turns out Mr. Giant Balls is a particularly stupid flavor of human. He left a remote sharing access point in the public-facing site, which also has an access point into Eternal, which..." She typed rapidly and sent off an attack she'd been coding up for the better part of the last 48 hours. Which was why she was short on sleep.

"Has a breach through the perimeter to DARPA?" Now Crunch was impressed.

"Maybe." They both watched as her code prompted for credentials. "I mean, it's a long shot, but it's possible he made a bunch of accounts and left one open."

"They have to have a zero-trust barricade." Crunch was back to skepticism, munching away on his snack. "This is DARPA. They're not stupid."

It looked like he might be right. Her code was ticking

through the possibilities and coming up with nothing. Then suddenly... a ping back.

Saanvi sat up straight. Then sent a command to reveal the directory listing.

The scroll was *massive*.

"What the—did someone just *let you in?*" Crunch tossed aside his snack and ported over a remote window to her computer.

"I don't know but grab everything!" Saanvi's heart was pounding. She started a root-directory scrape then sent a spider off to see how far it could go. She was in *deep*.

"Wait, what's this stash labeled *Renew?*" Crunch was paging through while she was busy downloading. "Slipper, there's something here about... I think this is kompromat."

"Just *download*, Crunch. We can sift through later." But she couldn't help scanning through the files as they downloaded. All different kinds—some were definitely drawings or tech spec sheets or something the folks trying to make their own ZPE reactors would find useful. She'd upload it all to the leak sites when she was done. No time to sift through everything when she could get a thousand allies to parallel process through in a fraction of the time. But there had to be, somewhere in this data dump, something about the physical key DARPA designed for Miller's quantum encryption. If she could score that, then even if Miller got all those contracts signed, even if the corrupt low-level officials in every country and their even-more-corrupt political bosses couldn't resist being the next big Energy Titans, if anyone had the key to shutting those down... or locking Miller out of his own machines... then none of their bullshit would matter.

Please be in there. She sent the silent prayer up to whatever goddess looked favorably upon white hatters trying to fight the forces of greed and tech-exploitation.

Suddenly, they lost access.

"Oh, shit, shut it down. *Shut it down!*" Crunch scrambled to cut their gateway connections and instant air-gap their operation, but it was probably too late. Someone knew they'd gotten in. DARPA probably let them download just enough to pinpoint where they were. But tracking a couple hacktivists didn't seem like reason enough to let them inside in the first place.

Which Saanvi was almost sure had happened.

Someone inside DARPA had let them in for reasons they'd probably never know.

She pulled her drive. "You have a copy?" she asked Crunch, already getting her bag slung over her shoulder and ready to go.

"Just the Renew files." He yanked his drive out of the computer frame.

There would be no coming back here. They'd have to find a new location for their cell. Might not even see Crunch again. Not that she'd miss him all that much, but he *did* have some of her data.

Saanvi extended her hand. "Nice knowing you. Don't get burned, okay? And if you find something, ping me."

He pulled her in for a quick hug, which was startling, but not enough to keep her from briefly hugging him back.

And then they were out the door.

———

Miller was surrounded by incompetents and fools.

"What do you *mean*, the production line is shut down?" he demanded from the Renew flunky finally returning his call. The man had been assigned to update him on the status of the manufacturing facility they'd tucked between the floating piers of Esbjerg. This ridiculous small seaport town was perpetually cold—he would give half of his first Tier 1 payment to have Southern California's scorching heat again—but Esbjerg was in the middle of exactly nowhere, where West Jutland met the North Sea, and that was the best place for the first EVEG production facility to be built, unnoticed until its debut on the world stage.

Once the money started coming in, there would be one in every major city.

"Sorry, but it appears there has been some kind of... accident."

"We don't have *time* for accidents." His raised voice startled a pigeon off the railing of his wooden terrace over-looking the docks. Renew had finally secured a luxury apartment for him, but the view was primarily the compa-ny's brutalist architectural disaster hovering at the water's edge, framed by cranes and cargo ships. Everything had been going precisely to plan not two weeks ago, and since then, nothing but an outrageous comedy of errors. He was so distracted by the absurdity of the timing of this delay he almost missed the undertone of the flunky's emphasis on the word *accident*.

As in: *it wasn't an accident at all.*

"What's happened?" A weird, discomforting feeling crept into his chest. He vaguely identified it as dread a moment before the man said the word.

"Sabotage." His voice trembled.

Danes were absolutely inscrutable to him. Miller couldn't tell if the man was worried about telling the truth or horrified by the unspeakable atrocity visited upon the plant.

"How can it possibly be sabotage?" His frustration was rising again. "The location is secret. Not even Esbjerg's municipal council knows the plant's purpose."

"It could have been an accident." The man was definitely hedging now.

Miller struggled to remember the man's name. "Okay, look, Eric—just tell me. How bad is the damage?" He realized a moment later he should have inquired about injuries first, but—

"Sorry, my name is Ulrik. Ulrik Oster."

Miller couldn't fathom why that mattered.

"And the damage is complete," Ulrik said. "The entire facility is engulfed in flames. You could maybe see them?"

The words baffled Miller until he remembered: the plant wasn't far, at the north end of town. He slowly turned in that direction, and sure enough, rising into the air was a massive plume of smoke. He would have smelled it, but the gray column bent out to sea.

For a moment, he had no words.

"I am sorry to report, also, there has been some additional damage."

"*Additional* damage? Is it engulfed in flames or not?" Miller's mind scrambled to calculate how much this would set him back. How quickly could they set up another production facility? And with what money? The Tier 1 countries were already demanding prototypes for inspection before authorizing the contracts, and he only had the two—

"Not here," Ulrik said, that tremble back in his voice. "At the island. A saboteur broached security and set fire to the ZPE device. They were apprehended—"

"*What?*" Miller saw literal red, a haze that clouded his view of his facility, and his plans, literally going up in smoke. One prototype at the plant, a model for production, and one at the island for inspections. *How could they both be gone?* Without the prototypes, he was catastrophically set back. It was impossible that this had happened. If a sea monster arose at this very moment out of the North Sea and dragged him to a watery grave, he would have been less stunned.

How? How could this have happened to him? He was so close...

"Sorry."

Miller hung up the call. And seethed and paced the deck until his vision cleared. He had a mole. *Obviously.* First the leak—schematics, data, everything they had—and now *sabotage?* He kept everything so tight. He trusted *no one.* And yet someone had gotten access to data Ellis swore no one could possibly have. And they gave it to the fucking IEC! Had that director simply *died,* this would have never happened.

But she was unimportant now.

Miller had to get ahead of this. Had to, somehow, force this whole fucking mess back on plan. Bury the fire, put out a press release saying the prototype was still in operation, despite fucking *sabotage,* then move immediately to get another prototype and production facility built, and come up with some plausible reason for delays in delivery. Delay. Deny. He could trot out Ellis, send him on a world tour to convince the politicians to sign their fucking contracts and *pay him.* Then he could make it all happen.

He stopped pacing and went inside to place a video call to Søren, his most reliable man at Renew. The man's pale face was even more pallid than normal. At least he understood what a fuck up this was.

Miller ticked off his demands. "Fire everyone at the

plant. And the island. I don't know who's responsible, but I want all of them on the street and signing NDAs on the way out."

"That is not how—"

"Norgaard, fucking *do it*." Miller sucked in air between his teeth. This was what he needed. Show people what a mistake it was to fail him. "Then we'll need new people to build another prototype. Renew will have to put up some funds. Eternal's dry until we get those contracts signed and the payments coming. But we can borrow against—"

"That won't be possible."

"What the fuck are you—"

"The insurers for the company will be investigating." The man's affect was entirely flat. "They have already, before the sabotage and the fire, threatened to drop Renew's coverage over the development of unregulated energy sources—"

"*Unregulated.*" It was so outrageous, words momentarily escaped him again. "We're developing *world-changing* energy here! We're inventing the future!" His voice was rising, the volcano of his anger ready to erupt. "I will *not* be held back by insurance company imbeciles!"

Søren gravely nodded. "It is an outrage. They do not understand your vision."

"*Obviously.*" But at least the man understood. And might still be useful. Even if Renew was getting cold feet. They'd always been weak, incompetent fools easily scared. Just like the rest of the so-called leadership of the world. Always worried about a few protests or the latest exposé on the news. No one with the intelligence or vision to do what was necessary. Men like Søren understood. "Do what I said, I don't care how, find a way. And see who we can pressure inside Renew to get us the money we need to fix this fucking mess. I'll send Ellis out on tour, just the Tier 1 countries—fuck the rest. If we have them, we don't need anyone else. Ellis will soften up the politicians with his techno babble, but it's time for me to lean hard on those idiots we invited to the conference. They need to come through with signed contracts, and *money,* or I will fucking ruin them. And they need to do it *now.* Before this gets any more out of hand."

He couldn't imagine what else could go wrong, but he wasn't going to let it happen. He had a world to save. An empire to build.

These idiots had better get with the program... or they would wish they had.

SEVENTEEN

Arminio Salles had remained at CarbonCon because he'd been convinced Brazil's fate would be decided here, at the IEC building in Los Angeles, not back home.

He'd sent his trusted assistant, João, back to the capital and Brazil's Ministry of the Environment to handle the fallout of the ZPE crisis. João was keeping a close eye on that absolute idiota Antônio Campos, who Miller had tapped for his clandestine conference, but who was better known within the Ministry for his close ties to Movimento Verdad. They were criminals, every last one, and likely behind the fires that had violated Brazil's emissions targets and threatened Amazonia itself. They called themselves patriots, but they were enemies of Brazil, and of the planet. Yet they still had support at some levels of the government. The fact that Campos stood to benefit personally from this obscene contract he had negotiated in secret on the behalf of Brazil made Arminio want to fly down to Brasília and strangle the man himself.

Or send João. That might be sufficient for Arminio's

frustration, and arguably make the world a better place, even if it would do nothing to stop all this madness.

Arminio wasn't against the ZPE technology itself. Campos had bid enough for them to be considered Tier 2 in Miller's scheme, which meant Brazil wouldn't be left behind economically. But he was sympático to the students and the protesters. Men such as these couldn't be trusted. When in the history of the world, Brazil in particular, had such men ever kept their promises?

Only when it made them rich.

Which invariably caused mass harm, to people and to the rainforest.

Brazil had worked so hard to put that way of living behind her. The only reason the Amazon had not already tipped into a dried-up savannah was the people who understood the stakes keeping people like Movimento Verdad out of power.

These were hard-won battles.

Yet the world, especially the vaunted D-10, a coalition to which Brazil had never quite managed an invitation, was rushing to give Miller all the power in the world. Literalmente.

Even within Brazil, Arminio's vote was the holdout. It was embarrassing to the politicians not to have the approval of their own Ministry for the Environment for a technology contract that would supposedly save the planet. Arminio could not convince them of their foolishness. João reported it was only a matter of time before they proceeded without his blessing.

But now, on the news, it appeared Miller had a setback.

"An anti-growth commons named Reset Humanity has claimed responsibility for two fires spotted via satellite in Denmark, one in a small coastal town and the other at the wind farm in the North Sea where the ZPE technology was recently demonstrated." The reporter was from a local station in Los Angeles, speaking Spanish, which was close enough to Portuguese that Arminio didn't need the translator. "Renew Energy could not be reached for comment, but Miller Zendek himself, the brilliant businessman—"

Arminio snorted.

"—who was responsible for the secret development of the ZPE technology denies that the fires were in any way associated with the production facility Reset Humanity claims to have destroyed or the prototype purportedly housed at the wind farm."

The newscast displayed an interview with Miller, a pasty man who wore his arrogance like an invisible crown. His English was subtitled, but the tone was clear enough. "People who want to stop this technology from giving humanity a future will say anything. Yes, there was a small fire on the island. It's an older farm with aging technology, and one of the batteries developed a leak. It was, quite fortunately, quickly contained and there were no injuries." He shrugged. "I don't know what happened in Esbjerg, but it had nothing to do with the EVEG device, Eternal Energy, or Renew Energy, as far as I know. Everything is proceeding according to plan."

One didn't give extended answers to low-level reporters when everything was *fine*.

Arminio was more than familiar with the ability of satellite mapping to determine the nature and origin of fires. The IEC still hadn't released their report on the investigation into Brazil's fires, although perhaps they were understandably busy.

But if the radical commons had truly disabled the ZPE prototype...

He swiped up a video call to João, who answered quickly, but looked ragged. "Alô?"

"Are you seeing this on the news?" Arminio asked in Portuguese.

"The fires? I don't believe a word out of Miller's mouth."

"What is the status of Campos's contract?"

João rubbed his eyes. "Moving forward. The robotics unions have examined the information the IEC released. They are working on a prototype, but I can't find anyone willing to say they can build it."

"They're afraid."

"Movimento Verdad is strong in that sector."

Arminio swiped away the news and rubbed his face as well. "Robotics is the future of Brazil, as much as securing the Amazon from abuse. If anyone can build this, it's us. Why sign our future over to the likes of Miller? It's insanity. If we could just convince the President to support joining the protocols—"

"*Arminio.* It's not going to happen. Not as long as the D-10 are still in play."

He had been tracking that, of course. Six of the ten—Canada, Germany, Italy, Japan, South Korea, and India—had already signed or were close. The remaining four were more influential than their number: Australia, France, Britain, and the United States. All eyes were on America with this. Their support would influence the D-10 to formally endorse the contracts. Even without the Americans, and despite the protests, there seemed to be momentum in the halls of power to give Miller everything he desired.

It made Arminio's stomach churn.

"How does it come to this?" he grumbled. "Miller probably has nothing but ash and yet over half the D-10 are ready to give him a trillion dollars just for the pleasure of being first in line for the grift of the century."

"Is it a trillion?" João asked, eyes suddenly sharp. "How do you know?"

Arminio waved vaguely to the conference happening downstairs, if you could even call it that. No business was being conducted. And why would they? The world was upside down. He had retreated to his personal room, which was still inside the quarantine perimeter. "The bids are open secrets at CarbonCon."

"But you're sure it's close?"

Arminio studied João's face. "You're thinking he's triggered the exclusion."

João stroked his chin. "I have an idea. It's risky."

"Let's hear it."

"Whether Brazil ratifies the contract matters a great deal to Brazil, but is unlikely to influence others. America will do as she pleases, per usual. *But...* if Brazil's pledge were to put Miller over the exclusion limit—no funds transferred, just promised—and we were to, say, *suggest* to Director Desai that Miller was in violation, they could petition the international court. If they accepted the petition, Miller's assets would be frozen pending an investigation."

"*Ah.*" It was a glimmer of hope. "Delay. Perhaps a terminal one."

"The IEC might express their gratitude in the form of a carbon limit waiver."

"That might be too much to hope for." But Arminio smiled. "Still, the IEC is embattled. A well-timed blow to Miller *would* earn some good will." He would take great pleasure in it, regardless.

"The international court might not agree to an investigation," João warned. "It's a risk."

"That is out of our hands." The knot in Arminio's stomach loosening a little. "This is good, João. And worth the risk. Keep working with the robotics unions. If Brazil can build her own ZPE, we won't need to worry about the IEC's report. I'll take care of the rest."

João gave a short nod and signed off.

Arminio had been right to remain at the IEC after all.

———

Gwen was technically on loan to the IEC—her real job at USEC working IT for LA Regional Director Zuri Hill-Gray was languishing at the bottom of her priority list—but this gig taking down bad-guy Miller and hacking DARPA's physical key for their quantum encryption was way more fun. Plus she'd gotten a ton of time with the delightful and lovely Lucía Ramirez, who was likewise on loan and tragically unavailable for dating but still becoming a fast friend. She had that combo of features Gwen got stuck on fast— whip smart and funny as hell.

Also cute. The kind of cute that shouldn't be all lumped up into one person. Not fair to the rest of humanity.

Gwen would be sad when the fun times were over.

Except Miller needed to be gone. Maybe not physically unalived, but if a giant sequoia fell on his head, she would give a eulogy for the tree. Exhibit A of his annoying habit of still being alive was his current media charm tour, which she was watching on a short break from all the fun times.

"I don't know what these students think they're accomplishing with these protests," Miller was telling a way-too-credulous reporter. "A few well-timed arrests would make them think twice about skipping class."

This fucking guy.

"Do it, asshole!" she said as she munched the cafeteria's sad granola. "See what you get."

"And they'll probably deserve it," said a voice behind her.

Gwen swiped away the news on her display and swiveled, but she already recognized the voice of her temporary boss, Ms. Nitara *No, You Can't Kill Me in Immersive, Fucker* Desai. Gwen didn't call her that to her face, but she felt like she should.

"Just taking my *talk back to the news* break. What's up?"

She had her hands primly folded in front of her. "Can I ask you a question?"

"I mean, you can ask anything you like. Might not like the answer, though." Gwen quirked up an eyebrow because that was a lot of hedging from Boss Lady. She'd jumped right back in the hot seat after cheating death, which was questionable from a mental health perspective, but she was chip-inactive and seemed steady for over two weeks now. Gwen was already a fan, but demonstrated badassery *and* releasing the ZPE data to the public?

Well, that's how you win a girl's heart. Might be hard to say no to whatever this ask was about.

"Did you have anything to do with the arson of Miller's ZPE prototype?" The steely-eyed look was back. Much better.

Gwen held up a finger. "First, I'm offended you didn't think I burned down the production facility as well."

"I was getting to that."

Gwen brought out finger number two. "Second, if I

were in charge, we definitely would have taken the ZPE with us *and* not gotten caught. Ergo, no. Obviously not involved. But if I were, 100% would not tell you. No offense."

Desai was fighting a smile, for sure. "Understood. I was hoping you could confirm the reports that everything was destroyed. That would help us."

"I'd say Miller's pathetic media tour is all the confirmation you need: *someone* broke his toys."

Desai seemed to accept that, which meant Gwen didn't need to tell her about the dark web chatter. Badass probably had a channel there herself. Her assistant, Ian, came trotting up, looking earnest, although it was hard to tell with him. Seemed perpetually serious.

He gave Gwen a glance. It was only the three of them in the tiny break room. "Got a very interesting visit to your office from Arminio Salles, delegate from Brazil."

Desai frowned. "What did he want?"

"To tell you that he's given his blessing to Brazil moving ahead with Miller's contract. In fact, he recommended increasing the bid to \$50B in U.S. currency. He specifically said to tell you that would put Miller over the trillionaire exclusion, which, and I quote, *you might want to do something about,* end quote."

Desai's eyebrows hiked up.

Gwen's grin threatened to break her face. "Malicious compliance! My favorite kind of subversion."

Desai swung a scowl her way. "You work for USEC."

"Just ignore that. Besides, technically, I work for *you* now." She would really miss this job when it was all said and done.

Desai shook her head and turned back to Ian. "If he's actually over the limit, it's time to petition the international court to investigate. Especially with Miller thinking he's got a loophole with Renew Energy—make sure that's included. With any luck, they'll freeze his assets. At minimum, an investigation at the international court should trigger a suspension of the contracts that have already been signed. The D-10 can't just ignore the court and still pretend to be a cohesive power. Get the team working on that petition right away."

Ian nodded and scooted off.

"Sounds like good news." Gwen finished the last of her granola.

"We need all the good news we can get. Tell me you have some in this data breach splashing across the news."

"Oh, that's a whole basket of puppies!" She motioned Desai to follow her to the tiny sink so she could talk while washing up her dish. Housekeeping took good care of the IEC folks, but it was just decent to clean up after yourself. "These dark web eco-hacktivists are the real thing, but hacking DARPA? Not their usual target, and out of almost everyone's league. So, the fact that they scored such a huge data dump—"

Desai folded her arms. "You think it's not real?"

"Oh no, it's definitely real. I just think they had help."

"Hm." Desai pondered that a second. "Maybe this is the Americans deciding to help us."

"Or deciding to fuck over Miller. Either way, nicely done." Gwen finished drying her hands. "The data dump is an absolute gold mine. You know I've been trying to crack the encryption on DARPA's kill-switch code or, failing that, reverse engineer the physical key, but the DARPA hack has *everything*. Schematics for the key, *the actual code,* the original quantum encryption key. It's literally unbelievable. Like too good to be true. But it works—people are already using it. And some Ukrainian apparently redesigned the whole device *without* the kill switch. Nerds with a little time, I swear. Turns out there's a hundred ways to make this thing, now that people know it's possible and have, like, even a sliver of information."

"So all these people making the device... they're going to make it work?" Desai seemed skeptical, but Gwen couldn't see how. It's not like Miller or Ellis or anyone, really, had a lock on genius. There were billions of people on the planet, everyone starting with the same basic wetware in their skull —there were geniuses everywhere. And none of them could individually keep up with what folks could do working together.

"Someone's making power out there already," Gwen predicted with high confidence. "We just don't know about it yet."

Desai's focus went to her ear clip for a moment then came back. "Matti says DARPA just released a statement confirming they were hacked."

"See? Inside job. No way they'd confirm if they didn't *want* that info taken seriously."

She was listening to the voice in her ear again. "Supposedly, there's a cache of Renew documents tying Miller to the immersive security breach?"

"For my money, that's why DARPA let the hackers in. To get that intel out there." Gwen stroked her chin. "Although, it could be disinformation. They might hate Miller enough to pin attempted murder on him. I wouldn't argue with that choice."

"I'll leave that to the proper authorities to sort out. I want Miller stopped for the *right* reasons."

"I'll take the wrong reasons as long as Miller ends up in

a tiny apartment in Siberia having to grow his own potatoes."

Desai was fighting that smile again. She tilted her head toward the door. "I want to check in with my teams, but if you're right about any of this, that means America's swinging to our side. Might be time for me to pay the American delegate a visit."

"I'll be sifting through the data breach, see if I can come up with some more puppies for you."

Gwen might have to see if Desai had any open positions on her IT staff. Working for the IEC was way more entertaining than she'd have ever guessed.

———

Gwen had gone on break, leaving Lucía alone with the newscasters. She cradled the solar mug Joe had given her after she'd complained her super-caffeinated Kenyan tea was always cold. The mug soaked up photons, both from the lights and sneaking in from the windows, and kept her tea perpetually warm. It said: *CAUTION: may start talking about battery backups.* She'd laughed a solid minute when he gave it to her. It still made her chuckle several times a day. Gwen said only old men talked about battery backups, which only made her laugh harder.

The rest of Lucía's team at the IEC had scattered to the winds.

Akemi was off to Europe, working with some international union of physicists to develop the protocols and now to convince people to sign on. The protests helped —those were a worldwide thing now. Governor Kipo'mo had left the IEC building to return to doing governor type things. The protests were demanding Kipo'mo's attention too, plus Cal Tech was getting real about making a reactor of their own. They'd already published some preliminary data but had quickly backtracked and fallen into line with the Physiverse protocols: no release of data to folks who weren't abiding by the safety plan Akemi had helped develop.

That left her and Gwen to help with the IEC's *all hands on deck* situation. The USEC IT department had a bunch of staff to fill in for Gwen, but Lucía had to recruit someone to run turtle bot checks and handle her other duties on the Island. She'd been bouncing all over since this thing started a month and a half ago. First at Zuri's Hillstead, then back home and working on the Island, then the quarantine hit. Maria had been exposed at the hospital in the H_3N_3 outbreak, so the whole family had gone on locked down. It gave Lucía time to get to know baby Eva, and the rest of the family, and she was actually sad when it was over. Then, just as she was returning to the Island, Akemi took everything to Nitara, and things got crazy again. The interim Island Designer, who had stepped in when Miller left, had been covering for her, but to go on extended loan to the IEC—three weeks and counting now—she'd needed to bring in another power engineer. Fortunately, Power Island One was historic. Folks were jumping at the chance.

But now their team at the IEC had dispersed, Gwen was absorbed in the tech and now the data breach, which left Lucía chasing loose ends to make sure nothing was falling through the cracks. Miller had tried to kill her *twice.* Sure, he'd moved on to trying to kill other people, but it wasn't like that made it better or made her forget. She was here to see this thing through to the end.

Then she could get back to turtle bot maintenance and

an ordinary life. Assuming the position was still being held for her. Power engineers had strong job protection, but things were fluid right now. If she couldn't go back, she'd find something else. No matter what, her work needed to be close enough to Huntington Beach for her to live with her family. *And Joe.* Because that was getting serious in a way she still had a hard time believing. But holding onto the fairy-tale in the Family Strong was non-negotiable—the rest could be sorted.

Nitara had returned from the break room with Gwen, which gave Lucía a chance to grab the director and give her an update before she got whisked off to another interview or strategy meeting.

"Hey," Lucía said to Nitara, giving Gwen a quick wave as she settled into whatever data thing she was doing next. "Got a minute?"

"Maybe two. How are you doing?"

"Me?" Lucía was thrown for a second then remembered Nitara relentlessly checked on their mental health. Such a difference from her prior disaster bosses, up north and then *Miller,* she still wasn't calibrated for it. The director had been that way even before the assassination attempt, which she seemed amazingly recovered from, although she took a lot of breaks now. Which Lucía was glad to see. She understood a little about how that messed you up, and she hadn't even been trapped in an immersive nightmare. "I'm fine. I take my frustrations out on Gwen, and she tolerates it reasonably well."

"Only because you're cute!" Gwen poked a finger at her without looking up, already deep in her data-crunching.

Nitara seemed amused but satisfied with that as an answer.

"A couple things, real quick." Lucía didn't want to take

too much of her time. "I saw on the news: the WSO came through with a belated ruling that the IEC has the right to claim copyright on the ZPE. Kinda moot since you've, you know, *released it to the world,* but I thought you might want to know."

"The D-10 was trying to bury it in subcommittee." Nitara tapped a finger to her lips, thinking. "I probably gave the WSO no choice. But that's good. Might help to get the D-10 to take a stand against the contracts themselves."

"You think? The news people all seem convinced it's a matter of time before the entire D-10 has ratified Miller's contracts. Despite the protests." This was her secret fear, the one she didn't voice to anyone, not even Gwen: that all of this would be for nothing. All the effort, all the risk, all the work to uncover Miller's plot and try to stop it. Part of her was afraid she'd been wrong. That the powerful were unstoppable, after all. They would have their way, despite lying, cheating, stealing, and trying to murder people. Maybe even because of that. There *should* be justice in the world, but it was a plain fact that life held no guarantees. She knew that better than most.

"It makes for great news, predicting the terrible people will win." Nitara folded her hands in front of her deep-blue sari, unruffled. "That no one will work together, come together, or do the right thing. Much less that *many* people will do exactly that. That's not news precisely because that's what happens every day."

"You're saying we shouldn't listen to the news?"

"I'm saying don't mistake their opinion for forecasting the future." Nitara smiled. "It's unwritten, even for them."

Then Lucía remembered the most important thing. "There's some guy on the news saying he can connect Miller to the attempt on your life."

Gwen's attention swung to them. "You mean the DARPA data breach?"

"No." Lucía shook her head for emphasis. "A bunch of Renew employees got fired, and this one's doing a tell-all to anyone who will listen."

Gwen's eyebrows lifted, and she gave an approving nod.

Nitara's smile grew. "See? Someone doing the right thing. And we didn't even ask." Then she was called over by another team and was off doing her important duties.

"So..." Gwen had swung in her chair to fully face her. "What're you doing after the party is over?"

"We're still neck-deep in crisis here, Gwen." She pretended to scowl.

"I know, I don't want it to end, either." Her faux expression of mourning made Lucía snort. "But seriously..."

"I only ever wanted to do one thing." Lucía sighed. "Not that returning to the Island was the fairy tale I expected, with Miller tarnishing it, endangering my family, and trying to kill me. I'm pretty committed to seeing him pay for that. Then we'll see if I still have a job. Or figure out what's next."

"Fair enough." Gwen turned back to her data display, massaging her hands for another go at data hunting. "Let me know if you need a ride-along on your revenge plot. I know some people."

Lucía gave a small laugh, rubbed the fatigue out of her eyes, and queued up more news to monitor.

They weren't forecasting the future—they were barely finding the news that mattered right now. That future was up to her and everyone else. Like Nitara said, each of them had a part. Sometimes it was big, like when Lucía shook off Miller's attempt to kill her and took all the crazy that had happened on Power Island One to Zuri, then Akemi, trying to find someone who could get to the bottom of it. That was a big thing, one she only could manage with the support of her amazing new family. Sometimes, your part was small, like watching the news and looking for something that could help with the cause. Big or small, what mattered was doing the *right* thing, when it was asked of you.

Lucía stretched out the kinks from sitting too long, sipped from her perpetually warm mug, and kept doing her part.

———

The world was always having some crisis or another—being Regional Director of USEC meant Zuri was constantly fielding some problem—but she could usually manage that from the Hillstead. She didn't want to miss those precious moments that fluttered by, like this morning when the kids foraged bright yellow buttercups from the Hillstead and bestowed them upon her with all the ceremony of royalty. The flowers sat on her desk, proud and tall in Auntie Vivian's hand-thrown vase. It was the kind of joy you grabbed and held tight because it made all the rest worthwhile.

She was blessed like this most days. Under normal conditions, she didn't have to go into the city to keep the power grid humming. Most of that work fell to her staff anyway, although they were a little short, given the IEC was trying to save the world from Miller and needed all the help they could get. USEC was managing, but *normal* was still a ways off. The WSO was dropping back to a Level One alert tomorrow, now that the outbreak had been contained, which was good for public health, but bad for the grid. Fortunately, the heat event had passed. They had enough capacity to run the city during a record heat wave *or* everyone cranking up their office air exchanges due to an epidemic, but running both had pushed the limits.

Which only made her hope this ZPE thing could be worked out *without* enriching the man who tried to kill her.

As her mother said last night over dinner, *That man deserves a lot worse.*

Life was too short for revenge, so Zuri didn't wish Miller to be dropped in the Sahara without a hat (Monique Hill's wishes were very specific). She did hope the Renew whistleblower on the news got some traction connecting Miller to that horrifying attempt on the IEC Director's life. Zuri couldn't prove Miller sent his thugs after her and Lucía but that didn't stop her from wanting justice. Preferably in a form where she didn't have to lay awake at night. Miller was the type who would want his revenge bloody and final, if he got the chance. She'd prefer he didn't.

She brought that whole business to Commissioner Sato for a reason. Miller's kind would chew up the world and its people, given half a chance. It turned out working this from the inside had been the right the thing to do. Akemi had taken it even further and managed to keep them all safe in the meantime. But she was still keen on actual justice. Or simply having Miller *stopped.* He would do anything to enact this plan he'd been plotting for a decade. At this moment, it wasn't clear how this would end. Not for lack of effort by a whole mountain of people. The IEC folks, of course, but Akemi had been swept up full-time. The man had been traveling the globe, trying to get these Physiverse protocols adopted by every country on Earth.

A message popped up on her display.

· · ·

Me and you, we got more yesterday than anybody. We need some kind of tomorrow. — Toni Morrison

Her assistant Jeevika and her relentless quotes. Zuri smiled and swiped the message away, but rather than bringing up Jeevika's usual morning report, it initiated a face-to-face call.

When her assistant's face appeared, Zuri asked, "Is something wrong?" She hoped her pleasant work-at-home day wasn't over before she even got to lunch.

"I thought you might want to handle this personally." Jeevika's pinched expression was uncharacteristically concerned. "Cal Tech put in a request to double their standard power allotment. They say it's for their ZPE experiments. They've supposedly signed onto the protocols, and you approved that overage from last week, but this is well beyond that. I've dropped the request in your folder, but they're very insistent they need it right away."

"All right. I'll see to it." Zuri was already opening her folder. "Everything else okay?" Jeevika's handling of demands on her time was the only thing that gave her space to do the mundane but still important tasks, like review that Santa Monica desalination project, which needed to move forward.

"Your calendar is booking up fast for tomorrow, but nothing else that can't wait."

"Thank you, Jeevika." She signed off and quickly read through Cal Tech's request. It wasn't like she wanted to hold back their progress—she was very much in favor of a working prototype built by anyone *other* than Miller—but the outages Miller orchestrated had cost USEC something hard to earn back: *trust.* She herself even had a moment of doubt. Were all the sacrifices they asked of people necessary? Specifically, the planned outages? She knew they were required for her region, but beyond that? Akemi had put her mind to rest, not just with assurances about the larger system, but the passion he put into stopping Miller. Her faith in Akemi was the bedrock upon which she kept doing her job. And she knew it worked that way, all the way down to the individuals going about their lives, trying to get by. Trust in the system was so easily corrupted, and men like Miller were smugly proud of their ability to do just that and get away with almost anything, no matter the cost. And that cost was always so much bigger than they even knew. Or cared about.

Zuri couldn't afford to lose any more public trust in USEC, not for a long while. And that meant not overextending the grid and making sure they had cushion for the unknowns that could pop up at any moment.

How important was this work at Cal Tech? She didn't have a good gauge for it. The IEC had its hands full, and Zuri didn't want to bother the governor again, if she could help it, which was why she sent off a call request to Akemi, hoping it wouldn't take long for him to advise her.

Plus she just wanted to check in on him.

He answered quickly. "Zuri, so good to hear from you. I hope nothing is wrong?" His tone was more clipped than normal, and he looked *worn*. Which worried her.

Zuri almost regretted the call, but she would make it quick. "I'm sorry to bother you, Akemi. But I need your advice, if you have a moment."

"Of course."

"Cal Tech's spooling up one of these ZPE devices. I can spare the kilowatts, but just barely, and I don't like keeping our cushion low like that. You understand. Can you tell me:

how important is it? Will it help you and…" She waved to conjure the right words. "…the larger effort here? I've been on the outside of this. I know you and the team at the IEC have been doing everything you can. We're coming off the Level Two alert tomorrow, so you know that means our margin is even less."

Akemi's brow wrinkled as she spoke. "If it were me, I'd give them provisional overages. They'll have to agree to shut down and let you claw those back in the event of a problem. But yes, it's important. Anything we can do to show it's viable to get a reactor going, especially with the prestige of Cal Tech behind it, will put pressure on these politicians to do what they ought to understand without my explanation." His frustration was clear, and she didn't want to poke it any further.

"That's what I needed to know." She scanned his face as best she could over the call. "Are you doing okay? Monique made me promise to ask if I saw you."

His expression noticeably brightened. "Tell her I'm fine. I haven't been able to return her messages. She said not to, but I wish I could. It's been hectic."

"I'll tell her you're thinking of her."

A smile broke out on his face. "Thank you." Then his attention shifted. "I'm sorry, I need to—"

"Go! I appreciate your time."

He signed off, hastily. But Zuri felt like he was better for the call. She'd made her peace about those two. It was only a matter of time before Akemi would be a regular at the Homestead. And he'd fit in just fine. Probably good for the both of them.

She modified Cal Tech's power request, making the conditions explicit, and signed off on it, sending it back to Jeevika with a note to handle it personally.

As she finished, Denzel peeked in past the mostly-closed door. "Kids want to know if you're joining us for grilled cheese? Just so you know, your mother is here. She brought Ruby. I can distract them with a game, if you need a minute..."

"No, no." Zuri swiped all her work closed. "Perfect timing. Besides, I've got news from Akemi, and Mama will kill me if I don't take it straight to her."

Denzel's eyebrows lifted, but he knew it as well as she did.

They were all blessed with an abundance of gifts—family and careers, influence and comfort—but everyone, even the lucky, deserved to have that spark that made you *want* to come home. Made you *yearn* to make the world a better place, if you could, given the chance.

That's what she would never understand about people like Miller.

It was like they were blind to the difficulties of the world they lived in. Cut off from it in a way that warped them. Zuri prayed his eyes would be opened. Or he could be stopped. The world needed to see the cost of a man like that having power before it was too late.

Meanwhile, she'd have some grilled cheese, count all her blessings, and do everything she could to keep the power on and the world running straight.

———

Akemi had never seen anything like the Palace of Versailles.

He understood its importance as a historic French landmark, and the art was intriguing, but he could not get past the D-10 choosing *this location* for their emergency session on the ZPE. France held the annually-rotating presidency, so there was a certain logic to holding it in country, but it was as if the French had suddenly become immune to irony. The proceedings were held in the Coronation Chamber, surrounded by gilt, from the intricate ceiling carvings to the hanging chandeliers and a towering column in the middle with a lone white-porcelain figure at the top. Everything that wasn't gilded was painted—enormous works covered the walls, depicting historic battles and Napoleon's seizure of power, including the crowning of the Emperor.

It was a temple to empire and emperors.

Which flabbergasted him. The optics on it were *atrocious*. Or perhaps it was even worse: maybe the D-10 had already decided upon a return to the time of kings. Then again, this very room was where rioters broke in, marking the start of the French Revolution.

Perhaps the French were more sly than he gave credit.

But he wasn't here to argue the aesthetic or political choices of the location but to somehow persuade the world's leaders to reject Miller's contracts and accept the Physiverse protocols in their place. A parade of eminent physicists, including high-ranking members from the International Union of Pure and Applied Physics, had been testifying all day, and now Akemi's chance had come.

It was not going well.

"The Physiverse is a worldwide commons coordinating the vast amount of research and testing being conducted on every continent. In the eighteen days since the IEC released the ZPE specifications to the world, an astonishing amount of knowledge has been gained." He'd repeated these same words endlessly, but they still held amazement for him. This spontaneous effort had happened via the actions of countless scientists. He was only the herald of it to the seats of power, not the originator, by any means. "The report submitted to the D-10 has already been fast-tracked through the United Nations Environment Programme." He didn't need to say it was stuck in committee, with the D-10 member states unwilling to let it proceed to the General Assembly until some resolution was made at the D-10 itself. "More importantly, it has the approval of every major physics organization on the planet. That's because the protocols are scientifically sound. They will ensure everyone who signs onto them will have access to the latest knowledge about the device, the underlying science, and how to operate it safely and effectively. And I would like to emphasize how quickly that knowledge is evolving. If you operate outside the protocols, not ensuring the highest levels of safety, you will not have access to that quickly-evolving knowledge dataset. That would put those outside the protocols at a serious disadvantage. Which is why I strongly advocate the D-10 invalidate these contracts with Eternal Energy and join the protocols. There isn't a sensible alternative."

Even as he spoke, the delegates were checking their displays, ignoring him. Akemi's chair was uncomfortable and utilitarian, and the room was overly chilled and musty, as if the air itself had been summoned from the past. He kept wondering about the choice of delegate chairs, high-backed and cushioned in red velvet, arranged in an imperious half-circle like a royal court. They didn't actually seat the leaders of the D-10 countries, but some lower-level representatives sent in their place. It was simultaneously offensive and perfectly symbolic of how Miller's entire enterprise hinged on people whose personal ambition was entangled with his.

Whereas Akemi would much prefer to be taking tea in his office and doing the ordinary work of ensuring the power stayed on in Southern California. Leo, his Chief of Staff, had to be tired of covering all his commission duties while Akemi traveled the globe, desperate to stop this disaster from unfolding.

His stomach was perpetually knotted.

"This is the perfect framework for formulating new theories and testing them," he continued, undaunted by their inattention, "with worldwide coordination of science on one of the most important technologies of our time. The majority of the effort initially will go to that—testing, safety protocols, general knowledge progression—and any energy generated will be used for recapturing carbon from the air, which needless to say, benefits everyone. Only once the device and its operation have passed rigorous safety checks, and we have plausible theories to ensure there's no greater harm, will those who have signed onto the protocols proceed with more widespread implementation."

The delegate from America, Anton Smith, smirked from his central seat. "I don't know about my distinguished colleagues, but I'm not inclined to trust a bunch of random people to hold the world's knowledge. Much less let them tell my country when it's safe to use the device."

Akemi had tried to look up Mr. Smith's background, but there was scant information on the delegates. Almost as if on purpose, although he couldn't imagine why. "We already use these kinds of protocols in many other sectors. The IEC itself is a model of that kind of worldwide collaboration in the development of green technologies..." He trailed off as a buzz went around the seated delegates.

Anton Smith spoke again but to his fellow delegates. "Given the news that's just been reported, I believe we should take a twenty-minute recess."

The knot in Akemi's stomach spasmed tighter. He

pushed back from the table where he'd been giving testimony and quickly swiped up the news to see what had happened. As he scanned for details, he rose and worked his way through the crowded press of the Coronation Room.

A ZPE accident of some kind in Ukraine. He'd heard some group had built a device and possibly made power, but it was now being disclosed that two people had been killed. *Sliced in half.* Just as the earlier versions of Ellis's work had done in Palm Springs. Akemi shuffled through the series of adjacent rooms until he emerged into the Hall of Mirrors, where he finally had a moment to read the details.

Reporters were already saying this would set back the efforts to convince the D-10 to sign the Physiverse protocols, which made no sense at all. If anything, this was an argument *to* co-sign the safety plans—the makers in Ukraine were operating outside the protocols—but speculation was already being made that the only "safe" way to ensure proper operation was to have Miller control everything.

Akemi glanced around the dizzying gilt and mirrors of the famous Hall, desperate for a restroom. His stomach was staging a revolution of its own. He was momentarily distracted by a tall older man with unkempt white hair striding with determination toward him. It spoke to Akemi's distressed state that he didn't recognize Ellis until he grabbed Akemi by the arm and dragged him toward the window, away from the few people nearby.

"I need to talk to you," Ellis whispered hoarsely, his gaze flicking nervously to the others.

Akemi was nonplussed, his outrage getting lost between his volcanic stomach and the preposterous notion that Ellis would demand to speak to him.

He yanked free of Ellis's grip. "How dare you—"

"Don't give me that." Ellis glowered, but it was shifty. "I

know you're connected to all of this. To *her*. You can get me in contact."

Akemi didn't know who Ellis was referring to and frankly didn't care. His outrage had found articulation in his brain. "How *dare* you betray... *everything!* All of science! The entire *world!* You want to be called a genius, but you're nothing but a..." Caution took hold and he lowered his voice. *"Murderer."*

"I *tried* to stop him." But again, that twitchy look, like someone might overhear.

What was this nonsense about trying to stop Miller? Ellis has been complicit all along: the attempted murders, the people sliced in half in Palm Springs, and now Ukraine. Ellis *knew* there was danger in the device. He could have released information on how to operate it safely. Instead, he was accosting Akemi, furtively, for his own reasons.

Disgust welled up and Akemi turned away.

"Dr. Sato, wait!" It was only the sound of true desperation that stopped Akemi.

He took a long moment before turning back. He couldn't—the *world* couldn't—afford to throw away whatever chance this might be. No matter his personal feelings and the clear knowledge that Ellis was a horrible human being. Akemi wrestled those thoughts aside and considered: *why on Earth was Ellis hunting him down in the Hall of Mirrors?* Akemi knew Miller's assets had been frozen by the international court. The hacktivist data dump and the fired Renew employee were all pointing to Miller's orchestration of the attempt on the IEC Director's life. It was looking bad for Miller, personally, and maybe Ellis by association. But when did the powerful ever fully pay for their crimes? Or even partially? And corruption and self-interest seemed to be driving the D-10, which *still* appeared determined to barrel ahead with Miller's contracts, despite everything.

Why was Ellis here?

Akemi turned to face him, giving his coldest stare. It finally clicked: there was only one *her* Ellis could possibly be referring to. "You're insane if you think I'll give you another chance to murder Director Desai."

"I don't want that. I never did." He looked increasingly desperate. "I tried to talk her out of this, tried to *warn* her—"

"That's absurd." Akemi couldn't know what had happened in immersive, but the facts spoke for themselves.

"That doesn't matter now." Ellis waved a hand through the air, but it was shaky. "This is too important."

Of course, it mattered. But Akemi held his tongue because Ellis needed something... or he wouldn't be here. The only question was: *what could Akemi get from him in exchange?* He couldn't trust Ellis, and there was no small amount of risk even talking to him, but the man knew how to operate the ZPE safely, and that might be key in all of this.

"Look, Miller is..." Ellis blinked rapidly. "Not making sense. He's saying and doing things that... it's just *crazy.*"

Akemi kept his voice cool. "You want out." He wanted to say *it's a little late for that,* but perhaps it wasn't. Maybe this was exactly the leverage they needed to push the powerful, the reticent, the greedy and the ambitious, onto the right side of things.

"He fired Astra." Ellis's voice was hushed. "I thought he'd cool down and bring her back, but now she's not responding to her messages, and she's just... gone." The man was truly spooked. With Miller's bloody track record, that at least made sense.

Maybe things had turned enough that Ellis wanted out.

He had been, at one time, a legitimate scientist. His dreams of glory surely hadn't included playing the part of mad scientist for a murderous tyrant increasingly reviled by the world. *Oh, look, the consequences of your actions have arrived.* Akemi kept that thought to himself. Conscience was *not* making a belated appearance in Ellis's psyche. This was something more basic. *Fear.*

"You want me to arrange a meeting." Akemi was already mentally scrambling how to make that happen.

"I have information you can use," Ellis insisted.

"Information about the ZPE," Akemi clarified. "How to operate it safely. How to tune it to keep these random bursts of energy from killing people. You'll tell me everything."

"I want assurance the IEC will protect me." Ellis said it like he was in any position to make demands. But he was agreeing to Akemi's terms. And Ellis understood this key part of the ZPE reactor operation better than anyone on Earth.

"We'll need to leave immediately." Akemi glanced around, but no one was paying them any attention. "Tell no one."

Ellis nodded hastily.

Akemi took him by the arm and marched him toward the exit from the palace. He had no idea whether this would work or even what the risks might be, but he could figure that out on the way. There was nothing more he could accomplish back in the Coronation Room.

This, on the other hand, might be a chance to turn the whole thing around.

EIGHTEEN

"I can't believe you're doing this." Matti's voice was perpetually in Nitara's ear clip these days, a constant open channel which she greatly enjoyed and which generally helped keep her anchored. Except when it sounded fearful, like now.

"I have an impressively intimidating security person with me." Nitara gave a grateful smile to the tall, well-muscled man striding down the IEC's second floor with her. She didn't know his name—she didn't *need* to know—but she recognized him from the hazy return boat ride across the North Sea. He was one of the special-ops IEC security that had hustled her off Miller's island. The Exec Director himself had assigned a whole group of them to protect her.

Her bodyguard gave her an assessing look and seemed to judge that a response was not needed. Then he returned his gaze to sweeping the hall with a level of attention Nitara admired... and would rely on to make this work.

"I don't care if you've got a bodyguard," Matti said. "If I were there, I'd be barricading the door with my own body."

"Sweet but unnecessary." Nitara stepped into the

elevator once the bodyguard had cleared it, and they took it to the floor where the meeting would take place. In a way, Ellis was a high-level refugee, if you could ignore that he was fleeing his own bad decision-making. The vast majority of the world's climate refugees were escaping the unlivable conditions the world had collectively created by pumping endless amounts of carbon into the air. And it was relentlessly true that the least responsible for climate change were those most likely to suffer from the carnage. But occasionally, the IEC brought in refugees who had a little more culpability in the mess they were running from.

She had to admit she'd never brought in someone who had personally tried to kill her. That she still couldn't turn on her chip and the nightmares were still haunting her sleep added a bit more spice to the situation. She had to admit it was possible that simply *seeing* Ellis might be a trigger. She couldn't care less about his demands to see her personally. No one was forcing her to talk to him. She *wanted* to be the one to do this. And if she literally couldn't make it work, she'd hand it over to someone else. Ellis could cool his heels in the secure processing room until it got sorted.

Before they turned down the hall to the IEC's Refugee Commission wing, her bodyguard motioned for her to stop. He was checking with other members of his team, who Nitara had yet to see, but then he seemed satisfied, and they continued.

Akemi was standing alone outside the room, the light on to signal the door's magnetic lock was engaged. The room was jammed, muted for speech and motion, and ran on self-contained power. Ellis wasn't going anywhere, and it didn't hurt to make him wait.

"Anything I need to know before I go in?" Nitara asked Akemi. They'd been in contact the whole twenty-four hours it took for Akemi to personally escort Ellis from France to LA, but there could be things he hadn't been at liberty to say.

"That I'm on record with how terrible this idea is?" Matti said in her ear.

Nitara's ear clip would be cut off once inside the room, and that was probably best. For both of them.

"I still don't know what Ellis wants, beyond his stated request for security." Akemi looked haggard but animated by an internal fire she could well understand. "He won't talk to me. And I still think it's unwise for you to meet with him personally."

"See?" Matti echoed.

"But that seems our only recourse at the moment," Akemi added.

"Thank you for saying that," Nitara said, mostly for Matti's benefit. "I expected you to come back from Europe with a signed accord, not the top scientist from the other side. Well done."

"The accord wasn't going anywhere." Part of the fire was directed at the world leaders Akemi had been trying to convince to follow the science of energy not the politics of it.

"You'd be surprised how often things that appear to be going nowhere are just about to go precisely where you've been pushing all along." Nitara understood the frustration, even if she'd developed a gigantic well of patience in dealing with exactly those glacial processes that eventually, one day, resulted in an earthquake.

Akemi might not see it, but *this* was the tremor before the big one hit.

Nitara just had to see it through. "We could easily lock Ellis away at this point. It wouldn't be hard to drum up any number of charges. And trust me, that would be very personally satisfying." That was for Matti. "But you've handed me a gift, Akemi, and I'm about to make the most of it. I would like to have you in there with me, though."

"Of course."

Nitara nodded to her bodyguard, and he disengaged the lock. Inside, Ellis stood with another of the IEC security team, looking disheveled and exhausted. Which worked well for this.

"Finally!" Ellis burst out, throwing his hands up. "I asked for security, not a jail cell."

"You're lucky we don't have any jail cells handy at the moment." Nitara kept her tone cool and kept her distance. The second IEC security person positioned themself between Ellis and Nitara, with Akemi barely inside the door as Nitara's bodyguard closed it from the inside and re-engaged all the security measures. Her bodyguard took a spot at her side, but slightly closer to the disgruntled Dr. Ellis.

Who was blinking rapidly and didn't seem to have a follow-up for his demands for better accommodations. "I need assurance the IEC will protect me." He flicked a look to the security person between them. "Not just a body-guard. I need something like witness protection."

"I'm afraid that won't be possible." Nitara arched an eyebrow. "You're no good to me anonymous, Ellis."

He gave her a pinched look. "What do you mean?" He was obviously operating on jet-lag because Nitara couldn't believe the supposed genius couldn't figure out this much on his own.

"I mean that you're going to be on a lot of newscasts," she said. "We can arrange for you to do that from a relatively secure location, but slipping off into obscurity isn't going to be an option for you."

He seemed confused, and it *should* throw him: she suspected that what he wanted all along was the glory of applause, from the scientific community and the world at large, and she was offering that to him. It galled her to not have Ellis behind bars, much less have him *win* this in any way. But this wasn't about winners and losers—this was about building a world that worked for everyone or one that enriched a few. And Nitara had been fighting that battle her entire life. Ellis was going to be the key to winning it, if he could manage to get out of his confusion fog and let it happen.

"What do you want me to say on these newscasts?" His eyelid twitched.

Nitara repressed the smile that threatened to burst forth. Now she wished Matti could hear this part. The secure room meant no one was privy to this conversation except the occupants, and that was essential. But she would absolutely tell Matti every detail later.

Because *this*... this was the moment they won.

"You've only got two things I want, Ellis: your knowledge and your voice." She laced her fingers and let her hands rest in front of her. This was the easy part. "Whatever key bits of knowledge you may have about the ZPE—how to operate it without slicing people in half, how to *stop* it should that become a problem—you'll share immediately with the Physiverse. They're probably ahead of you by now, so I'm not sure your knowledge isn't dated already, but we'll take whatever insights you have about the technology. Then you'll officially join the Physiverse—in an emeritus and advisory-only position, mind you—and continue to lend your open support to their efforts. Next, you'll go on a media tour, starting with the D-10, and explain how you understand the IEC owns copyright and that you support the IEC's efforts to coordinate with the Physiverse to enact the worldwide, safe, and ethical use of your technology. Most important, you'll disavow your association with Miller, Eternal Energy, Renew Energy, and any other shadow corporations Miller's set up in his attempt to annex the world energy market."

Ellis was slack-jawed listening to her, and she'd probably have to repeat it, but when she paused, he sputtered, "Miller will kill me!"

"I personally think Miller's motivated by greed and ambition, not revenge, but you know him better than me." She let that sink in. There was still a tiny possibility of Ellis panicking and backing out. But she put those odds at low single digits. "This is not a negotiation, Ellis. Those are my terms. You'll be welcomed back into the scientific community, you'll do your mea culpa tour rejecting Miller and endorsing the Physiverse protocols, and you'll have a chance to contribute to the worldwide implementation of your research. Or I tell Miller to come get you."

His eyes actually bugged out.

Nothing like staring down the consequences of your own poor choices.

It took a moment of tormented expressions and no words, but then Ellis let out a shuddering breath. Nitara would like to think it was regret for everything he'd allowed to happen—all the harm he actively or passively caused, including *specifically to her*—but she knew it was only him being resigned to his fate.

That was all she needed.

"All right," Ellis said. "I'll do what you say. But I want protection."

She smiled. "We'll want to keep you as safe as possible for all those media appearances you're going to make." She flicked a look to the two security folks, belatedly noticing Akemi standing behind her with his mouth agape. "Keep him here. Make sure our guest is comfortable. Dr. Ellis could probably use a good meal and something warm and caffeinated to drink. I'll send someone in to brief him, shortly." She gestured for Akemi to follow her, deactivated the door, and let herself out. Her bodyguard shadowed her silently.

As soon as the lock was re-engaged—not locking Ellis *in,* but then he didn't know that—Akemi burst out, "I can't believe he agreed to all that."

"I keep thinking I should have asked for more." Nitara gave him a small smile. "He wasn't in any position to refuse." She had been right to do this personally. It settled something deep inside her to face him again, this time from a position of power and safety.

"What happened?" Matti demanded, back in her ear clip once more.

"I got what we wanted," Nitara replied, indicating she was talking to Matti. "Akemi will fill you in, but it's basically what we discussed. I need you two to coordinate rolling that out, as soon as possible. I have yet one more thing to take care of."

"What's that?" Akemi asked, the surprised expression still occupying his face.

"Matti will brief you." She turned and strode down the hall, bodyguard still keeping pace.

"Are we leaving the building?" he asked.

"Nope. Just one floor up." Her steps were light and unhurried, yet powered by a tremendous surge of adrenaline. There was only one essential piece left to secure. "Matti, I'm going off comms for this."

"As long as you're not going back to see Dr. Murder," she grumbled.

"Promise."

"All right. I've got my hands full anyway," Matti said. "But I want to hear everything when you're done. Give the American delegate hell for me."

"Yes, Ma'am." Nitara smirked. This part wouldn't be so easy, but she was pretty sure the ball was rolling downhill and gaining momentum. The kind which couldn't easily be stopped. Delegate Rodriguez could get on board or get squashed, and if there was one thing she could generally count upon, it was political types having a finely-tuned sense of self-preservation.

The American delegation had been reliably camped out in one of the CarbonCon conference rooms furthest from hers. It took a minute to get there, but when she did, Rodriguez was at his makeshift desk with a couple aides perched on the edges. They weren't talking, each absorbed in their displays.

Nitara strode up with enough confidence to commandeer Rodriguez's attention. Or maybe it was the burly and broodingly silent bodyguard at her back.

Rodriguez half rose from his chair before thinking better of that and sinking back down, leaving her to stand on the other side of his desk, flanked by his minions, with her bodyguard an arm's reach behind her.

"Director Desai," he said. "You're looking well."

"I'm hard to kill." No sense in playing this soft.

Rodriguez cringed and his aides were startled enough to back off a little and give her some room. A part of her gave a moment's notice to the young Mr. Thomas Green being one. Good. Maybe he'd learn something about how the world worked—something he could tell future bosses when they second-guessed what happened here today.

"What can I help you with?" Rodriguez asked, with a tone that said he would be as little help as possible.

"I have Ellis in a secure location."

"I'm sorry, what?" Rodriguez almost rose out of his seat again, but aborted that motion, and it was faintly amusing to watch confusion ricochet around his body in a series of terminated impulses to move.

"Dr. James Ellis, inventor of the ZPE? Perhaps you've heard of him." She needed to give him a second to catch up.

Rodriguez nearly snarled and finally gave in to his need to stand, maybe to tower over her, a clumsy physical attempt at intimidation that certain types defaulted to. It always struck her as a show of weakness—the real kind, not the gentleness or softness that was a sign of strength and decency in an oft brutal world.

She didn't need a bodyguard to fend off Rodriguez's kind, although it was still nice to have one.

Rodriguez attempted a glare. "You're holding Ellis captive?"

She allowed herself a laugh. "Hardly. He came to us, wanting to break with Miller and support the Physiverse protocols. My people are making sure he's safe, which was a top priority for him. You can imagine why."

Again, shock rippled across the man's face. Nitara glanced at Mr. Green, and there was a kind of awe on his face that said he might be coming to work for the IEC soon. She might even allow that. It would be good to have insights into the power struggles inside America in the days ahead.

"Look, I'm doing you a courtesy here," Nitara said, turning her attention back to Rodriguez. "You can get ahead of this by moving now or you can wait for the fallout. But Ellis will be making statements soon, and you might want to get there first. By the way, we know about DARPA's intentional leak. And Cal Tech is officially making power. Your move, Rodriguez."

He was sputtering now, and maybe she overestimated his ability to keep up. "What exactly do you expect me to do?"

"Well, I'd think *you* would want to let your bosses know Ellis is about to make a fool of America dragging their heels in the D-10 emergency proceedings." She laced her fingers again, this time behind her back. Not that she was signaling that she could do his job with both hands tied behind her back *or anything.* "It's pretty obvious they'd want a heads up about that. The real question is: *Where is this headed?* And I'm here to let you in on that as well. If you're ready." Okay, that was a little much, and the changing colors of red suffusing Rodriguez's face said she *might* be enjoying this a bit too much. "If you have time in your schedule, that is."

It took a moment, but Rodriguez managed to compose himself. A little. "You're telling me Ellis is going to make a statement in support of the Physiverse protocols." His tone was flat, angry of course, but implying she was trotting out some grand misinformation.

Nitara shrugged one shoulder. "If you're not going to take this at face-value, then we're done here."

"*Wait.*" He had his hands up to stop her from leaving, even though she hadn't moved a muscle.

It took serious effort not to smile, but she managed it.

"I just want to make sure I'm clear on what you're saying." The calculations were visibly whirring in Rodriguez's mind. *Finally.*

"Of course." Nitara nodded like this was entirely

reasonable. "Let me be clear, then. We have Ellis safely tucked in a secure location, per his request. He will soon make an announcement disavowing Miller and embracing the Physiverse protocols. He will take a position on their advisory board and will contribute to the effort to enable safe, *free* worldwide usage of the ZPE technology, per the protocol testing plan. I fully expect the D-10 to stop quibbling and back the protocols as well, recommending invalidation of Miller's contracts. I suppose some countries might still want to get their ZPE tech straight from Miller, but given his, um, financial difficulties and the loss of his genius inventor, that doesn't seem like a prudent path to go down."

Rodriguez's eyes narrowed. "And the IEC will be running all this."

She allowed herself a small smile. "The IEC has released copyright on the technology. We will not be directly involved with the Physiverse—they're a new commons that's operating independently of everyone. And I must say: *good for them.* However, I fully expect the IEC to propose a doubling of our Global Energy Tax, specifically earmarking those funds for ZPE research and deployment. We'll be passing those funds back out to the wide-ranging efforts to contribute research and testing results to the Physiverse database. And you can count on those funds being conditioned on an inverse-tier order, making sure the countries most impacted by climate change will get the most funding, for research as well as deployment of the device, once proven safe. And only, of course, to countries that sign onto the protocols."

"You think this is going to be your new fiefdom." The accusation was nasty but not entirely unwarranted.

"I think the IEC will do as it has always done: coordinate global green energy research and development. And that has always rightly benefitted severely-impacted countries more. America will get their share, but it can afford to fund Cal Tech's research on its own. You should have plenty of funds once you cancel payment to Miller."

And there it was. Would America get on board with this? It wasn't even Rodriguez's call—all she needed from him was a little self-motivated urgency to get ahead of this and help his country look like a leader instead of being dragged into reality by Ellis's surprise betrayal. But where America went, many others would follow. All would eventually see that this changed the game.

Sometimes, you don't have to defeat the bad guy. You just have to make them irrelevant. Which was really the worst punishment for men of ambition.

Rodriguez didn't strike her as someone who would welcome becoming irrelevant overnight. By the tormented look in his eyes, he was catching up to that reality too.

"I need some kind of official statement from the IEC." Rodriguez's torment had settled into a steady hatred for her, which neither pleased nor bothered her—as long as he got the job done.

"I'm giving you an *un*official briefing right now, Rodriguez," she said lightly. It was absurd of him to ask. Likely a delay for him to get his mental ducks in order. "You can thank me now, or you can wait to hear the official one with the rest of the world."

"*Fine,*" he spat out. "Anything else? I have a few calls to make."

"Have a nice day." She smiled broadly, winked at Mr. Green—which she thought might cause him to have an actual heart attack—and turned her back on the American delegation.

Her steps barely seemed to contact the conference floor.

Her bodyguard shadow was inscrutable as always, his attention solely on possible threats, not her triumph in the conference room.

She would give Rodriguez a half hour head start. Then she'd start working through the rest of the D-10 representatives at CarbonCon. Eventually, before they fled home for the power-brokering that would happen there, she would talk to the reps from every country. She'd make sure they understood the IEC wasn't *stopping* this world-saving technology... they were saving it. From the catastrophe that Miller's mismanagement and financial extraction held out like a nightmare they'd long-ago awoken from and no one sensible wanted to return to.

For all its promise, technology wasn't what would save the world. Or destroy it. It was, and had always been, *people.* The messy, hectic, often horrifying struggle of the world's people to figure out how to live with themselves and all their inventions.

Nitara was simply doing her part.

NINETEEN

The weather was blissfully cool on the IEC's rooftop garden, and Nitara couldn't be more pleased. Matti deserved all the good things for her nuptials with Anthony, and for once, Southern California's weather delivered its legendarily gentle blue-sky warmth. It helped that it was still early on this gorgeous Saturday morning. A full month delayed but perfect timing.

The bot-tended garden, shaded by a soaring white solar sail, was a popular spot for diplomatic gatherings but was also open to the public, now that quarantine had ended. Yet the attendees represented a good part of the IEC's organizational chart. One could be forgiven for thinking this was a gathering of the now-disbanded CarbonCon conference, except for the extra festive attire and delicate white-lattice arch trimmed in flowers. The garden itself was in full bloom, with rooftop views of both the mountains and the sea. More décor would only detract, and she knew Matti's preferences were toward the simple and breezy. It was special to have her back in the building, although that was as temporary as the weather.

Nitara wanted to make the rounds before the ceremony started. She started at the back, easing up with a smile for Lucía and Gwen in the very last row of chairs.

"Hey!" Lucía said. "I was hoping to catch you. I have some news."

"You can stop updating me now, Lucía," Nitara replied with a wider smile. "I've heard you returned to Power Island One." It had been less than a week since the D-10 had invalidated Miller's contracts, but the IEC's emergency level effort had quickly wound down. People were tired and deserved their much-needed break from all the intensity. Still plenty to do, but not enough to commandeer every hand and brain she could find.

Time to return to the blessings of boring, normal life. And weddings.

Gwen leaned forward. "She's *Island Designer Ramirez* to you now. I expect her to become far too important to talk to the likes of us."

Nitara's laugh came from deep inside. She missed a lot of the crew who had helped keep the whole thing afloat. That's what happened when you came together in a crisis. "Well, I hope that's not true. I might need to visit our most-historic Power Island soon. I hear you're going to make some history of your own, renovating Ellis's old lab to house the new ZPE research and development center."

"In collaboration with Cal Tech and the Power Engineering Institute," Lucía confirmed. "Everyone wants to be in the Physiverse these days."

"Well, congratulations on your promotion." Then Nitara looked to Gwen. "I keep expecting to see an application from you."

"I know, I miss the fun times too." Gwen pulled an exaggerated look of sadness but then smirked. "But I'm still catching up on all the drama I missed at USEC. Once things settle down, though, I'm thinking the Physiverse might need some IT help."

"On Power Island One?" Nitara's eyebrows lifted. These two certainly seemed attached.

This appeared to be news to Lucía as well.

Gwen was decidedly non-committal. "If they're lucky."

Nitara grinned. "They *would* be lucky to have you." And she meant it.

She left the two of them arguing over this possibility and eased down the rows, greeting friends and colleagues. She spied Zahara and was surprised to see her back from Denmark. Then again, there was a lot of turnover in political offices right now, the fallout from Miller's rather rapid descent still rolling along.

Nitara tapped her friend's shoulder to gain her attention.

"Hey, you're alive!" Zahara said, popping to her feet.

"Doing my best." They embraced, and it was an unfortunate collision between the prickly gold embroidery of Nitara's sari and the wondrous cloud of billowing white chiffon of Zahara's sundress.

As they chuckled and detangled, Zahara said, "I'm just in town for the wedding. But then I gotta decide whether I want LeBlanc's job."

"Is he out?"

"Oh yeah." They were finally detached. "He booked it out of there, once things started to fall apart for Miller. I heard Miller's run off to Siberia."

"Really?" Once the man was out of play, Nitara had literally stopped thinking about him.

"Mm hm. It's nice and green there now, and I hope he

catches one of those new pathogens that keep getting released from the melting permafrost."

Nitara laughed. "I'm just happy no one wants to do business with him." She was honestly surprised she wasn't obsessed with putting Miller behind bars. Maybe because she'd let that possibility go for Ellis, and all her spare bandwidth went into staying anchored and waiting for the nightmares to fade. She hadn't had any for days, so maybe they were done. If so, maybe she'd start to have energy to care what happened to Miller. The most important part had already happened: he was permanently unable to exploit his way to riches. The international court investigation had collapsed when the D-10 canceled their contracts. The remaining countries quickly followed. Many, like China, already canceled once she'd released the IP, but they were still waffling about joining the Physiverse. She was confident they'd come around. Meanwhile, Renew Energy had declared bankruptcy, trying to reorganize and purge the stain of Miller's involvement. She didn't know what the man was living on these days, but she didn't care.

"That's nowhere near enough for me," Zahara said, making Nitara smile. "I want his ass in jail. I think he killed that Astra woman. No one can find her. Eventually, the man needs to get put away. In the meantime, I want to see him broke and starving in the middle of nowhere. And I want all his toadies like LeBlanc scurrying off and hiding under rocks again. I've been tracking the attendees of Miller's secret conference, seeing how I can help them get fired. I'm petty that way."

"I expected no less." Nitara was grinning now. "You should take LeBlanc's job. They need someone competent for a change."

"I'm actually thinking about returning to the Corps.

They've got a new ZPE deployment mission. That's where I really want to be."

"You'd be fantastic at that." Zahara had always been more comfortable in the Pandemic Corps than either her or Matti—and that was before the fire. But Zahara wasn't the only one buzzing about the possibility of ending energy poverty in some of the hardest-hit places on the planet. Green energy had already made so much progress in pulling up living standards around the world. The potential for ZPE was truly exciting. "Look, I'll see you after the ceremony. I need to check in with Matti, make sure everything's okay."

"Let's catch up later." Zahara squeezed both her hands then returned to visiting with another friend from the Corps. A whole cohort of them had shown up for Matti's wedding. She'd kept more in touch than Nitara had, and she was glad they were here for her.

Nitara scanned the crowd and found Matti up front with Anthony, off to the side, out in the sun, looking luminous in her wedding finery. Unhurried, Nitara worked her way that direction, shaking hands and performing her informal job of greeter. It was all so calm and beautiful, joy suffusing the air, she simply wanted to soak it up.

Nothing was normal anymore, but every small good thing that came her way seemed extra bright. Matti had taken to staying with her, helping her to re-anchor when she awoke in a screaming panic. It was so like those awful days, long ago, when Nitara was the one holding her through the night. But her trauma wasn't the same—both briefly more severe but also not as tenacious in its hold on her mind—and Nitara had set a cutoff to the sleeping over. Once Matti was married, she needed to be with her husband.

Nitara would be fine. Months, the doctors said, but she already was well on her way.

When she reached the soon-to-be wed couple, Matti's face lit up, her creamy-white knee-length dress more hippie love trance than wedding gown. Anthony was more fancy with his all-white attire, but the open collar was probably less formal than he normally wore at the UN.

"You two have something special planned for today?" Nitara asked. "You're looking pretty dressed up for work."

"Ha ha," Matti said, but Anthony at least cracked a smile.

"Everything looks set." Nitara swept a look over the guests still milling around their seats. "Anything I can help with?"

"Well, there is one thing." Matti flicked a look at her fiancé, and he gave a small nod.

"All right." Nitara couldn't think what it would be. She'd already signed up to be the witness for the religious part of the ceremony, but there was literally nothing she wouldn't do for Matti.

"I need you to hold this for a minute." Matti held out a small black box.

Nitara suspected it was their rings, but they were already wearing their thin black bands etched with each other's names. Maybe they had separate ones for the wedding? She opened the box to be sure. "Why is there only one?" It was the same as theirs, except both Matti's and Anthony's names were etched on this one. Nitara looked up. "What is this?"

"We got ours changed already." Matti was holding her gaze, intensely.

Nitara's heart squeezed. "Changed to what?" *What was happening here?*

"To have your name on them as well," Anthony said with a bright smile.

It was like he was speaking in a language she didn't understand. She knew Anthony well enough. They'd socialized a few times. The only thing that mattered was that Matti loved him. And that there was still a place for her in their lives. *But this...*

"We want you to be part of our family," Matti rushed out, nervous, which made no sense because it was Nitara's heart that was beating out of her chest. "Or rather, you *are* part of our family. This is just acknowledging what's already true. So, it's no big deal. Right? And you'll also say yes. Right?" She was gripping Anthony's hand like she was about to fall off the edge of the roof.

But it was Nitara who was in free fall. And she had no words at all.

"Oh, and the contract!" Matti released Anthony, fished a folded half-sheet of paper out of a pocket hidden in her diaphanous dress, and handed it to Nitara. It was the script for a legal proceeding. Matti fussed with her display, her hand shaking. "You can voice print through your ear clip. I checked, and that counts. You don't have to have a chip."

The rooftop suddenly felt crowded. These people were here to witness Matti and Anthony publicly confess their love for one another, their commitment to form a family, and here she was staring at a legal script that included the words: *for better or worse, in sickness and in health...*

"It's to... to... make it legal." Matti was a mess, although Nitara could barely tell through the blurred vision brought on by tears that had no business being in her eyes.

"You want to make a family." The words were thick in her mouth. "With me."

"Please say yes before she crushes my hand." Anthony's

words were comprehensible again. Matti was back to gripping him like her life depended on it. This was really happening. This thing she had avoided for so long because she was terrified everything would disappear was suddenly coalescing at the top of the IEC building with Matti trembling in fear that Nitara might turn her away. *Them.* They were a package deal now. She understood that. And it didn't matter in the slightest.

"*Yes,*" Nitara breathed. "I want to make it legal."

"Oh, *thank God.*" Matti dropped her hold on Anthony, who was grinning wide now, and rushed to embrace Nitara. Her hug was fierce and pure and full of love, just like Matti. She pulled back and held Nitara by the shoulders. "Is the ring too much? We don't have to do the ring. That was Anthony's idea."

Nitara glanced down at the box still in her hand. "The ring is perfect." She met Anthony's beaming gaze and said, "Just to be clear, I'm not having sex with you."

He saluted her with two fingers, and Nitara about melted with laughter.

"Oh my God, *what?* No. This isn't that!" Matti was horrified.

"I know. I was joking. You do that with family." Nitara's heart had swelled to an impossible fullness. Then a flash of fear sliced through her. Strong emotions cracked through the barrier, and she was still navigating how to manage that. But this was all goodness and light, and her mind did nothing but sing with the joy of it.

"Not to rush this along or anything," Anthony said, "but there's this other gig we need to get to." He meant the wedding. Which was for everyone else. But this... this was for them. Anthony swiped to start the proceedings through his display. "I, Anthony Gutierrez, being of sound mind, do legally agree to form a family with Matti Richards and Nitara Desai. In family, we pledge to care for one another, for better or worse, in sickness and in health, until that bond is legally dissolved by a court of the state of Southern California." He gave a small nod to Matti.

She stepped back from her grasping hold on Nitara's shoulders and activated her own entry, repeating the vow for the AI attorney. Then it was Nitara's turn, and she surprised herself by being able to speak, clearly, through the whole thing. Her ear clip apparently took the voice print and vow just fine.

The tears didn't return until she put on the ring.

The next minutes were a blur of hugs, the next hour one of ceremony and more tears, and by the middle of the day, Nitara was exhausted, utterly spent, even more than after nearly dying and then traveling across the North Sea and half the world. But her heart was full in a way she couldn't remember ever feeling.

It turned out Anthony was moving to LA—something about all the exciting work now being at the IEC's new Division of Zero Point Energy. Meanwhile, Matti had already joined the nascent Physiverse Office at Cal Tech, in her new position as liaison to the IEC. Nitara would continue, of course, as Director of the IEC's Office of Multilateral Funds and International Agreements, despite many offers that were substantial steps up the power ladder. She didn't need any of that, and with the dispatching of CarbonCon and a wholesale reorganization at the IEC to focus on ZPE work, they needed her to stay put.

And her family was here.

It was time to return to boring old diplomacy, the building of relationships and managing of points of conflict, and simply the maintenance that kept the whole thing moving forward. There were still tipping points to stave off, biomes in need of rescue, and a hundred other challenges beyond renewable sources of energy that would be necessary to live sustainably on the planet. But they'd survived this challenge, this deeply dangerous time, when the lies of the past threatened to rise up and drag them back under. Lies that said nothing mattered, everyone was collectively helpless in the face of change, and the future was hopeless. The hubris of that certainty—that anyone knew what the future would bring—had always been used by the powerful to underwrite cynicism and despair. Hope was the only sensible response to the reality that the future was unwritten.

And everyone had a hand in writing it.

———

HALFWAY TO BETTER

Solarpunk Anthology

A collection of short stories, each exploring a near-future where we're struggling to survive the climate crisis and build a better world.

———

To be notified when I have new stories out,

subscribe to my newsletter:

http://smarturl.it/SKQsnewsletter

NOTHING IS PROMISED

Hopeful Climate Fiction

In a world beset with climate-driven plagues, power engineer Lucía Ramirez just wants a family to join...but she finds a mystery on Power Island One instead.

Book 1, Book 2, Book 3, Book 4

———

HALFWAY TO BETTER

Solarpunk Anthology

A collection of short stories, each exploring a near-future where we're struggling to survive the climate crisis and build a better world.

———

CLOSET FULL OF TIME

Black Mirror-esque Anthology

The thing the machines consume is *us*.

———

SINGULARITY

Hopepunk Sci-Fi

Eli is a legacy human, preserved for his genetic code, but he would give anything to ascend with the rest of humanity.

———

MINDJACK

YA Sci-Fi

When everyone reads minds, a secret is a dangerous thing to keep.

———

ROYALS OF DHARIA

Alt-India Steampunk Romance

The Third Daughter of the Queen must go undercover as the fiancé of a barbarian prince to find a weapon of war.

———

DEBT COLLECTOR

Cyberpunk

When your debts exceed your potential life earnings, debt collectors come take your life energy and give it to someone more "worthy."

———

FAERY SWAP

Middle Grade Fantasy

Finn becomes stuck the Otherworld when a runaway faery prince steals his body.

———

BRIGHT GREEN FUTURES: 2024

(Edited by Susan Kaye Quinn)

Solarpunk Anthology

A collection of short solarpunk stories from guests of the Bright Green Futures podcast.

Podcast: BrightGreenFutures.wtf

———

Most of SKQ's books are available in audiobook:

http://smarturl.it/SKQAudio

———

Get a free box set of Singularity novellas when you subscribe to SKQ's newsletter:

http://smarturl.it/SKQsnewsletter

ABOUT THE AUTHOR

Susan Kaye Quinn is a rocket scientist turned speculative fiction author who now uses her PhD to invent cool stuff in books. Currently writing hopeful climate fiction and solarpunk, but her works include SciFi, YA, gritty cyberpunk, steampunk romance, and that one middle grade fantasy. Her bestselling novels and short stories have been optioned for Virtual Reality, translated into German and French, and featured in several anthologies.

---

www.susankayequinn.com